THE SUIT OF NUL - A NIGHT ON A RIVERBOAT

The Suit of Nul - A Night on a Riverboat

Samuel Henry

Copyright © 2024 by Samuel Henry
All rights reserved. No part of this book may be reproduced in any manner whatsoever without written permission except in the case of brief quotations embodied in critical articles and reviews.
First Printing, 2024

Cover illustration by Ruxandra Onita (@hogfaerie.ink)

Layout and map design by Sam Medlam

To Sam.

Contents

I	A Suit	3
II	A Town	19
III	A Barrow	33
IV	A Fish	45
V	A Single Tooth	59
VI	A Woodland Walk	85
VII	A Scry	109
VIII	A Sea of Bluebells	133
IX	A Castle	149
X	A Cell	167
XI	A Mouse	185
XII	An Escape	201
XIII	A Hillside	217
XIV	A Realm of Fog	233
XV	A Moment at Court	259

Act I

A Town

I

A Suit

A dark gauntlet stood, half buried, in a circle of cracking and blackened earth. The clearing was wide. The sky was blue. Distant hoof beats rolled down the valley. Moisture hung in the air, trickling down grass and from the curled fingers of the gauntlet. Soon, came a rise. A cloud of birds flitted from the tree line, crowing. Beneath them, a man surged with fear in his eyes, followed by another and a third. They looked beaten, sporting torn red clothes and broken armour. One runner carried a sword and another a spear. The last carried nothing at all. As they neared the centre of the clearing, the runners saw the perfect circle of scorched earth, and in the centre the standing gauntlet.

"What's that?" one said, but the wind caught his words and whipped them into the air. His companions had no moment to reply as behind them came a greater sound. A row of cavalry appeared from that same tree line. The spearman turned and raised his arm, but in an instant, he disappeared into a mass of men and beast, maille and green cloth shirking with every beat. Blood fell on the grass and in the time it takes to sigh a slow sigh, the three runners lay dead. A commander atop a green-barded horse raised his visor and looked out across the field, curling his lip at the butchered three.

"We go north," he said, his voice the bark of a tree, "nary a message is to cross the three corners."

The Braelian horses turned, the cloth of their trappers shifting in the breeze. As they did, one filly stepped upon the burned circle. As is often the knack of animals, it felt a thing, a hint of a thing, a thing it could not understand. It panicked. Rearing, it tossed its rider to the ground. The falling cavalryman cried out, but the sound was cut short as the earth arose to meet him. He rolled over in wet dirt, sputtering, and with one eye he spied the half-buried gauntlet. Black metal, caked in mud. He eyed it curiously but at that very moment, it stirred. It made a fist, and with fearful speed, it tore upward from the earth.

The cavalryman scrabbled back, crying "What in the fade?" as the other men pulled reins and made low sounds in their chests to steady their mounts.

The metal fist was followed by a cuff and vambrace, a pauldron, and breastplate. Finally, a helmet rose from the ground, and with a groan that rolled through the Hounskull as steam, a suited knight stood out of the tumbling earth. His armour was bashed, scorched, and black, and was covered head to toe in innumerable inscriptions and runes. A prominent mark in the centre of the breastplate depicted a candle flame. The gauntlets were covered by yet more runes, partially obscured by mire, and on the helmet was the unmistakable symbol of Darbhein peace: a reptile hand with a perfect circle on the palm. The knight stood up, and the fallen man stood as well, tremoring as might a wood mouse before an ashtail.

A horn sounded and the cavalry surrounded the two. Pointed lances and panicking mares eyed the iron-clad stranger. "You there, ser knight," the commander barked, wariness stark in his voice, "Whom do you serve?"

"*Molag of Nul,*" the knight replied with a voice that was as cold as the air itself.

A flicker of recognition passed the commander's eyes. No longer hateful, but somehow warier, afeared even. All knew the name of Nul, and all knew what it meant. The Nul Kevar fought beings of the fade, and ancient rights separated them from ordinary folk. From wars, kings, and the rule of law. "Be on your way then," he said.

"*Way?*" the black knight said. He looked up at the cavalrymen and yet more steam, or ash, billowed from his visor.

"Go. Walk. If you've finished your... *task*, then you must leave."

The knight turned and reached into the disturbed circle of dirt. He grasped at something weighty and heaved. A greatsword like those used by the Pallid clans came free in a shower of blackened earth. It is said that one Pallid swordsman has the strength of ten Braels, though only a Braelian deep in his cups would admit that such a thing could be so.

The knight said nothing more, turned south and began simply to walk. He dragged his blade, leaving a deep cut in the land behind him. The commander waved west and the rest of the cavalry followed.

With a hollow mind, the knight of Nul began a slow trudge. He walked through hills and forests. Ash fell from chinks in his maille, as clouds in rivers, and as dust on the underbrush, whirling like thoughts of the ether, specs catching slants of light through canopies and water surfaces. Each step was heavy and metallic. His visor betrayed nothing. His sword left a mottled gash in the ground in his wake. Soon, the forest lessened. The trees became sparse, and the knight crested a valley to see a string of smoke rising from a small hamlet.

Sitting on a great rock, overlooking the scene, was a wiry young man smoking a pipe, as was his habit. He was clad in a musty jerkin and his brown hair was cut to his shoulders. He had a wry grin, much like the grin of a fool, although he thought himself wise and witty. He was strong of arm, and brass of tongue. He couldn't fight well; though he occasionally tried, he couldn't argue; though he often tried, and he couldn't think as deeply as he would've liked. Yet these things would change with time. Kief Stroongarm he was called. Walker of the fade, singer of songs, picker of tales – though he had not yet earned those titles.

He could pluck a lute with skill and tell a joke with ease. He laughed, ran, and hungered. There was an easiness to his surface that could be mistaken for foolishness, but Ser Keif was not foolish. He was young and bashful, and he went unnoticed by most. Indeed, he was not noticed by the black knight on his solitary march.

Hearing the metal trudge behind him, Kief turned. To Kief, the knight was a warm embrace on a cold night, walking straight out of a hearthside tale. He felt a tugging in his chest and was glad at the sight.

He looked at the knight, looked down at his pipe, gave it a sniff, and then looked again at the knight. "Good morning," Kief said, with warmth in his voice.

The knight did not reply and did not look up, as he continued his solemn walk, dragging his blade.

"What's a lone knight doing here?" Kief said. "Are you on a quest?"

"No," the knight said.

"Where're you going?" Kief stood up, tipped out his pipe, and started to follow.

"Leaving."

"You look exhausted. Come inside, get out of that armour. Tess'd be beside herself if I let a knight go without a bit of hospitality."

The knight grunted in response. Kief fancied he saw ash spill from the thin slits in the helmet.

"Who are you, then?" Kief called after the stranger.

The knight stopped again and looked out across the valley as if pondering something dark and unknowable. He saw the green hills and heard the gentle sounds of people and livestock in the hamlet below. *"I am a task,"* he said, turning to the boy.

Kief felt a coldness in those words but did not know why. "Task? You're on a quest? Like from a book?"

"Book?"

"You know, books? Reading? I thought all knights read?"

Reading was uncommon in those days, but it was known that knights were required to learn the gentle arts: the poetics, inking, the murmuring of philosophies, and other such things. Kief himself could read, as well as write, albeit in a near illegible, chicken-scratch letter style, a rarity. The local farmers often required his efforts as a scribe, though most times he worked in the tavern. Earning two copper pents a day but having to always return one for room and board.

"I am a task," the knight said again, irritation in the voice. No, not irritation: frustration, uncomfortable and strange. He stood in stark contrast to the natural hillside, the swaying ferns, and gently drifting clouds beyond.

"What's your task then?"

The knight seemed hesitant, staring over the vista. He finally said, *"The... suit."*

"You think your task is to wear a suit?"

The hounskull turned and looked at Kief, the slits over the eyes and mouth were dark, terribly dark, all-consuming, all-encompassing dark. The knight looked unto Kief, and as the moments stretched into millennia, he finally spoke; *"I... do not think."*

"Concussed," Kief said, wondering whether it was that or whether the poor sop had lost his mind. It was known to happen following a battle, soldier's shudder, as a certain physik had coined it in times gone by. However, something in the way this knight held himself told of a stouter constitution. What's more, this knight was sure to carry news of the capital, or of the recent battle, in that iron head of his.

In the past few days, the tavern had been abuzz with tales of Braelan forces marching from Rustgate to the Leubar Bridge. Kief was curious. He wanted the knight to stay. He wanted to hear a story. He wanted to be taken away from this place, from Mondar village, with its sheep and mud and prattling tongues.

"What's your name? Were you at the battle?" Kief asked with foolish curiosity, something he'd always had, and could never lose. Something that would earn him all manner of grief and would take him to places no man had seen before.

The knight stopped in his tracks, *"I am the Suit of Molag Nul."*

"The *Suit* of Molag Nul?" Kief ran his fingers through his hair and frowned.

The knight began to walk once again, still dragging the great blade. Kief jumped up and followed on his heels, descending into the valley. "Why're you dragging that sword?" he said, "You're making a terrible line."

The knight stopped again, and a skeeter of pebbles rolled down the hill ahead of him. He looked at the blade, and then back to the trail. *"This is... wrong?"*

Kief had always been interested in blades, in knives, as is the way of many young kin. He used to sneak into his pater's chambers when he was small. There had hung a certain long sword of Braelian design over the fireplace. Kief remembered the sheen of its blade, remembered how easily it cut his hand when he tried to hold it, hot pain and a clatter of steel as the killing metal fell against the floor timbers.

He remembered the sharper words from the Lord Stroongarm's tongue.

"Don't you have a scabbard?" Kief said to the knight on the summer hillside.

The knight stopped once again, put a hand to his back, found a crevice in his shoulder, and pulled out a half-burnt length of leather. He looked at it for a moment and then let it fall to the ground.

"No."

The knight then hefted his sword over the same shoulder and continued his march. Kief, of course, followed close behind as a pup is want to do. This knight was the most intrigue the lad had seen in months. The man was a full head taller than he, the armour was filthy mud-blotched black, and the sword was the same. The steel was covered in symbols that Kief didn't recognize, and there was a faint, burnt smell drifting in the air.

He followed the knight into the hamlet. They stepped onto a wider carriage road with deep marks for spokes, tufts of grass along either side, and some few walkers with carts, donkeys, and hounds. Some stopped to stare as the pair walked, some frowned at Kief, and others ignored them completely. After a few more yards the knight, with boy in tow, came upon The Lone Horseman.

The tavern had been Kief's home for long, scarcely counted years, and it was the first building on the road through Mondar. The proprietor, Tess Monteith, was a rigorous sort. She didn't suffer fools and had no fear of clapping Keif over the back of the head when he did or said anything foolish, but Kief liked her, admired her even. The Horse, as the locals earned it, was cosy and thatched. In front, on flattened earth, there were three rows of wooden benches and potted plants in a line beneath the windows. As they passed, a muffled shout suspended the quiet scene and birds alit from the rooftop. There was another shout, followed by a woman's scream, and then a bucket exploded through one of the tavern's low windows, the wicker lining splintering and falling away. Some townsfolk turned to gawp with their sacks of grain and hand carts.

The knight stopped in his tracks.

"It's those liegemen again," Kief cried. He turned and looked over the square and the same townsfolk who had stopped lowered their eyes and continued about their days. For many trihads, men had been coming to levy taxes twice as often as they should. While he would have liked to have seemed selfless and courageous in his next request, it was curiosity that led Kief to speak up. "Our men are away fighting. These take advantage," he said, his heart racing. He recalled the day the men came to round up churls, how he and some of his friends had slunk away and spent days in the wood hunting and camping. The memory made him wince.

"Any chance you'd say something? Being a knight an all?"

"I am not that which you think."

"Please. What about chivalry?"

"Molag Nul said nothing of... chivalry," the knight said. He stepped over the splinters and continued down the road.

"You're a knight!" Kief called after him. "Knights are supposed to fight. Don't you fight?"

"*Aye.*"

It was night. The knight of Nul could feel the heat of the Baoleth's breath. The rune on his breastplate began to glow. A chaos creature rippled in time and a smouldering claw reached through the blend.

There was a scream and another crash. The knight turned and looked at the tavern.

"Help them!" Kief cried. Still standing by the splintered wicker of the windows, hearing feint sounds of a scuffle inside the tavern.

The knight sighed. Steam, or ash, fell from his visor. "*That is not my task.*"

"Well... I'm asking. I, Kief of Mondar village, am giving you a task!"

The knight sighed again. He turned and then leaned his sword against a low fence. He crossed the courtyard and pushed through the doorway to the tavern. Kief followed at his heels, a wicked grin on his teeth.

Inside were five armed men. Tess cowered behind the bar, her blonde hair misshapen and her eyes fearful. Old Belroy, one of the village elders, was pinned against a stony wall by a man with a curved dagger. Belroy was grey and balding, with thin piggy eyes and a scowl that could and did make children cry. Kief hated him, but at that moment, he felt nothing of that sort. Today, naught but fear held old Belroy. Not the shocked, outraged sort of fear that you may see at the side of the road, in ditches, and in those fleeing war in long western trails. This was different. This was regular fear. Fear that had been felt so often that it was like one's own skin.

"You were warned, Belroy. Fifteen geffers a month. I'm a reasonable man. Am I not a reasonable man?" The reasonable man was in rusty maille, a ragged cloak, and he had a pockmarked face. Another one, the one pinning Belroy to the wall, grinned and licked his lips. This man was stockier, with a bent nose and missing teeth – little doubt as ugly within as without.

"This is a book?" the knight said. The room was dark, and the roof was low.

"Who the shiteteeth are you?" the reasonable man said, turning around.

The knight looked to Kief, *"You wish for me to kill them?"*

"Uh..."

"Kill us?" the man with the curved dagger dropped old Belroy and turned.

"I have never been inside a tavern before," the knight said.

Kief began to say a silent prayer and stepped back into the doorway.

"Has this knight had a knock to the head? Get a move on, ser. We are liegemen to Caspian of Monterio. This is his fief and we've come to collect taxes."

"I have been told of taxes, they promote public health, yes?" the knight said. The bar was dimly lit aside from a pillar of mid-day glare from the broken window. The room felt compressed, as if the roof, held up by an oak beam, was too heavy, causing the stone walls to slope gradually inwards. A few stools had fallen to the ground and there were several

barrels upright across the floor serving as tables. A flat, polished bar was the centrepiece. *"I am the Suit of Molag Nul and this... serf"* he pointed to Kief, *"says my task is to fight."*

Kief bristled.

"This *elder* is refusing to pay his taxes," the reasonable man said, stepping forth. He was shorter than the knight, but he looked strong and frightening. "I don't like all this talk of killing. I don't care what you're wearing, five to one is a loss in my book."

"Loss?"

The reasonable man hefted a great mace from his hip, four ridges in a shallow cross. It seemed to vibrate slightly. There was a rune on its crown of a bird's foot.

"I see," the knight said.

"You see what?"

"You have no choice. The crane demands blood."

Something shifted in the reasonable man's eyes and indeed like the darting neck of a still crane, he lunged, but the knight stepped back easily. The weapon sparked as it grazed the black breastplate. The rune on the knight's chest began to glow. In the centre of the etched candle flame a thin scratch, unseen until that moment, too began to glow. The suit stepped forth with terrible speed and struck the reasonable man hard in the face with a steel fist. With an eruption of blood at the nose he fell back, and his companions surged to his defence. The knight turned and swept a metal leg, crushing a shin, and then with the same impetus he launched another man over a stool.

The Baoleth's breath was hot. The gap in the Fogkeld had been shifting for trihads, following the lay line between forest and grassland. A natural barrier turned transient. Molag Nul stepped into the clearing, pulling his sword free from a leather scabbard over one shoulder. In the wind, there was a hiss.

The man with the mace pulled himself up as the knight hit another liegeman in the stomach, lifting him clean off the ground. A fourth man drew a short sword and brought it down on the knight's back. A hollow, shuddering *clang*. The knight whipped around and seized the sword by the blade and with his other gauntlet, he smashed the assailant's head into a sloped wall. The man crumpled, blood dripping from his ears. The reasonable man came forward, swinging that mace, but this time the knight was too slow. The mace sparked as it hit. A choral sound. A perfect tone, like a bell. The knight fell to one knee, a low groan in his chest. The reasonable man cried out and brought the mace down on the armoured head.

The Baoleth laughed, hissing into the feeble darkscape. A strange sound, quite unlike a Humaine laugh, or even a Darbhein laugh. Falling water, rising steam. The beast stepped out of the vapour before Molag Nul, armoured in black, with steely eyes. The Baoleth defied understanding, defied the eyes of countless devoured witnesses. It was a thing of claws and disdain, fire and formless ash-black smoke. It threw back its head and laughed deeply.

"Ahh, runic knight. This hast been waiting for thee." *Its voice was a crackle of thunder, a sigh through the trees.*

Molag Nul grunted. He leapt and swung his blade, cutting a great line in the Baoleth's spectral shape. The beast disappeared into smoke, laughing. Molag touched his forehead and from it a streak of white light cut through the smoke, emanating from the peace rune.

The Baoleth's form shuddered, its essence became solid in the white light. It hissed, saying "With finality. A meal worth remembering."

The reasonable man swung, but the knight rolled to the side. A rune on his cuff lit white, and in a blink, as if time stood still, he was behind the reasonable man. He drove a fist into the enemy's ribs. The reasonable man grunted, and the mace came around again, the air crackling.

The Baoleth laughed as the sword crossed its chest. More spectral fire came away. A great, black claw swung at Molag Nul, but he ducked. He fell to one knee and pushed his blade upwards, deep into the Baoleth's chest. It screeched and the grass at their feet lit up. Two dark figures in a pillar of fire. The candle rune on Molag Nul's breast glowed, brighter and brighter. Beast and knight disappeared into the blaze. A spectral finger reached out and touched that same rune, cutting a thin line over the flame at its centre. Molag cried out and drove his sword deeper. The Baoleth laughed, spluttering. A pained laugh, a fearful laugh. Its great eyes flickered and then it was gone. Fire rippled across the clearing and the knight fell. Ash poured through gaps in his breastplate, through holes in his visor, from his wrists. The suit fell back, one gauntlet reaching for the Baoleth as the last strand of it faded into the Fogkeld.

The mace connected with a deep metallic sound. The knight's helmet flew free and skittered across the room in a hail of dirt and ash. Beneath the helmet was nothing at all. A headless suit of armour stood up, ash billowing, hot and black from its gaping neck. The reasonable man screamed and fell to his knees, but the sound was cut short as a gauntlet grasped his throat.

There was a crunch and the mace fell with a weighted tone to the tavern floor.

II

A Town

"Saph, are you listening?"

Grappy, as the girl and Timmin called him, was sat on a low bench on deck, grasping his staff. He had a long beard and overgrown eyebrows and beneath those a pair of sharp grey eyes wreathed in sandy lines and furrows. The night overhead was soft. The sound of the water alongside the riverboat was gentle, and there was an occasional, rusted creaking of a lonely lamp hanging by a hook above them. The river Peden was one of the creeping calm rivers of The East Ward. It was wide and well-sailed, and Grappy knew it well. He was sat a mite uncomfortably with his back to the bow. His cloak flapped in the breeze. His hands tremored and he let out a little sigh into the night. His two grandchildren were at his feet, chewing at duhl biscuits, their eyes hollow. Grappy looked down on them with pity. They were lost, small, listless. Escaping things not meant for children's eyes. Saph was but ten and Timmin sixteen summers. They had dark hair and thin faces, much like Grappy had looked at their age. Timmin was tall for his years, and Saph wise, but still they were young. Though the night was wearing on, Grappy knew it was not a time for sleep or silence.

All the while he'd been spinning his tale, Saph had been fiddling with a long blade of grass that would occasionally flash a pale silver with the passing of the distant moon between overhanging branches, but now her gaze met his. Saph had the same eyes as her grandfather, near grey and glistering in the night's ebb and flow.

Grappy listened for a moment to the rolling sounds of the water against the side of the boat, the Adder, and to the many sounds of the crew pulling ropes, oars, or occupying themselves with any of the thousand tasks that keep a vessel afloat. The boat rocked lazily through the darkness. It was an old, converted raider's ship, though all its armaments had long since been removed. Now it sailed out the last of its days along the great lakes, coasts, and rivers of Brael.

"I was listening," the girl said. "I was just watching the moon on the grass as well."

Grappy looked at Timmin, who raised an eyebrow, and then settled his gaze on Saph, "You know, they say the moon was once a scale from the mother's back. It shines today as her entire self once shone."

Saph looked at her feet. Grappy sighed again and stroked at his beard for a long moment. "You know, this is an old story – older than me, and in parts even older than Molag Nul himself and so I'm prone to losing track of the ore of it, of the mineral parts, but it surely can't be so dull that a piece of grass better holds your interest?"

Timmin adjusted himself and hugged his knees tighter. He was wearing what little clothes he had from his home, and he shivered slightly. "I have a question," the boy said "Why did the men on the horses kill the others? Could they not they have simply spoken with them?"

"At the time, the men of Redheim and the men of the Braelian Empire were locked in a furious and bloody war – spanning the longer end of forty years, with neither side gaining more than a few miles in either direction in all that time. It was an era of fear and violence. Many died who didn't deserve to."

"What about that symbol on the knight's armour? The candle flame?" Saph said.

"It is the symbol of Nul. You would know that if you were listening."

"I am listening," Saph said, although her gaze was once again fixed on the blade of grass.

"I hope so. This story isn't simply about my father, your great-grandfather. The noble Kief Stroongarm. This is a story of all of us. This is about where we came from, and how we came to be," he gripped his staff tighter, the wood giving slightly to his grip, "therefore, my tale must drift onward across hill and dale, to another place, another person. Entirely different, but in many ways the same..."

* * *

A crow's flight away, at the base of The Copper Mountains, in a small bakery beside the refractory of Bastaun, a girl gazed out of a window. Not a glass window, this was nought more than a shuttered hole in a wall. The girl was curious and amused, eyeing the world like some half-slumbering candlecat. She was black of hair, and blue of eye, which was quite an unusual visage around those parts. Most near The Copper Mountains had copper hair and copper eyes. They say the copper gets into the soil and the crops, but Sen didn't tend to give it much thought. As she gazed out of her window, other thoughts crossed her mind, like the striking of great hammers on steel, sparks showering endlessly into the paving stones and gutter ways. Sen thought of faraway places and faraway people and of those terrible, secret things hidden beyond the doors of the refractory. Behind her, an older woman worked at turning dough. Her copper hair was tied neatly back, and her copper eyes were fixed on her task. She was quietly complaining to herself about one thing or another, as was her way. The sound was comforting, if a little irritating. Sen listened to the complaints, yet her eyes remained on the window.

This was her way.

Sen liked to watch the metalworkers in the morning, their wooden boots clacking on the cobbles outside the bakery and sinking into the mud as they neared the refractory. It was an obtuse-looking building, almost resembling some crouching beast on its haunches, tapering upwards in a somewhat unsound fashion. It had great stone walls, old as mankind itself, or to the religious, perhaps older still. Thick black smoke poured from a mess of chimneys, as spines up its back. Atop the roof and through portholes along every side of the building, a lattice of wooden pipes criss-crossed in all directions, taking sweet-smelling smog from the bowels of the stone.

Sen had never been allowed inside, never so much as spoken to the metalworkers, but that was their way. They were cautious, as their runework demanded. They were quiet. They would always give their orders on paper when they entered the bakery. Sen would take the leaves of crumpled parchment and pin them to the overboard, and she and Mog would set to arranging and passing pies from the ovens to the workers. Mog always said, "They daren't utter a sound, Senhora, lest their utterances turn to runes in the air. They also wear no metal or animal parts lest any latent runes in the smog stick to 'em, breathing arcane life into every which object, causing *terrible* consequences." At the word *terrible*, Mog would always grin fiendishly, the whites of her eyes stark as she raised her copper eyebrows in mockery.

"Like what?" Sen would ask, "Like what could happen?"

But Mog would smile and tell her not to mind, "Forget all that. They take precautions is all. Nothing happens, so there's nought to fret on."

The only talking that ever took place in the hillway of buildings that surrounded the refractory came by way of fellow shopkeepers and farmers, or travelling merchants or artisans, who came to buy the metalwork or bring supplies. That day was grey, as often is the case in The West Ward. Smog rose into the greyness and seemed, as soon as it were to trace the sky, to melt into rain, wetting the fields and the cobbles, running into the grass, and forming mud by the entranceway to the refractory.

Sen would stare out of her window, watching the metalworkers walking to and fro, carrying their bastal wood hammers and wearing their bastal wood shoes, made from cuttings of the ancient bastal trees that grew in a kind of orchard behind the refractory. The wood was so hard and heavy that it almost resembled metal. It was impervious to flame and impossible to scratch, and so it was impossible to lay a rune onto. Stories told of how the mother of all, Mesuda the Lonely, had laid her great body down as she breathed her final breath unto this world. A spine from the tip of her tail took root and from it grew the first bastal tree. They looked akin to fir trees, sharp and tall, with soft red bark, and needles that fell in a blanket all through the year. The needles made a fine restorative tea and when on occasion a full branch would fall it would be collected and treated with due care, and with the tears of giants and the blood of thieves, if such stories were true. All to craft the essential tools and protective garbs of the metalworkers. It was said that this had to be the way, for it was impossible to cut the tree with mortal axes and saws. The bastal trees were protected day and night, and a tall wall encircled their orchard. None were allowed in or out and from her vantage at the front of Mog's bakery, Sen could just see their tips tracing the soot-stained cloud cover.

Like most everyone in Bastaun, Sen wore a rough spun cotton overskirt and leggings, thicker cotton for the boots which had bark soles – for much the same superstitions as the metalworkers. Though the shoes of the townsfolk weren't made of real bastal bark, merely the bark of the surrounding pine trees. Bastaun lay deep in The Den-Woods, sprawling over two-thirds of The West Ward, and halfway up The Copper Mountains to the north. The woods stopped only for the river Brenn, which runs from the Grey Lake to the sea. Day and night the metalworkers filed in and out carrying sacks and tools, metal, and charcoal. Sen longed to look inside, to see them at work, or even to be given some clue as to what it looked like inside, but whenever she asked metalworking folk about it, they would make the sign for *patience*. Three fingers tracing a line on the palm of the left hand, slowly. The slower the trace, the more patience was required. Sen knew some signs; she knew patience, and she knew all of those relating to the sale of pies. She knew the signs for vegetables, pastry, bread, soup, and thank you. She also knew hello and goodbye, and one she suspected was a curse word, but Mog hadn't had the decency to clarify that for her. The rest of the silent language was a secret, it seemed. Mog knew more, of course. Occasionally, Sen would catch her having silent conversations with some of the older metalworkers when they thought Sen wasn't looking.

Mog said that Sen had been named for Senhora, the messenger hawk. Not that Sen had ever seen one. Mog always said, "They're the pride of the three kings, and even the secluded masters of Kammar love them. They're wild and free, but once you build a sky rune to call them, they'll take a message whenever and wherever you wish. They know the ways of the arcane words, and the ways of the wind, carving runes into the beaks of their own young, without a thought at all. They're beautiful and fierce, just like you." And then she would usually prod Sen's belly in a good-humoured fashion.

The girl turned from her view of the smog and the village, the trees and the faraway sounds of metal tapping, and runes being carved, and as was her way she resolved to ask Mog a difficult question. Each day Sen would ask a question intended to be more difficult than the last, ever questing to pry some new secret from the old woman's mind. Mog had a mind full of vibrant thought that seemed locked behind meaty doors of bastal and piecrust. Mog had a remarkable ability to talk for hours without saying anything at all.

Sen had been thinking of this latest question for a while, seeing statues and tapestries in the Bastaun Chapelry, and on elder carvings on the outer walls of the refractory. Finely hewn artworks, showing mythic scenes of the lost folk, and their many fables and knowings. It was a topic that most adults seemed hesitant to speak on because none appeared to know the whole truth of it.

The girl turned from her window and said, "Would you tell me about the Darbhein, Mog? Were they frightening?"

Mog looked up, pausing in her task for the barest of moments, "Well, I suppose. Had you not seen 'em afore they may be. Great scaled men, long rows of sharp teeth, but back when I was a lass they were everywhere, lived among us closer than other menfolk oft."

"Were they nice?"

The kneading of dough resumed, "They was like men in that regard; some was nice, and some was not. The real trick was getting to notice which were which. They didn't have the same expressions as us, see. They talked in the common Braelian tongue, but they wouldn't smile or cry. You had to look at their eyes, at the pupil."

"Like in a school?"

"No, the pupil's the black part in the middle of your eye," Mog grunted as she hefted her slab of dough, folding it and then pushing her palms into it. "But I'll tell you, they had little trouble speaking, friendly on the most part, particularly this one, Fenteh," she lingered on the word, *Fenn-taey*. "He had a lovely row of spines up the back of his head that shined like pearl, charming man. He used to sit as he ate and tell us stories. When I knew him, he was young, at least by their standards. Painted a fine picture with his words. He didn't work in the metal yards like most round 'ere, his brood owned Darson's farm. He was always on about Styrios, thought we'd like to hear about it since the Humaine weren't allowed to go there."

"What happened to him?"

"Well, none know. Last I saw him, he was sitting there in the window box, exactly where you are right now, eating a pie. He and the rest of his broodgang went off to the farm and didn't return the following day. Word is they were all called back to Styrios, some Darbhein politics, or some pox gottem. Truth is nobody knows where they went. Every last Darbhein soul vanished, and now it's been fifty-odd years and nobody knows if they's gonna come back."

Mog always had something to do, whether it was counting the change, cleaning the decks, polishing the bottles at the back of the bakery, measuring and collecting flour, wood, and yeast cake, or scraping dried dough hard as rust from the base of the rows of kneading trays. Behind her counter, Mog picked up a shapely wooden bowl and wiped out the middle of it with a rag. The counter was a firm timber piece with a wire rack for freshly baked goods. Mog wore a heavy apron, a pale blue that made the copper of her hair seem brighter and more cheerful. "When I knew him, he hadn't yet completed The Right of Stone. Word is they were always quieter after that. It was a ritual involving–" Mog seemed to catch herself there, "Well let's just say it was rather difficult, and not something for young'uns to hear about." She grinned, and hefted the dough into the bowl, placing a length of cloth over it for rising.

Sen often spent time with the other youngfolk in Bastaun. There was a school of sorts that ran twice a trihad, set by various members of the community taking turns. Most recently it had been Mr Fentshcook, the weaver, who'd been showing them how to work an abacus, giving the children sums and counting to attempt, "Say we have three apple pies from Mog's bakery and they're selling for half a pent each, how much do we need to buy all the pies?"

Sen didn't mind Fentshcook. He was a quiet man, like most folk in town, but there was an air of kindliness to him, for he had three children of his own, not like Miz Gabs, a mule-like woman who'd decided they were to learn dancing a few trihads before. Sen had hated every moment of that with every fibre of her being.

After the classes the children would always find a little time to play games such as twenty-rocks or gablefist, chasing each other around and roaring battle cries in the mud. Sen got on fine with them, though she'd always felt a little different, and it was more than the way that she looked. It was in words and moods. In the names of da and ma, and other such things the young called their parents

You see, Sen didn't recall her mother, whom Mog guessed had died in childbirth. Sen's father had been some trader who'd one day come into town and left the child behind by the bakery. One of the metalworkers, old Raggedy Ralfo, as the locals called him, found her by the horse trough, and brought her in asking for her to be fed. Mog said she'd been looking for a shop assistant, so she didn't mind letting a littleun stay, provided she'd help watch the shop. Mog always told that part with a wry grin, as if it was some firm and secret joke that Sen wasn't to be let in on. Mog herself had never had a child but had taken to mothering quickly. She'd always wanted a daughter, but never much had an eye for men, never sought any suitors, and never married. "Didn't see the attraction," she'd said when Sen had asked, another difficult question sometime before. Mog had said that she saw no use in marrying men, or women for that matter. "Load of faff for nought."

Though something about it evidently fascinated Mog, as she was never shy to share gossip from the town: like how Tetcher the farrier had been spending an awful lot of time with Jen from Fentshcook's weavery, always sneaking off together for walks. Especially since Jen was promised to that young soldier, the son of O'Leary from the pig farm. But all this had only complicated the idea of family in Sen's mind. She regarded Mog as a kindly auntie, which was comforting, but it did leave her with a somewhat uneasy feeling, not knowing who she was or where she came from, none even could recall her trader father's name. For all she knew, he'd died in some war, in faraway Redheim. There, Sen thought, that's it. There's a difficult question.

"What can you tell me about the war, Mog?"

Mog was busy pushing more dough into a crust tray. She flattened the edges and took a fork to mark the rim. She then draped a cloth over it and looked up. The question hung in the air. "Now why might you wish learning on a thing like that?"

"I thought…"

Mog sighed, "The war's been a great source of misery for a lot of folks for a very long time. Your questions made a pair today. I've always thought this war came about as a result of the Darbhein leaving. Humainekind vying for territory, power, and whatever atonement can be found at the end of a spike. It's a great pity and I'd rather not talk on it."

She kissed her thumbnail, the sign of Mother's cleansing. When Mog petitioned the Mother, Sen knew better than to prod for more. Mog was a devout follower of Mesuda, and the girl knew well that an evocation of her was doubly a call for silence. Mog would always tell a prayer or two before mealtimes and sleep, and would always recite the line that to hold an untruth was the gravest of sins, to hide thought from our fellows was unkind and unnatural.

Sen always found it an odd thing to say, as surely there had never been such a one, a soul without secrets. Even Mog, especially Mog. In fact, it seemed that she hid most of her secrets behind The Mother herself. It was something Sen had noticed in most adults she came across. There was always something hiding behind the eyes, always some word that could fray a mood. Looking up, Sen saw a hint of pain in old Mog's copper eyes. She looked back to the window, better to leave slumbering dogs.

Sen sat for a while, watching the metalworkers trudging through the mud, watching birds flit overhead. At one point, she even fancied she saw a Senhora hawk, but it could have been anything. The day wore on, Mog bustling about, occasionally coming up behind Sen and giving her some chores to do like fetching water or stoking the ovens, turning bread, or weighing the remaining dough. Before lunch arrived, Sen had finished with her tasks, and without thinking, she sat back in her nook by the window, the nook that once held a young Darbhein by the name of Fenteh.

But then something changed. There was a shift in the wind, and all the townsfolk looked up from their tasks. Breath was bated and there then came a flurry of movement up the main road into town. Metalworkers and traders all swept to the side in a worried silence, and a group of green-clad soldiers marched into the square, clearly visible from Sen's vantage. One held a banner, which fluttered violently. He was followed by a dense group of spear men, stamping their feet in a frantic, uniform march. Behind them were two horse riders. To see so much metal, and to hear so much chatter was deeply unusual. Sen had never heard of an army coming into Bastaun. Any metalwork that the king required was sent by carriage to Kendar, the city on the river. The metalworkers were mostly left well enough alone. One soldier in less armour than the rest, and in an ornate green tunic, stepped down from one of the horses with a long brass horn in one hand. Sen remembered her lessons on music with Miss Daisy and thought about the little sketch she did of a military horn. The man put the instrument to his lips and a sharp sound rang out clear, loud, and grating all at once.

All the folk of the town stood and stared, mightily disturbed by this uninvited metal music.

III

A Barrow

"Who was Senhora?" Saph said, splitting her grass between finger and thumb, an even seam, and then she separated the two ends and examined them in the moonlight. Below them, the water rocked and whispered.

Grappy pulled his cloak tighter around his bones and leaned back against the bench. "Did your father never mention her?"

The two children shook their heads.

"How am I to describe a person in a few words? Senhora was a great friend and ally of Kief Stroongarm, your great-grandfather. Great-Grappy Kief, you may have called him."

"Did she follow Mesuda?" Saph asked.

"Not as far as many do. I would even argue that most so-called followers of She Who Sleeps, are fools and opportunists."

"Even Mog?"

"No. Not Mog. Not in that moment, or in the moments which followed. The moments with our metal soldiers, hoof beats, brass horns, and spear tips, all marching into the tale of Sen, set to alter her life for good. And as that moment was fired in time's kiln, so too did the moment my father met the Suit of Molag Nul..."

*　*　*

Miles to the east, in a wicker tavern, a knight's shell stood up. Blood dribbled down the metal of its breastplate and rolled down its blackened greaves. Its movements were fluid and lifelike, and yet within the suit of armour, crusted in dried mud and ash, and spattered with fresh slickenings, was nothing. It stood there, reeking, tense, devoid of life, and with no head. It was as if there was some unseeable man within, with translucent skin and organs and mind, and yet even that was not right. There was something knowable in there, something which had shape and form, but nothing so mundane as a man. As the suit moved, ash spilt from the neck, small amounts, gently trickling, like the last morsels of flour at the bottom of a sack, floating into the nether and the warm air of the tavern. The suit took two steps. The first took it over the body of the reasonable man, and then the second towards its helmet. Tess stood there, aghast, stripped of her normally boisterous ways. She seemed under some spell, transfixing her in place behind the bar, old Belroy too. He lay where he'd fallen against the far wall, one eye watching the suit.

"And so, the claws of the Mother wrought up the earth, and from it, trees sprang," Kief muttered, but in the silence, his voice rang out. He was breathless, his chest was racing.

In the days to come, when he asked himself why he didn't run, first at the sight of the violence and second at the sight of this steel abomination, he couldn't say. There are many times in life when there's nothing to do. No action, no words; nothing.

Kief looked down at the blood and mess. He looked up at the knight, at the emptiness within. Kief was afraid. He realized at that moment that he'd never felt true fear before. He'd felt glancing fear of a beating, lively fear when talking to a pretty lass, and hungry fear at the end of a dry summer. He had felt the same fear as anyone else of his ilk, perhaps more so even, for Kief in earlier years had been torn from one life and deposited in this one. In that parchment moment, he'd felt a rolling stomach and a stone in his throat, but that fear could not compare. It was never fear of something before him. It was not visceral. Kief was responsible for this. He could have stopped it. He could have made a different choice. He could have stayed on his rock, smoking his pipe in the sun.

Kief's legs were shaking, his palms hot with sweat. He opened his mouth. Kief did not intend to speak, but speak he did. It was a talent that he had, one that would one day be honed into razor steel and stoked flame. He would one day learn the power of simple words, and when he did, he would think back to this moment, back to the way the words came freely and without thought.

He asked the only question there was, "What are you?"

The suit paused, standing over its helmet. The bascinet had rolled across the wooden floor and stopped slightly in a puddle of black blood from one of the fallen liegemen. The suit looked at Kief, or it would have had it still possessed a head, though the boy did feel as if it could see him in some manner.

"I am The Suit of Molag Nul," it said in its deep and hollow voice, radiating from somewhere within. It was then that Kief realised that when this suit had spoken on the hillside the words had come from within, from someplace impossible to tell.

The colour of the world drained around Kief, "You are truly nothing more than a knight's armour?"

"That, and a task."

Kief knew of many tales of arcane forces in the world with the power to bring metal to life and breathe thought into that which has none, and so another question sprang to mind. "Who is Molag Nul?"

The suit continued its stare, headless and dripping, and finally it spoke; hollow and metallic, *"Was."*

"Was?"

"He ought not to have died."

"Where is he now?"

The suit reached up, into the cavity of its neck and pulled out a fistful of ash, letting it drift from its gauntlet, the black powder falling slowly to the floor like a terrible hourglass.

Kief watched the falling ash and became lost in it. The tavern was forgotten. The stone and wood and blood. All of it was gone. He and the suit stood on a dark lake, expanding forever in all directions, nothing but it and nothing but them. "And where do you come from?" Kief said, his voice echoing into the darkness.

"I do not know."

Kief could have blinked; old Belroy groaned, and as if nothing had happened the two were again in the tavern. The suit turned and reached towards the bloody pool, grasping for its helm.

"The done thing is what I'm talking about, do you understand?" That's what old Sandy always said, sitting in her rocking chair by the fire. It was a grand wooden chair, with images of ornate grapes carved up the side, the legs thin and curved, and the back made of woven wicker. It was frightfully comfortable and endlessly tempting. Kief had in fact sat on that chair on one single occasion, only to be cracked sharply over the back of his head with Sandy's walking cane, her grizzled voice crying out, "That chair is not for the likes of you!"

She was a violent soul, always grinning wickedly when the mood struck her – when the mood to strike struck her. Kief thought about the chair, in the comfortable sitting room attached to her chambers on the west wing of the clan house. Kief could have sat there all day, swinging and rocking, reading, and enjoying the fire. That chair was likely burned to a crisp by now. "And when something isn't the done thing, it's not the done thing. You need to know the difference, toe rag."

"What do you mean, it's not the done thing?" Kief would always ask. It was a game they would play. Sandy was the name they had for their granny, but Kief could never remember why. Perhaps it was her sand-coloured eyes or the way she spoke, the way her voice seemed to slide through your fingers like dry sand, swirling and rolling through the air, catching in your throat, and stinging at your eyes. She always sat in her chair after the evening meal, telling tales. Kief and his brothers would sit, sometimes patiently, most times impatiently, for her to begin. She would smile, stir at a clay cup of tea and her rasping voice would fill the room.

Sometimes she'd tell a tale of someone they knew. Other times she would tell stories of folk far away, or of folk from ancient times. Rarely, she spoke on scripture. Sandy would speak on the ins and outs of the done thing, and why each thing was or wasn't to be done, and then she would tell a story about someone not doing the done thing. At that moment, in that tavern, Kief did not think of any of the hundreds of stories he'd been told. All Kief could think was that he himself had become a character in one of her many fables.

Sandy's work seemed to have done the trick, for every time Kief did anything wrong, he heard creaking in his ears. He felt the heat of the hearth, the spectre of a raised cane ready to strike, and Sandy's warm words, "Was that the done thing, young'un?"

At one time, the done thing had been to sit patiently and listen. At another time it had been to take the long journey toward the scribe's Oratory of Jeffet to learn the trade. At another, it had been to halt that journey and to spend nights in a tavern weeping, only to be offered a job by a rude and overbearing woman by the name of Tess. The done thing had then been to clear tables, carry drinks, and polish the flat wood of the bar. To bow one's head when Monterio's liegemen came calling. The done thing had been to take a quiet life and be grateful.

The suit collected its helmet, lifting it clean out of the blood, dripping and scarlet in the glare from the broken window. The body to the left stared vacantly upward, his head smashed, grey and pink matter oozing free. The suit turned the helmet over and put it on, or rather placed it over the rest of its armoured body.

Kief was still standing in the doorway, looking at the scene. It was almost beautiful in a way. There was a subtlety to each piece of destruction. The speed at which the suit had dispatched the men. The silence from both Belroy and Tess. Kief took a step forward. He was about to open his mouth again to speak, but that was when he saw it. The mace, shimmering slightly in the shadow of the bar and half-covered by the reasonable man's body. Kief bent down, admiring its strange beauty, the delicate craftsmanship that must have gone into its creation.

"Don't," came the suit's voice, somewhere in Kief's periphery, but it seemed so strange, so far away. It was an unimportant sound in the background, like the rush of a familiar river, or the sounds of a caravan on a distant road.

Kief reached down, grasped the mace by its handle, and lifted. It was surprisingly light. The head was made of two crossed flanges, pieces of metal the size of one's open palm down the haft, with a strange scene etched into them. An archer by the water's edge, reaching for a crane. On the next side, the archer shot a woman with his bow. The third was two archers sharing a drink. On the final side, the archer held a dripping heart in one hand, raising it into the sky. The metal was solid but strangely reddish, like rust. It was smooth and well made, not decayed in any sense but the colour.

"Don't," the suit's voice came again, but the handle seemed perfectly sized to his hand, there was a belt hook below suited to just his belt, and above the grip, below the heavy top was a single rune embossed in silver. A bird, a crane's foot. He tasted rust in his mouth, metallic, like blood.

"PUT IT DOWN," the suit bellowed. Kief looked over at the hulking, armoured form filling the room. Kief tried to drop the mace, but he couldn't. It was warm and safe, and something about it reminded him of home.

The knight, strode across the room in two short steps, reaching out for the weapon, but then something happened. It shuddered and then fell. The legs went first, unhooking and dropping to the floor. Then came the breastplate, the arms, and the helmet. The suit fell apart and clattered lifelessly to the ground, a cloud of ash rising in its wake.

Kief stepped back, looking down at the pile of armour and the corpses littering the room. Tess cried out, her tone cutting through the silence. She was young for a tavern owner, in her thirties, flaxen-haired with a long, hooked nose. She was tough but fair and had a way of brightening any room she was in, but that natural glow was gone that day. There was a note of fear or shame in her voice, a mingling of the two.

"What in the bleak was that?" she said, striding out from around the bar, "What devilry is this? Have you brought fade magic to our door, Kief?"

Kief had a deep anger within him, as is true of many normal folk, doubly so in those who think themselves more than they are, and at that moment this drop distilled. His hands began to shake as Tess continued her tirade, her words fading in and out of hearing. "They're dead," she reached down and put a hand on a crumpled form on the ground. All the liegemen of Monterio lay still, almost peaceful. The gentle sun filtered through the broken window. Kief's knuckles tightened on the mace.

Tess stepped over to old Belroy and bent to help him up. "Kief," Belroy said, looking up at him. Belroy was an irritating customer, always expecting more for less, but he had accrued certain privileges because of his status. He was a speaker on the village council, making mundane decisions like the time to bring the grain in or when a thatcher was to be hired. To his credit, he'd evidently been the only one to speak up against the unfair taxing of the liegemen who now lay dead and scattered at his feet. He was bald and had a grey, wispy beard. Thick arms from years at the fields and a voice like chewed leather. "You need to leave this place and take *that* with you." He gestured to the pile of armour. "A hung boy will do none of us any good. Where did you find this... thing?"

Kief stammered, "I... he was walking on the road, and I asked him to say something to the liegemen... I thought he was a knight."

Tess barked, "You thought you'd ask a demented arcanist to help us? Good god, boy. Look at this horror, look at what you've brought to my door. You think Monterio won't wish to know what became of his men? You don't think they'll come looking? You think no one in the village will speak?" And almost in answer to her words, there came outside sounds of village folk murmuring and approaching, surely in response to the ruckus within the tavern. Tess moved sharply and bolted the front door, glaring at Kief as she did so.

Tears appeared in Kief's eyes, to which Tess' view softened. Kief said, "I didn't know he'd kill them, I just thought..."

Then Belroy spoke again, "This is not fade magic, Tess. This is runic working. None that I've heard tell of afore, mind you." He gingerly kicked at an outstretched gauntlet. It made a clattering sound against the floor, but did not come alive, "We cannot be accused of cavorting with powers such as this, and neither can you, Kief. Monterio has spoken ill of soothsayers and arcanists, folk have been burned for making simple poultices or for owning twinning sheep. Take the armour to Rustgate, they may know something there, or to Bastaun. There they surely will, but the journey is greater. Rustgate is close, and they do have metalsmiths there, ones who work with runes, though they don't have the same mastery."

It may be difficult to understand the motives of Belroy and Tess at that time. They must have thought that sending Kief away would protect him. Perhaps they also feared to be near him now that he had been in contact with arcane forces, or it could be that they were all simply tugged by the winds of fate. All that can be said was that they judged it wise to get the boy and suit well enough away, hoping Kief would find safe harbour with runesmiths better qualified at identifying such an item as this armour, and to take care of the matters of murder on their own.

Kief swallowed, his fury bottled, hidden. Belroy continued, "Go outside, take the barrow, put this in there, cover it, and be on your way. You can make it to Rustgate within two days if you hurry. Tess, grab the bucket. We will set to cleaning before anyone thinks to come looking for these men."

Tess opened her mouth, clearly affronted at being told what to do, but then she closed it again. She walked out of a side door to the kitchen and pantries.

Kief went out the back door and spotted the barrow, an old, rusted contraption with a wooden wheel on the front. It was sitting by the pig trough. He wheeled it inside, past the bar, and began to lift the suit into it, each piece reeking of blood and woodsmoke. The armour was oddly light. He carefully placed a cloth on top and stood there shaking at the knees. Tess appeared at the door with the mop and bucket and a small woven sack. "Take this afore I change my mind," she said, putting it on top of the barrow. Kief looked inside; a loaf, a parcel of likely morid cheese, and two clay bottles of ale. He looked up at Tess, her earlier rage seemed to have simmered down to grim resolve, "Thanks, Tess."

"Be on your way, boy. Yer better not coming back for a while, but I wish you the best." There was a sadness to her voice now, the sharpness somewhat dispersed. Old Belroy nodded, and Kief breathed out heavily. He lifted the barrow and started out the rear door, once again bumbling on the step.

The village backed onto a birch forest, one where Kief had spent much of his time over the years: hunting, fishing, and playing at soldier with his friends. He thought of his closest companions, and how he hadn't said goodbye to them. He pictured the gentle breeze rolling through Ursille's hair, the curve of her neck, and the feel of her breath on his ear. She was a girl who lived a way along the road, and he knew then that he may not see her again, though he hoped to, once all this was straightened out. His grip tightened and he heaved the barrow over an upturned root, a lump in his throat. He felt the weight of the crane's mace on his hip. He didn't recall hanging the weapon's hook on his belt, but nevertheless, it was there.

It was strangely reassuring.

IV

A Fish

"We'll pass Neuport soon."

The riverboat captain, Kraf-Krak, had a hoarse voice – no doubt due to long years of drinking and smoking and heartily singing shanties: The Sharp-Toothed Sailor or the Maiden of Kingsport. Kraf-Krak knew hundreds of songs, more than most: The Quiet Blacksmith, The Fool of Bastaun, The Tears of the Grey Lake, and The Ghoul of Styrios. Music made him feel alive, and like he had company even when alone. The wise captain had tense arms and the darker shading common among Kammarites. His hair was tied back into the three braids of a learn'd man, and he had something of a wily shrewdness. He had, up until this moment, been at the back of the boat manning the tiller and giving occasional instructions to the familial handful of misfitting crew members who were busying themselves taking and giving yards, arranging ropes, and waxing oars.

The Adder was a long boat with a flat hull and finely hewn birch seams and slats. It had a broad sail for catching the lesser river winds, and when at sea the keel could lowered and pushed back through a clever knocking mechanism for stability in the chop. It also had seats and slats for four oarsmen like most rivercraft. Any sea journeys would hug the coastline, for there was little chance the Adder could survive a lengthy deep-water voyage. There was a single level below the rear of the deck with cabin quarters, storage, a poor excuse for a kitchen, and the captain's bunk room. At home on the river Peden, it slipped through the water as a serpent's tail. It was nothing so fine as what Kraf-Krak had once been used to in Kuh-Dul, but it was his.

He'd taken the small family aboard some hours ago, in Brill. The three, the old man and his two grandchildren looked ragged and blemished, but when the old man offered three golden braizen for their passage provided they left within the hour, Kraf-Krak made no qualms. Indeed, he made a point of not asking anything at all. Kraf-Krak did not enquire as to what their hurry was, where they were from, or even what their names were. He decided that it was perhaps best he did not know in case the need to feign ignorance arose further downstream. Besides, he doubted an old man and two young'uns could likely be involved in much bother. He told them to get comfortable at the boat's bow, then set sail along the Lower Peden, watching the dangling willow branches tracing both banks for much of the way.

When the willow began to part for jagged cliffs, the captain knew Neuport was looming. Kraf-Krak wished to take some time at the river town, a favourite stop of his for profit and amusement, and so he cat-limbered to the foredeck and voiced his intentions to the old man, who had been all the while sitting and sharing stories with the children.

"So long as it does not take long," Grappy said, looking kindly and humble.

"Needs must." Wants must. "I did not have time to get certain stocks in Brill, and we may not get the chance when we drop you at Remtaun. The guard tend toward moving passing vessels there. However, the night is still young, and I suspect I could gain what I need in Neuport." He put one foot up on the railing, every bit the striking sailor. "Any merchant is only as good as his wares, and if I do not have what my buyers seek, I may not be able to regain favour with them."

The captain didn't tell the old man exactly what stocks he was interested in. Le'ed blue rust plates. A most special metal made near the water wheels of Neuport, using the natural salt mined from the nearby Bell's Cavern. Through a part alchemical and part natural process, the rust formed thick and blue atop base metals stored like beeswax shelves in jealously guarded enclosures. It could be used for many sorts of wares, potions, and elixirs. It wasn't illegal per se, but its sale and acquisition were carefully controlled through long-standing arrangements and mercantile currents – in which the likes of Kraf-Krak had no place. Beyond their rare and protected status, if but a drop of water were to touch the plates in their raw and most valuable form, they would foam and spit and devour both flesh and stone. These Le'ed plates were the lifeblood of Neuport, as they had been since its founding some centuries prior – when the town had presumably been new.

"If you need supplies, you need supplies," Grappy looked up at the captain with a certain glint, and if Kraf-Krak hadn't known better, he would have guessed by that the old man knew fine well about blue rust plates, but of course that was nonsense. The codger was unlikely to know much about alchemical matters. In all his voyages, Kraf-Krak was yet to meet such a poorly dressed alchemist.

* * *

The captain returned to his post at the back of the boat, and Grappy looked back to the children. To his surprise, Saph piped up and said, "Could we get a blanket, Grappy?"

"Yes, could we?" Timmin said, putting an arm around his sister, who shrugged him off with a grumble.

Grappy grinned: a true grin, not a forced one, or a pitying one as most of his seemed to be that night. "All right," he said, "at the port, I will ask the captain to return with a blanket. In the meantime, shall I continue with the story?" Timmin sat back down, and nodded, "I'd like to tell you about the third piece of this puzzle, the strand that binds the cloth as it were; the thread that ties the blanket. She was sitting on a riverbank, much like this one, holding something wriggling and squirming in her hand…"

* * *

"It's hot and dry and there's nothing in my gills, there's nothing in my gills. I can't feel anything in my gills," the squirming

thing said. The riverbrook stretched far to the west, running slowly, and meandering tongue-like down sloped hills.

"You're a talkative one, aren't you?" said Drelle. She had madness in her voice, wildness even, but not as if she were quite lost to lunacy. Drelle was seasoned, road-hardened, and wrapped in a thick woven cloak. She was at a small inlet on the river Brenn, which followed a course from the Grey Lake, high in The Copper Mountains, rolling west through the valleys and hills until finally tending southward to the sea. Drelle had chosen a spot on a lay line, at a point where hillside met forest, and had scrabbled down a pebble-strewn riverbank to perch herself on a large flat rock on the water. She then called a fish into her open hand. The fish ceased flapping and squirming for a moment and looked up at Drelle with one glassy eye. It shrieked into the thrumm. *"It talks, it talks, it talks."*

It was an old salmon, chosen for its bravery and intelligence, its thousand scales glittering in the sunshine. The river made a gentle babbling sound, in wet contrast to the fish's cries of fear, pain, and surprise. The trees behind Drelle sighed discontentedly.

"I don't like doing this – but needs must."

She flopped the gasping salmon onto the rock and opened her satchel, pushing several vials of powders and liquids to one side. She produced a small crystal bottle, removed the wooden stopper, and out came a glass straw with it. She let out a shaky breath and dropped an inch of foul-smelling tincture onto the wriggling water kin.

It was a fine day, too fine for such work. The fish's voice was clear and shrill in the midday sun, *"It's hot, it's hot, it talks, it talks–"* but as soon as the drop landed, the fish shuddered. Its eye glazed over, and it lay still.

Drelle rested a grimy hand on the scaled and lifeless muscle and uttered a rune. The fish shuddered again. She could feel its silvery soul beneath her fingers. "I wish I could have done without." Drelle sighed again and produced a knife, slitting the fish's belly in one fluid movement. Blood mixed with the damp on the slate stone, and she reached in, felt around, and then there, hard and circular: the ovulum. She pulled it out, a perfect sphere of blue gemstone, a faint glow in the light.

"Mmm," she said, "a wise fish makes a large stone."

She put the ovulum into her satchel with the rest; dune-fox, robin, and pine-lizard. She stood and called out, "Pecham," and down from the woods flew a crow. His ink wings shone in the light in many colours. He circled once and then landed on a nearby root, which twisted thick and gnarled from the riverbank.

"Pecham," the crow said, regarding Drelle with a stern eye.

"I wish you were so wise, Pecham," she half-smiled and then reached again into her bag. She brought out a single corenut and unwrapped it from its green spined shell.

"Wise Pecham," the crow said, *"Drelle is a fool."*

"Just tell them that I've found the final one. We may begin tomorrow." The trees groaned their satisfaction, and the bird lifted his wings. He eyed her sullenly and looked at the nut in her hand. "And this is for your trouble." Drelle reached out and handed the nut to Pecham, who took it greedily, dropping it on the rock to peck it apart with several sharp jabs. The crow swallowed mashed nut and then looked back at her, cocking his head to one side.

"Pecham will tell."

"Thank you, Pecham."

"Thank you, Drelle. Thank you, Pecham."

Pecham was a rude crow at the best of times, but he was loyal. A rare enough trait in any bird. He'd been with her for many years, carrying messages, spying, and making light, if frustrating, conversation.

Pecham flew off. Drelle leaned back on her rock and closed her eyes. She had a sharp jaw and ragged, wind-strewn hair that seemed, ever so slightly, to change colours in the light, from black to brown to white – it was even said to occasionally resemble green. Drelle hummed a song of the forest, and the forest hummed back, and she sat for a while lamenting the lives she'd taken. It pained her, but a promise was just that, and her word was as true as any knight's. Truer even, for untruths might break the forest's faith in her, which would spell misfortune for many, especially her. After a time of sitting and breathing the sweet river air, she sat up and once again lifted the lifeless fish. She gently placed it in a shallow eddy and watched it drift downstream, its blood following in a cloud of maroon. "Life to life," she said and stood up.

Drelle of Coldharbr could count the number of animals she'd killed on one hand: five to be exact, three of which had been in the last trihad. They – she, for she took this work alone, needed the ovulae to build a scry. A promise not made by her but by her master, and one she intended to keep. Time was known to pass differently in the Fogkeld, but the Kammar master's arithmetic was exact. They'd agreed that fifty years would do. To Drelle, that time had been all her life and then some, but to the masters, with their infinite writings and scrolls, time meant little. "I hope you finished it, Nul," Drelle said into the wind. "We don't do so well unwatched, do we?"

At that, the forest laughed.

Drelle stood up, hefted her staff, and looked westward. She knew she could make way before nightfall if she walked all day.

Following the river Brenn southwest, it was impossible to mistake the ancient road to Bastaun, marked by signs and the constant trail of smoke from the refractory. Drelle hadn't been for many years, because it was a place she did not like, with its iron smell and silent smiths, mud, and cobblestones. It was in the heart of the forest, but it was also so far removed from the forest. The thought of it tightened her back teeth – but needs did, should, and would, must. Drelle was used to walking and so she went on her way, admiring the river and the sun, the trees, and the wind. She started to whistle, and the birds trilled along with her.

Her path was long, and the hours dragged. Dusk was nearly upon her when she made it to the Bastaun road. She took a moment's rest at the crossroads, eating some wild raspberries she'd found and some bread she'd kept, and she breathed once more into the forest before turning north. She'd been on dirt paths and forest ways for most of the journey, but she was now on a well-walked cart road, covered in horse leavings and wheel tracks. It already reeked of iron and steel, but unabated Drelle continued her solitary march, the weight of the ovulae on her hip.

The Bastaun road was long and was broken only in the middle by a brick well as old as the road itself. At this well, Drelle had resolved to take a sip. She rose over a small bluff and looked down on it. A simple brick well, ancient and well-used. To her surprise, in the near dusk, she saw a young man splayed, with his back against the worn brickwork. He was whistling to himself, but the birds did not join his song.

Drelle continued toward him, unenthused at the sudden company, but still, she was thirsty. As she neared the sitter, a wren swooped down and said, *"Beware this one."*

Drelle knew that wrens were marked for their honesty, and so she took heed, putting one hand on her knife, and gripping tighter her staff. The young man looked up at her, with not an aggressive look. He looked more in the way a farmer looks at a cow at market. He looked up at her cloak and her boots, her staff, and the long dagger on her belt, and his eyes finally settled on her satchel.

"Afternoon ma'am," he said, cheerily. "You from 'round here?" He had a homely accent and spoke in a homely way. His eyes even seemed warm. He had long, matted copper hair and old dusty clothes. He smelled much like a gutted thing, festering, unclean. "See I was on me way into town, and I sprained me ankle, mayhaps you'd lend us an 'and?"

Drelle looked him up and down and said, *"Kulcak kruah glrven?"*

"What was that?" the man said.

"Oh sorry, I sometimes forget which language I'm speaking." She smiled, "You've injured yourself, gimmie a look." She stepped to him in two short strides, and he pulled up his hose to reveal a long gash in his leg. It looked dark and bloody, shallow, bloat flies hovered above singing their hungry songs, and maggots groaned within with the pain of their feast and their growth, and of their coming change. To most, it would have seemed like an awful wound starting on gangrene, but not to one such as Drelle. She could smell the corpse of the rabbit in the bush, she could hear the voices of the tiny worms moving through its flesh. She could smell the filth and gut life in the wind. She reached down, grasped at the edge of the man's wound with finger and thumb, and pulled up with a twist.

"Hold a minute," the young man started, but Drelle was too quick. The wound peeled off, a piece of rotting rabbit skin, and underneath a dirty but otherwise unharmed leg. The man scrabbled to his feet and produced a thin knife from one sleeve. From the bushes behind him, two more appeared: a girl of younger years holding a haggard crossbow and a burly man with a carpenter's hammer.

"Give us yer goods or there'll be trouble," the larger man said, stepping toward Drelle.

Drelle sighed, "Any other day, I'd have given you anything I had. All I have is of the wood anyways and may be replaced, but today I carry things much too valuable to lose."

"Ma'am, I think you misunderstand your position 'ere," the girl said. There was a bolt ready in the bow, and her finger quivered on the firing lever. "Give us the bag, the cloak, and the belt. Drop the stick, drop the dagger."

Drelle took one step back onto the road and said, "I am sorry, little one, but we're a little pressed for time. Let go of the bow or it will hurt."

"Excuse me?" the girl raised the crossbow to her pinched eye and so, without wanting to, Drelle whispered something into the wind. She asked the wood to kindly grant her a favour. As usual, the forest agreed that this favour was a fair request, and it did as she asked. Roots sprouted from the bow and wrapped the bolt and string. The robber cried out and dropped the seething crossbow, horrified. The large man ran forward, hefting his hammer, and Drelle hummed another fair request. This request was larger but still fair as fair goes, so once again the forest agreed. There, of course, had been times the forest had been in disagreement with Drelle, but with all that was at stake, it seemed pleasured to oblige – though its response was unusual in its sardonism.

Drelle didn't often ask the forest for violence. It was a difficult thing to ask as the violence of the forest was never vicious, only of beginnings and endings, of the growing and falling away of things, which is why on that day, and on many days when Drelle asked it such things, the answers were as uncouth as they were.

Two blue jays flew out of a nearby tree and buried themselves in the eyes of the man. He screamed, dropping his hammer, and fell back, scratching at his eyes, but the birds only dug deeper and deeper out of sight, writhing and squirming, screeching, blood-maddened. The man fell on his back, and after a moment of unpleasant struggle, he fell to the longest sleep.

"*Metha-dusa*," Drelle said, "I didn't ask you to do that."

Not all forests speak in the same voice, though Drelle knew the language of them all. Some were more forgiving, some were kind, some were brutal, and some had a sense of humour. The forest at the base of the Copper Mountains was one such forest. It had a name, long before it was named by Humaine and Darbhein, and Drelle knew this name, but she didn't care to share such things. The wind whistled laughter through the trees and the girl with cut hands from the crossbow turned tail and ran. The boy with the fake wound kept his grasp on his knife, despite the urine sweat on his palms.

"Come now, I didn't want to do that," Drelle said to him, herself irritated by the mess the forest had made at her request, "though, I have to say it pained me less than the fish."

A wet patch appeared on the trembling boy's hose, and he dropped his knife, still frozen to the spot. Much like a rabbit, Drelle mused. The forest surely liked that. She knelt next to the large man, dead on the ground, his head twitching as the birds ate their unnatural meal and said a quiet offering to She Who Was Lonely. Drelle also spoke to land and beast, and the elder trees. Gratefulness was another thing most forests listed on.

Drelle, somehow no longer thirsty, walked past the boy and continued on her way, seeing for the first time the great pillar of smoke from Bastaun. Today, it seemed thicker and darker than she recalled.

She could smell calamity in it and so she hurried along.

V

A Single Tooth

The Adder rocked gently and Grappy sighed upward. There were clouds of weatherbugs flitting along the riverbanks catching the moonlight and the occasional eelbird would dive like an arrow from the cliffs to catch them with a swoop of paper wings.

"It is said that Bastaun was founded long before the empire of Brael when the peoples of the lowlands were disparate, split by riverbanks and rock ways. They didn't like to speak of this much in my father's days, but there is an old tale of the origins of the Bastaun refractory. It was a sailor who regaled it to me when I was little older than you are, Timmin. I was on a barge down the river Ael, and myself and my companions would share stories by the light cast from spitting oil burners. The tale is of an ancient Darbhein scholar. A story of a storyteller. A telling shunned by nobility for it paints a different picture of the Darbhein than what they would have us think of them. The scholar's name was Gil'denon. One tooth, smooth of scale, sharp of pen.

He was a chronicler of the Hevamir, those very first Darbhein called to life from ash and blood. It is said that they lived thousands of years ago, born in a time older still. They were wise and noble, and almost godlike. Since their creation, they had lived as immortals until begging Mesuda the Lonely, the creator and redeemer, to live as men, and to love and hope and die.

"Mesuda granted their wish and laid down to sleep, as she will until the end of days. It was Gil'denon who first placed the tale into runes. This first generation of mortal Darbhein began as a peaceful people until the time came for their immortality to end. As is the way when life and death are at stake and all things gain value, they soon devolved into bloodshed. The first war, the war of the legion, lasted for fifty years, so it is said. It is also said that this first horror and destruction was what created the Fogkeld – the fade – a place borne out of fire and hate. Another world layered over this one, there and influencing, but to us unseen.

"The Darbhein Gil'denon, with his feather quills and runework, was peaceful and detested this bloodshed. Yet for all his wisdom, his words would make no mark on the hearts of his kin. He begged both sides to lay down their arms, but they were similarly proud and fearful, and so they would not. Gil'denon asked a Humaine man in a Humaine village in the Den Woods, who called himself Brael, for the Humaine were a new race and they possessed a certain innocent wisdom that Gil'denon saw as boundless. Brael was lythe and quick and he lifted his hunting spear that he used to guard his family from wolf and bear and said that Gil'denon should make the greatest weapon of all to cast fear into the hearts of those born into violence and to bring safety to those who were not. Gil'denon pondered this, as his mother Mesuda once had pondered before her tears became the Grey Lake. Gil'denon sat in a cave for thirteen days and thirteen nights, the first trihad, until finally, he stood up. He begged his mother to awaken and tell him the course to take, but of course, her slumber would not be disturbed, as it won't be until the clash of the world.

"So, Gil'denon stepped out into the night, and in a voice inherited from Her, called down a star and made a sword from its glowing metal. He took the words for peace and justice and carved them into his blade. He then put fire into its pommel and strode out to meet the armies of the feuding Darbhein.

"Five hundred met twenty score and ninety-nine. Gil'denon walked out onto the field holding his sword ablaze, but the quarrelsome Darbhein would not be stopped. A great many vengeances piled atop one another had led to this battle, and so hatred had turned the godchildren into beasts, reptile jaws thirsting for blood, scales shining in the moonlight. They charged one another, and Gil'denon remained in the middle, vacant as butchery erupted around him. He cried silent tears watching his brothers and sisters warring every which way. Finally, he raised his star sword and brought it down with a terrible crack of thunder. Thought strode across the sky and the clouds opened. Rock and metal, fear and fire rained from the heavens. Many thought it was the breath of the mother, and dropped their weapons, falling to their knees. Those in the eye of the storm knew the truth, that it had been the runework of Gil'denon that had called such fire from the sky. Many of the Hevamir died that day, and those who remained promised never to allow themselves to war again. A foolhardy promise, and a promise broken time and again as new generations mingled and conquered the middle plane. And so Gil'denon walked away from his fellow folk and instead chose to live with Humaine kind."

"Is there a town close by?" Timmin said, looking over the side of the boat into the darkness. He had his long tunic pulled over his knees, with his flank braced against the side. He shivered slightly.

Grappy almost seemed not to hear him, "Gil'denon built the refractory from fallen stars and taught his friends to work metal and runes to aid and protect their folk. He taught them to carve stories into iron, air, and stone, and with these stories, he gave a final warning; the Charcoal Law. When working at runes, to never speak, to never wear metal, and to never dislodge the keystone. The stone was smooth plinth that he erected at the very centre of the refractory. After Brael, his most loyal friend among the Humaine, had mastered the craft, Gil'denon knew his work was finally done. He laid down to rest at the foot of the basal tree grown from his mother's tail and breathed his last. With no carving or tracing, not a hand touched the keystone, and yet within it, at the very heart of Bastaun, his likeness appeared, etched in the pillar of stone. Watching and guiding, and taking note, as was his way."

Saph looked out over the black water, broken and swirling in places by unseen rocks below the surface.

Grappy continued, his voice merging with the hubbub of the river. "I do not doubt that you've heard the song, The Fool of Bastaun, or The Burner from Skike as they call it in Pallid. Well, on that fateful day, as Senhora looked from her window at the soldiers and the hornsman, and at the one still atop his horse – she saw history and song with her very eyes..."

* * *

The refractory of Bastaun groaned and a black plume of smoke rose from its pipework as if it were sighing its sullen dislike of the soldier's brass horn. The townsfolk gathered outside shops and on street corners, all eyes on the men in the square. The horn finished its crass tune and then with a flourish, the player produced a letter from a thin wooden tube on his belt. His untarnished maille and soft leather boots spoke of an easy innings. He also wore a pointed woodsman's hat, as was the style in the capital. The player cleared his throat, unfurled the letter, and held it ceremoniously in front of him. The rest of the unit shuffled, and the other, still mounted, horseman rested a hand on the pommel of his sword. Sen couldn't quite see, but she fancied it held a large gemstone, a ruby or an ashrock. The hornsman, with the distinctive air of one unused to stepping outside of castle walls, eyed the town with disdain and then cried out the contents of the letter.

"From the great halls of Lord Julais, the sixth of Braden, Lord King of the Brael, second Arbiter of the Covenant, Watcher of the Western Isles, and Sword of the Night. The following words are his and his alone."

The man cleared his throat again, peering out at the gathering throng over the tip of the parchment, "For the past one hundred and thirty years, the refractory of Bastaun has been allowed a certain leniency and deficiency of taxation. This has been historically unchallenged and respected due to ongoing relations with *heretical* peoples and unfounded superstitions. However, the people of Bastaun are citizens of Brael and therefore have always been under the king's guardianship. Therefore, it is with great regret that I, King Julais the sixth of Brael, send this missive. With the recent loss at the fields of Yonn, the plague of Redheim ever grows across the land. It is therefore pertinent that all the fiefs of our noble kingdom send appropriate support to the war effort. This means that a guard is to be stationed in Bastaun and that martial law is to be put forth. Furthermore, mayorship of the town is granted to the right honourable Lord Divish of Skike for the duration of the war, in its entirety."

At that moment, the other horseman kicked at his steed's hind quarters with a near-comical roughness, and the poor beast lurched forth into the square. Lord Divish was handsome, and as clean as his noble hornsman. He wore a shining breastplate, likely an heirloom piece that had never seen warfare. He was sporting a sword that did indeed have a gemstone as its pommel, though not one Sen could name.

The new mayor ran one hand through his tight blonde curls and surveyed the scene. The Bramleys from the greengrocers across the way were standing under the stoop of their shop peering out at the soldiers. Beyond, closer to the butchers, a group of metalworkers had stopped in their daily trudge, hands touching wooden hammers on their belts.

The blonde man opened his mouth and said something to the crowd, but his voice was nowhere near as finely piercing as that of the hornsman, so Sen couldn't quite catch what he said. It seemed he expected a certain response from the onlookers but, receiving none, he again kicked at the tired old horse, and it rattled its bones towards the group of metalworkers. He said something to them, but of course, they said nothing. They stared back at him blankly for a moment until the youngest of the group, Finn-Bar pointed at the bakery. Sen remembered his name, and his handwriting from his pie orders. The new mayor then turned in his saddle and caught Sen's eye through her low window. She ducked behind the wall and looked at Mog, who'd been standing at the other window nearer the counter. Outside, there came a chorus of clinking metal, as the soldiers crossed the courtyard.

"Get behind the counter, girl," Mog said quickly, and Sen scurried around, taking her usual position by the ovens. A moment passed, and then the door flew open to show the handsome blonde knight, the new lord mayor, followed by a group of weary and irate soldiers.

"What the bloody hell is wrong with these people?" Lord Divish said in a voice that was undeniably high-born, and unquestionably grating. Close up, he didn't appear nearly as regal as he had atop the horse. He had a plump face, which Sen suspected matched a podgy belly beneath his honey-gilded breastplate. He had thin wrists and a thin neck that seemed well suited to holding and swallowing rosy wine in fluted glasses, and under his mess of golden hair was the only true beauty of the man, a pair of deep blue eyes.

"Good day m'lord," Mog said, her voice taking on that familiar timbre it always did when serving a passing merchant or noble. Mog understood that such people required a certain finesse and sweet handling.

"Good day to you, good woman," his voice softened for a moment, but then grew weasely teethings again, "I seek lunch for my soldiers, what do you have?"

"We have ale, apple, beef, lamb, and vegetable pies. Yolked just this morning to gold the crusts, hearty and delicious. How many are you?"

The gracious veneration that Mog was giving him seemed a might surprising to the new mayor. He, as befitting his standing, had been affronted by the quiet, surly ways of the metalworkers. He relaxed and leant over the counter. He looked down at Sen and held her gaze for a long moment. He had a strange look on his face, a look that Sen didn't quite recognize. A hunger, almost. It gave Sen a certain flesh-crawling sensation, like a horde of wry geeters in heat on the cloth of a tent. The mayor's gaze flicked back to Mog, and he said, "We need a meal for twenty men, a selection if you please. And could you do me the honour of telling me who in this town is currently in charge? I should like to speak with him on accommodations for me and my men, and the legislature that the king has called upon me to instigate here."

Living in a town where words were scarce had taught Mog the value of them, the true understanding that only one with a lack of something can have. She could say in a few grunts what choice people could say in a grand admonishment, and so she set upon this so-called mayor with a familiar and sharp tongue that had often lashed Sen, fellow townsfolk, or merchants alike. "The leader of this humble hamlet," she said in a voice that was somehow both accommodating and, to Sen's well-trained ears, dripping with rudeness, "is the head metalworker, Fache Ironpiece. You can recognize him for his great beard. And if I may, I would take this opportunity to humbly apologize on behalf of the town for your welcome. You see, the people of Bastaun do not often speak aloud, least of all the metalworkers. The runework they do is highly dangerous, and so they daren't utter words in case their utterances meddle with the runic powers. It is of course far too complicated for a dame such as myself to fathom, but I do not doubt that his magnificent lordship could grasp it wholeheartedly. Education comes more easily to bluer blood in my experience."

The new mayor grinned and then held out his hand, not for a handshake, more with the back facing upward. Sen had never seen such a manoeuvre before and so stared on, baffled as Mog curtseyed deeply, took the man's hand, and gently kissed his signet ring. Sen would have laughed if not for the dozen or so hardened soldiers standing before her.

Mog then turned to Sen and said, "Fire twenty pies then lass, quick pace."

Sen wobbled but would not move. She was staring at the lord and his entourage, at their weapons and the steel. Metal in rings on their bodies, in beaten lengths on their arms, shining in the low light. Sen was transfixed. She'd never seen so much metal as wearings and adornments.

"What's the matter with you, girl?" the mayor said, fixing on her once again. She felt his eyes trace the nape of her neck, and then sink lower. She shuddered.

"She's merely unused to seeing such weapons, your grace." Mog said, and then she put a hand firmly on Sen's shoulder and whispered in her ear, "Get started."

Sen didn't need telling thrice so she opened the cupboard below the counter to pull out a tray of ready-made pies. They always made a stock in the morning and then they would batch cook throughout the day as needed. Sen lifted her tray and pushed it into the oven. Then, with a practised flick of the wrist, she pulled the wood out, leaving the pies behind on the hard stone over the fire. She then double-pulled on the bellows.

"Unused to seeing weapons?" the mayor was leaning more heavily on the counter now, stretching in a way that to him may have been an attempt at graceful manliness, but which only succeeded in showing the sag of his gut. "Surely the refractory of Bastaun sees weapons? Don't they make metal here? Surely metal makes weapons?"

"Unfortunately not ser – the work of weapons has been disallowed for a hundred years in Bastaun. Did the king not inform you of this?" The lips of Mog quivered, "Surely if they were made here, they'd be far more common."

At that, the mayor scoffed, "Unfortunately the king has more pressing matters than catering to the traditions of common artisans. Though, I suppose it's true. I for one have never seen a runic weapon, aside from the king's noble Chandiar blade, not that it's ever been drawn in my presence. Perhaps now that I'm mayor that may change. Some runic workings could turn the tide of this war, I say."

Sen took another tray, a nicer, polished one for serving, and placed it atop the counter. The mayor again looked at her with his hungry eyes and said, "You there, you've never seen a sword?" Sen had a sudden urge to run or to take the bread knife and plunge it into the man's bobbing throat, letting the juice run like pie sauce.

"I have not, m'lord," she said. Though in truth she had, merchants commonly had one or two guards with a short sword or a club, but in that instant, she judged it wise to fein deeper ignorance.

Lord Divish grinned, and her skin crawled all the more, like a pod of galfish in a froth, devouring a deer fallen in a river. With a fluid movement, the mayor drew his sword, and the men behind him silently groaned. The blade was polished so bright it was near white. Sen could see her face in it, her hair misshapen, her skin grubby. Divish hefted the weapon and then whirled it once, causing a soldier to step back. The mayor then threw it up, flipping it in the air and catching it by its bending blade. He passed it across the bar to Sen, as casual as if it was nothing more than a bunch of flowers. Mog gave her a look, but ignoring her, Sen reached out to grasp the sword's handle. It was heavier than it looked, immediately sinking her arms, but it was truly beautiful. A seam divided the blade of it, rolling down to an enamelled cross guard and finely wrapped, blue-dyed leather on the handle. The pommel shone a dull green.

"You like it?"

"It's heavy," she said.

"Perhaps a rune could make it light." He turned to the rest of the boys. "A runic knight in the making, don't you think? I heard in the times that they were common, even women could be runic knights."

"Return the mayor's sword, Senhora," Mog said, there was a warning in her voice.

"No, no. I like the way she's holding it. You will be my sword-bearer for today. What do you think about that?" He grinned a sharp-toothed grin at her, and Sen almost dropped the blade. A difficult question arose in her mind, *how hard is it to push this into someone's throat?* But she stifled the thought.

"Perhaps while the pies cook, you could show me to the refractory. You don't mind, good pie wench?" he said to Mog.

"I need her to see to the meal for the soldiers," Mog said, flustered.

"Ah if they're late, they're late. What's a late pie to the company of a charming woman," the mayor reached around the counter and took Sen by the arm with gripping fingers. Before she could protest, he quickly led her out of the door.

"Now, to the refractory. Let us see if they truly work magic within those walls."

The lord mayor led Senhora and his group of dishevelled soldiers across the village, passing townsfolk and metalworkers, curiosity and trepidation painted in equal measure on their faces. There was a certain stillness and expectation to the air, and as they continued onto the mud-speckled road to the refractory, a feint murmur grew amongst the folk behind them. Sen carried the sword in her arms. It was heavy, too heavy, making her shoulders and back ache, but it was beautiful. Sen kept glancing down at it, flashing with flowing reflections as they walked.

At the entranceway to the refractory stood two of the largest metalworkers, one held a hand up to the new mayor and his entourage. "You cannot enter with metal," he said. Rom, as he always signed his pie orders. Up until that moment, Sen had never heard him speak. He had thick arms and greying hair. Intelligent copper eyes, as well as a larger hammer than most on his belt. It was a sign that the bastal trees favoured him, giving him rank amongst the workers. He liked apple pies with extra honey slathered on the top. Sen could picture the sauce dribbling down his beard.

"I am an envoy to the king; I will enter as I like," Lord Divish said, his tongue slithering betwixt his teeth. "This town is a fief to the kingdom."

"You are as you say, yet still you cannot bring metal," Rom said. The other metalworker to his right breathed out slowly through his nose. "There's danger beyond these doors," Rom continued. He was huge, towering over the little mayor.

"Nonsense, and superstitious piffle. You will let us in, or you'll spend a day in the stocks."

Still, Rom would not move, the mayor's bluster washed over him as eddies over rocks. "No ser, I cannot endanger those at work by carelessly bringing in foreign materials. You may only enter if you remove the armour and the blades." It sounded like a most reasonable request to Sen, but Lord Divish was not to be denied anything.

"If I remove my armour?" the mayor turned back to his men, some of them snickering. He turned back to Rom, "Fine, perhaps I shall remove my armour and any metal in my possession, but on the condition that you place a rune of lightness on my blade. What about that?"

Rom frowned, "We do not work with blades."

"Well, now you do," he commanded, pulling at a strap on his breastplate to loosen it. "Gregory," he barked, and a young soldier scurried forth and began de-armouring the mayor. A few moments passed of grunting and ungainful exclaiming and there stood Lord Divish in his fine, florally embroidered underclothes.

"You will work at my blade, or there will be a punishment for all of your men. Are you in charge here?"

"No," said Rom.

The moment boiled and bubbled to the brim, but then behind mountainous Rom, the great doors of the refractory swung open. Steam poured out, and then came a large man wearing a wooden mask and a thick flaxen apron. He was slightly shorter than Rom, elder, but still greater in size than the mayor. He also had a gravity that Rom lacked. He stepped forth and the mask came up to reveal a jovial face over a tumbling, bouncing copper beard. "Greetings, I am Fache," he said in a voice as low as summer thunder.

"Finally, someone with some authority," the mayor said.

Fache spoke as if he hadn't opened his mouth in tens of years, "Blades are banned, but I suppose I could take a moment to ensign a sturdiness on the handle." It occurred to Sen that he may have been listening at the door before making an opportune entrance. "What say you to that?"

The mayor grinned all the wider, "Fine, that'll do." He leaned closer and spoke in a quieter confidence. "Now, are you aware of the meaning of my presence here?"

"I am informed."

"In that case, I should like to tour the refractory, and my sword-bearer here shall accompany me." He gestured to Sen, who felt as out of place as one could. Rom, behind Fache, wrinkled his nose at her.

Behind the mayor, a group of six or so men had removed their armaments, making a pile on the ground, and they came to their lord's side. Sen considered turning away and running, or dropping the sword and refusing to go in, but as ever she was curious. She'd always wanted to see inside. She'd always wanted to learn the refractory's many secrets. She met Rom's questioning glare and resolved to follow this incident to its conclusion. Curiosity and cats, as they say.

Fache sighed. "Come this way," he said, looking to get the unpleasantries over with as soon as possible.

Despite the many questions Sen had thought to ask Mog, she was still ignorant of the true history of Bastaun's founding, and so she didn't know the meaning of much of what she saw that day. The entranceway to the refractory was made of polished bastal wood, a long corridor which was the carved-out interior of an enormous fallen tree. Once they passed through, they came into a grand stonework chamber with its roof sloping to a point, with several doors along each side. The sounds of tapping and steam blowing could be heard from beyond. At the very centre of the courtyard stood a stone pillar with the face of Gil'denon, one-toothed, staring savagely out at the room. Sen wilted, tiny and adjunct amongst it all.

"Why are you here then, in your words?" Fache said, quietly. Barely a whisper.

"On orders from the king, I am to take charge of this entire region and provide the empire with funding for the war effort," the mayor said, meeting his pitch, but with a note of threat.

"The king's father knew better than to meddle with Bastaun," Fache said.

"The king's *late* father, Julais the Fifth, named his son king, and so his wisdom lives on," the volume of the mayor's voice raised a little.

"The king's wisdom should leave dangerous things out of the way of ordinary folk."

"The war is a dangerous thing indeed," Lord Divish said loudly. His voice echoed out unnaturally into the chamber, "and I'm starting to feel a sense of heresy on your tongue."

"You come here seeking riches, and blood. You shall find none." Fache said.

Sen looked around the room. The brickwork was clean and smooth, and in rows on each wall were three bastal wood doors, each with exquisite metal hinges and trappings, leading somewhere unseen, unknowable. Mingling with the distant sounds of tapping there was a low, almost imperceptible hum. Senhora had often dreamed of this moment, and yet she had never envisioned it so utterly peaceful and not, sterile, clean, but also murmuring with life. She deeply desired to slink away and get lost within the smoky chambers and iron stores and to leave these talks and frightening men.

The men before her continued to argue, their voices echoing strangely into the stonework. "Not riches, nor blood. This is to protect our hinds," the mayor said curtly. "Though if you would seek it, we can show you the strength of the king's arm tenfold. We are here by edict, to establish new tax relations and to bring news of new laws. And, as I'm sure you also have heard, as per the king's decree this dawn-summer, as per their historic betrayal to the empire of Brael, all Darbhein iconography is to be removed and destroyed, and a guard is to be set up here in Bastaun, all of which I will oversee."

"Betrayal? What do you mean?" Fache said.

"If you had taken the time to read his decree, if you can read at all, you would understand. When the Darbhein left to cross the sea fifty years hence, bound for some new land that they chose not to share with us, they allowed our kingdom to fall into disarray. The nobles that vanished, the warriors, and the soothsayers – because of their betrayal – are exiled from this land, and their iconography is to be destroyed. Your foolish superstitions are yet another example of their idiocy, rutting fiends that they were. And calling them mothers and fathers of Humainity is heretical and nonsensical. The mother created us Humaine to cleanse the world of their wickedness."

"To destroy Darbhein iconography?" Fache said. He glanced at the central column and then looked back to the mayor.

"That, for instance, will have to go," the mayor gestured at the ancient face of Gil'denon and then motioned to two of his men. Fache stepped forward, putting his hand on his hammer, which was paler than most, well-worn, and well-used.

"That would be unwise," he said slowly. "This stone binds the entire refractory, and the town itself. This is a most powerful rune, and you must not damage it."

"I am developing a certain distaste for the manner in which you are speaking to me, *blacksmith*," the mayor stepped forward.

"We were two halves of the same coin," Rom said in a low grumble behind them "half Humaine, half Darbhein. We walked the earth, they the sky, and where we met, the sea of thought." Sen hadn't noticed him behind her and shivered at his quoting of Laegoth's Tale of the Mother. Rom pushed through the fidgeting, under-clad soldiers and took a stance betwixt them and the statue-faced pillar, his hammer hefted.

"You raise that hammer to me, serf? Hand me my sword." The lord mayor turned to Sen, who hopped out of his reach. One of the guards grasped her shoulder and wrested the weapon roughly from her and then handed it to the mayor. Divish pointed the tip at Rom, but Fache quickly put himself between his friend and the blade.

"He does not mean offence," Fache said, "but we cannot allow this stone removed. Any other Darbhein images in town you may destroy, but this must stay."

Perhaps the mayor considered accepting this, perhaps at his heart he was simply fearful, and these strange people were merely a bewilderment that he was attempting to understand, or to bring to heel. Perhaps he was so ensorceled with his power that he needed to wield it, needed it coursing through his veins as cachtail through a beggar's. Perhaps he was taken by some fade thought at that very moment. Over her lifetime, Senhora recalled this happening many times, and under many different lights. The horror of it and the way it seemed so simple, and easy to the well-fed lord. Of all the things this memory became in Senhora's mind, the most fearful aspect of it was its suddenness. When terrible things happen, they do not always do so in laboured moments. The worst things happen quickly.

In one smooth and relaxed movement, Lord Divish punched the tip of his sword into Fache's neck. Sputtering, the old metal worker fell back, and the end of the blade came off with a slopping sound. Blood swam from the wound and his mouth, and he fell to his knees. Fache's great beard was quickly crimson-drenched, the warmth of it rolling down his chest and onto the floor. Then Fache, the hardiest and stoutest, the kindest and wisest of all the masters of Bastaun, collapsed to the ground, his eyes agape.

After a moment's grief, Rom roared and knocked the sword away with a mighty blow of his hammer, and then he drove a thick fist into the perfumed jaw. The mayor's head cracked back and two soldiers tackled Rom to the ground, while a third took Lord Divish by the arm, helping him to recover his senses. The mayor leaned on his dripping sword, gingerly touching a sweltering on his face, and then he said. "Tear it down, use hammers if you must."

The soldiers took Rom's great hammer. At the sound of the commotion, drips and then gushings of metalworkers appeared from swinging doors and iron-steamed surrounding chambers. They drew their tools and flew into the fray at the sight of their fallen leader. One of the nimbler soldiers dipped and ducked and scurried for the doorway. Hammers beat heads and folk clashed in the echo hall. Seconds hence there were sounds of swords being unsheathed, metal boots in the entry corridor, hard on the bastal, and vicious into the melee. A circle of soldiers gathered around the pillar, slipping in Fache's bloodways, and one brought the hammer of Rom against the one-toothed carving. A ring like a low gong resounded through the building as it struck.

Sen could only stand there in horror, watching the fray, and in the midst of it, on the floor, the light leaving the eyes of great Fache, who'd been partial to a pumpkin pie. Always smiling, and writing in an exceptionally small, lyrical font. Mog said that he was too cheap to buy more paper, so he used less. Sen thought he was funny.

The hammer came down again and everything seemed to hang in the air. The room felt hot, and the air thickened as if they were in a translucent sludge. The soldier wielding Rom's great hammer seemed not to notice as he swung again, striking the stone pillar, making another bell-like ring. The face of Gil'denon cracked with a piercing note that cut through the sounds of the battle, metalworker's hammers and fists baring down on the metal-clad soldiers. It all seemed so slow and strange to Sen, who had backed into a wall.

Rom, still held on the ground, screamed, "Your petty blood and petty wars weaken the lines to the fade!" And as he spoke, the words and the air they were made from seemed to shimmer.

The mayor cried out, "I have been given a *task* and I mean to see it through." The word *task* too hung in the air, vibrating, and the torches on the walls began to glow brighter in their glass cases.

The hammer struck the pillar one final time, and all of everything unfurled.

As Gil'denon's reptile face shattered, Sen watched as every brick, every speck of dust, everything in their close vicinity, rose slowly into the air as if pulled by strings. A line of light appeared through a crack in one wall and whipped across the room, cutting two soldiers and two metalworkers in half as they fought. Their bodies separated and they slumped into many pieces on the floor. Shouts became screams.

The chaos deepened and light and form seemed to twist and hammers and dust and salt whirled into an unnatural yet entropic rhythm, pinning and unpinning moments and whiles in time. Rom barrelled out of the rising madness and pulled Sen like a child by her hand down the wooden corridor, which was beginning to rotate. Men and tools, weapons and works, falling and stumbling. Rom charged forth and, with the end of the hammer in his hand, he pushed open the main door. With that gentle tap, it lifted off of its hinges, floating upward and outward. Behind them they heard the shrill cries of the mayor, the fool, the burner, calling on his men to fight on 'til the death.

Some soldiers were chasing and fighting metalworkers out onto the mud-slicked streets. All had become bestial in their fury. Hammers crushed breastplates; swords plunged with sickening short sounds into fallen folk. People screamed. Sen saw old Medu, a merchant from Kammar, her black hair tied in two braids. She raised a sword to cleave at an attacking soldier. They were out of control, metal warriors going in all directions, blood-maddened, sacking the town. Medu was struck in the chest with a spear, and she fell back. She liked her pies cooked for longer, a few extra minutes in the oven until the crust was almost black. She said the charcoal was good for her stomach. Always lamb for Medu. On the other side of the square, Kerd was running, a young apprentice metalworker who'd been a few years Sen's senior at the school. A shy and unassuming boy now nearly a man, with long thin legs that were carrying him well up the road. A ribbon of light curled after him, and like a cheese wire it dashed through his body, and he fell into two pieces. He liked apple pies, steak, lamb, and vegetable. Kerd always ordered something different, grinning and making a peculiar hand sign that Mog had told Sen meant *variety*.

Behind Rom and Senhora, the colossal refractory bricks floated higher and higher, almost like a landslide into the sky, and streaks of light erupted from within, cutting down nearby trees and buildings with equal ease. The only things unaffected were the bastal trees, which were motionless amongst the chaos. People screamed. Soldiers, metalworkers, merchants, and townsfolk alike ran for their lives, although they knew not from what they were running, only that death chased close behind.

Rom suddenly stopped, and as if some unknown string had tugged him. He took a right, dragging Sen. The ground behind them rumbled and then split. The entire main street was swallowed by the earth. They raced between houses, down alleys, amid the crash and sea-like turmoil of great waves of sound and light shuddering across the road. Spheres of fire floated, growing and bursting as bubbles in a froth, melting thatch and cobble alike.

"Wait!" Sen cried, catching one last glimpse of the bakery. The roof was collapsing, and her window was already crushed closed. Sen couldn't tell if Mog was still within. She tried to stop, but Rom dragged her around another corner, following some invisible path, darting to and fro, avoiding arcane wrongness at every turn. Quickly, they made it to the edge of town, sprinted up the hill into the forest, and ran further still. They ran until their legs ached and they could not breathe. They ran until all the light had left the sky and only then did they finally look back.

"I didn't ask her about the charcoal," Sen said, vacantly. A difficult question that she had saved for a long time, *what is the charcoal law?*

Rom, choking on his breath, either didn't hear or didn't feel like responding. The forest was peaceful, undisturbed. They could see a distant light and a pillar of smoke rising from the direction of Bastaun. Rom made the sign for *rest* and sat down next to a dreng tree. He took his hammer from his belt, which Sen now saw was the pale hammer of the great master Fache. Not Rom's own, not the hammer that had destroyed the statue. Sen started to cry and sat down next to him.

Rom set to building a fire.

Act II

A Road

VI

A Woodland Walk

A crewmember rang a bell somewhere in the eaves of the Adder and there came a not-so-distant response from the shore. The cliffs sloped into steep riverbanks and there soon appeared a thin jetty on the port side. Captain Kraf-Krak appeared from his quarters, Grappy ceased in his story and he, Saph, and Timmin looked up expectantly. The night wind ruffled their hair.

"Here are we," the Kammarite said, the deck creaking beneath his feet. To his right, another crewmember was untying a rope from a metal stirrup at the edge of the boat.

"Good ser," Grappy said, his voice taking on a frail note, "when you go ashore, would you mind terribly acquiring us a strong blanket, and perhaps some oatcakes?"

The captain grinned and said, "Aye, that can be arranged."

The rope was tossed and caught by a shoreman, and the riverboat was pulled in against the current with much huffing and calling. The old jetty extended for a few feet and then rose into a set of wooden steps up a hill. Hanging lamps decorated the path into the darkness, and further they could make out the many lights of a small town.

"Welcome to Neuport, dock fee's seven pents a day," the shoreman said across the narrowing gap in an unusual accent. He wrapped the rope thrice around a hook at his feet.

"Seven pents, is it?" The captain said, stepping down easily onto the jetty.

The shoreman finished his knotting. "Thought that was you, Kraf-Krak. Your price is five, of course."

"And yours is one, as I recall." Kraf-Krak grinned and produced a leather purse, counted six pieces, and dropped them into the expecting hand of the shoreman. Grappy watched taught-faced, as if expecting something suddenly to appear out of the encroaching darkness, to claw its way down the duckboard and rend the wood of the boat to chips and steam. He said nothing as the captain followed the shoreman up the steps, quickly disappearing from sight.

"Have you been to Neuport afore, Grappy?" Timmin said, after a while.

Grappy smiled and replied, "Indeed I have, in younger years. Most every learn'd man passes Neuport at some junction. I'm not obliged to step foot on shore tonight, but mayhaps in the future, we will return and I'll show you the second-best pie shop in all of Brael."

"After Mog's?" Saph said, her voice thin in the night air. Grappy couldn't help but think of the way she'd looked when he scooped her up out of the hay in that wood shed. Deadly still, deadly calm. The way Timmin had started back, eyeing Grappy's staff. The old man stifled a pang of regret. A lifetime of such pangs had taught him to push the useless feelings downward, to allow them to harden into stones, and to carry those mineral forms in his chest.

"Mog's were indeed said to be the greatest pies in all the land, but I never had the pleasure of tasting them. I'm speaking of a Rustgate pie, from Old Shann's Tavern. Delicious. Gravy: warm, salty, and filling. Crust soft on the bottom, yet meltingly crisp on top. My stomach croons at the thought. And, speaking of Rustgate, or rather its surrounding lands...

* * *

Far enough away, in Brael's eastern regions, Kief may have heard a distant rumbling or a small shake of the earth, but the distance to Bastaun would have made it seem more like a falling tree or some other such sound scarcely worth paying attention to. Besides anything else, Kief's mind was on more current matters as he left Mondar village and began his trek, pushing the wheelbarrow containing the armour of a Nul knight. Kief left the village through the woods and then walked along the Yonn River which fed the Caliphar valley.

He was in shock still, a stunned ringing. A time not committing itself to memory. Kief pushed his barrow for a long while, barely noticing as the miles fell away beneath his feet. He walked over hill and dale, through streams and over scolding roots. The knight's armour for the most part lay still but would occasionally groan, or seem to, to the ears of frightened Kief. When the boy lifted the blanket, the pieces would still be in their clumbard pile. Motionless.

The forest that stretched from Mondar to the plains surrounding Rustgate was bisected in part by the Yonn, before the turn that led it back to the falls below the Gray Lake, the home of all the rivers of Brael. Kief knew the region well, being partial to disappearing into the valleys and woodland that mottled this worldway. For many years it had suited him to disappear for lengths to hunt or walk or read. He'd always enjoyed the time alone, but this was not so that day. The solitude Kief often craved over his many years living in The Lone Horseman had been a loneliness of choice, and that type of loneliness is well sought after by most folk. When loneliness is forced upon a soul, or when it's a result of one's own actions, it takes on a different flavour. Thoughts of sudden violence and the pained eyes of Tess filled Kief's mind like disturbed river dust. His heart fluttered as he pushed his metal load, not knowing what he would find in Rustgate. Not knowing if he would ever be able to return home. Lamenting that once again his home was lost to him. Twice now he'd been exiled. Twice, a place he'd once called home he could no longer return to. Twice he'd felt the blame for the events that had caused such things, but as they say; nought is real until it appears thrice.

Upstairs, in Kief's squat tavern room was a cheap lute. A shabby thing that had been bought as a gift the past spring solstice. It was carved and moulded of rosewood, with a warm tone and taught gut strings. Kief had been working the tavern for nary two years at that time and after a turn on a passing bard's instrument one night, during the mid-spring festivities, Tess fancied she had herself her own player. Kief had learned the strings many years before on his father's estate. Unlike his brothers, Kief had taken to music with ease, almost as if he only had to be reminded of it. Of course, after, he'd had no way to continue his practice so the joy of Tess' rosewood gift had been true. He remembered the way his heart had ached in his throat when he held it, plucking simple chords from its wooden frame.

Kief's mind went to his first night in Mondar. The stir within him. He'd been set to meet a caravan that would take him south to the sea, to study scribing, as was commonly the fate of second sons. In the late afternoon on his second day of swilling, a horseman arrived with a letter penned by one of his father's men, Riktor, sealed hurriedly with a thumb. The letter carrier, a merchant who had been passed the note from another, and another again, knew nothing of its contents, only of the coin Kief would pay for it. He'd been handsome and smiling, not stepping down from his horse.

Kief broke the wax over a mug of warm ale and his tongue had become stone. Riktor's letter told him that his father had been executed as a traitor, his lands had been stripped from him, and that the then king of Pallid, Femmek the Wise had called for the traitor's bloodgeld. The genus punishment. It was ordained that all those of the Stroongarm clan were to be executed and that their lands were to be burned.

Kief thought of Sandy, and his younger brother Teffin. He thought of the sounds of his mother's voice and finally of Creng, his elder brother and heir to the Stroongarm clan holdings. He was brave and noble, and at times cruel. Kief knew in that moment, as he grasped the thin parchment, that he would never see any of them again. The letter also regaled to Kief that the funding for his education would no longer be possible, and in fact, told him in no uncertain terms that his name was no longer to be uttered for fear of bloody consequences.

Though the truth of his father's so-called betrayal would not become known to Kief for some years, he still held on to the belief that one day he would learn of Stroongarm innocence.

It was a brand on his thought as he carried the accursed suit of armour. Many times, he considered dumping it in a ditch, a river, or scattering it in bushes across the forest. At one moment he even considered donning it but thought better. Arcane forces had already done something that he could not explain, and fear stopped him from meddling further. The horrors he had left old Belroy and Tess cleaning could not be forgotten, and so if something could be done to rectify it he would try.

Kief walked, grunting, and heaving, not stopping for midday or evening meals. He avoided the roads and paths and instead made way through dense forestland, following the line of the river, awaiting the fording bend, whereupon he would turn northwest and continue to the plains. There was wisdom in avoiding people and traffic, and with any luck thieves and cut-throats, which were plentiful. Exiles and deserters, or oftentimes benighted soldier folk, all wandering the last lands of Brael. The forest continued for a full day, as Kief knew it would for another half-day still, and then there would be the treacherous march through the Raegar plains. Kief had taken a journey there just once with Tess. They'd needed new taps for the tavern and the local smiths hadn't the patience for anything more delicate than horseshoes. They'd gone by carriage, and it had taken just one day and a night, with the two sleeping in the back of the wagon. Despite Tess' vigorous snoring, it had been a calm journey.

Long after night fell, Kief decided he should rest and so he stopped his barrow at the base of a sprawling oak, a tree known for its luck and pride, and so he was wise to choose such a shelter. He parked his barrow, almost hearing another groan from the suit, but looking beneath the blanket he saw only blackness. He hurriedly returned the cover and set to make himself comfortable. He gathered some brush and obscured the barrow as best he could, and then he thought of eating.

He made a small fire and took out Tess' sack of dried foods, but even as he examined each morsel, all he could think of was the stench of dead and dying. He thought back to the mess of the tavern. He drew in his thoughts images of Tess dragging those bodies out and burying them in the wood, cursing him as she did. A while passed of sitting in silence, feeling the throb of his feet and aching of his chest, watching the wander of his mind's eye. He began to think of rabbit, how delicious and filling a fresh rabbit would be. He thought of how it would feel to slide a blade into its squeaking ribs and feel its little lungs collapse. To watch the panic in its eyes.

Kief paused, staring into the fire. That thought hadn't been his own. Taking such pleasure in killing a rabbit was perverse. His stomach leapt, his throat lit afire and he fell forward, retching, nothing coming out. He sat back, trembling. He could not stop it. It began in his legs and came to his chest, his mind, his thoughts. His heart danced within him and his tongue twitched on cluttered words. His hand went to his hip. He'd almost forgotten about the mace. As he touched it, his trembling stilled. A delicious feeling of wrong-rightness, of stealing and sneaking and making others afraid. Kief's heart calmed and his breath slowed to a ready pace.

It was a curious thing.

He lifted it from his belt and held it up in the diminishing light. A cloud passed the moon and he almost saw blood running laminar down the cross at the top and the crane's rune, but with a passing breath it was gone. It seemed lighter than it had before, slimmer. Better suited to Kief's smaller stature. It vibrated slightly. He could feel its wanting, its hunger, and so Kief dropped it with a weighted thud to the leaf-strewn ground. He finished his dried dinner gifted to him by Tess. He stamped out the fire and laid down behind the barrow, hiding from all the world. Coldness arose from the damp earth. When he finally slept, shivering, his last thoughts were of frightened rabbits.

Kief Stroongarm dreamed that night of men with wide grins, many of them. All standing in a circle, with bows over their shoulders. The ground was littered with bodies, and beyond, there was a broken castle wall. The men drew daggers and raised them, stepping closer, grinning, firelight flickering across their eyes and the glistering white of their teeth. Kief looked down and saw a boy in his arms, his face a pulp, shattered, broken, bleeding. In Kief's hand was something heavy.

He woke with a gasp and cast about. The tree behind him was sighing in a breeze, morning light was white and low in the air, and just like that the dream slipped away. His hand went to the mace on the ground. It seemed elegant, smaller even, as if the cross at its head had shrunk. He ran a finger along the flat edges and was surprised to find them sharp. Not enough to draw blood, but each of the four sides had a definite point. He was sure the edges of the mace had been flat before. Kief sat up and pushed away the branches, ferns, and moss he'd used to cover the barrow. He then lifted the blanket off the top of the armour. It lay in a pile, still covered in blood and ash. The helmet stared out at him.

Again despair crept into Kief's soul. None of it should have happened. It shouldn't have been possible. But despite all he thought he knew of the world, it was real. The suit lay there, and Kief had been given the task to take it to the rune workers, whoever and wherever they may be.

He lifted the mace, a swell, a rising pitch, and without thought he struck hard against the oak's trunk. The blow split the bark and showered the soil with chippings. Kief found himself once again thrusting the weapon onto his belt. He could see no sense in letting it go, though it disturbed him, though it enlivened him. There was nowhere else to go and nothing else to do, so he lifted the barrow and continued on his way. There was half a day's walk ahead of him, and he suffered it in silence, crossing through thick forest, trundling between treelines and bluffs, his arms and legs aching, then burning, then smouldering to an accepting throb.

Once or twice, a strange feeling came over young Kief in that forest, a phantom of that misdoing to that oak trunk, or something else. A prickling on the back of his neck. A feeling of being watched. He would turn and call out but there came no reply. Spurred on, he hurried towards the plains. He made a quick pace, pushing and panting until he reached the edge of the forest and looked out on a wide expanse of grassland.

Rustgate, the most northerly city of Brael, had stood vigil for centuries against invasion from the clans and raiders of the north, its towering city walls a grey mass at the far end of the Caliphar expanse, and beyond it roared the river Brenne. Humaine and Darbhein had once worked together during the building of the city to dig a deep moat around the outer walls, directing water from the river. Kief looked out at the beauty of the scene and knew that he could no longer hide in the forest. He would need to walk the road.

Bracing himself, he lifted the barrow and rolled it down the grassy hill, angling toward the city until in the distance he could see the way, already brimming with afternoon traffic. Across the sky were clouds, streaked like spilt paint. Churls and serfs walked with packs, horses pulled carriages, and groups of soldiers marched along. Kief carefully joined the throng, which seemed to deepen as more folk joined from the mess of paths and buildings and farmsteads at every crossroads on the plains and soon they approached the city gates.

It was named Rustgate after an old tale. An ancient lord of the keep – the mighty warrior hand of Brael, Tumbar, had been away seeing to a marriage for his daughter in the South Ward. In his absence, and by some feat of ingenuity or treachery, depending on the storyteller, a group of ravaging northern kingar-men took the city for themselves. It had another name then, but it has been long forgotten. Lord Tumbar and his men returned soon after the city's capture and, knowing the secret of the runework on the metal gate, they scored through the arcane lettering. The runes that had assured the gate's strength for a hundred years then saw to its destruction. The gate fell into rust and the Lord Tumbar fought a glorious battle, winning back his city and henceforth naming it Rustgate.

Kief, following the throngs of artisans and common folk, entered the city and came to a great square. There was a pillory, empty that day, but stocks could be seen, and a hangman's noose swaying in the breeze. Every which way hundreds of folk went about their tasks, wheeling carts, and carrying all manner of produce. They called out to one another and drove livestock. The ground was cobbled and littered with debris, and not a soul had a care for one boy with a barrow. Kief stood in awe of it all: at the square, the rows of ancient buildings surrounding it, with hewn stone pillars, and more towering behind. He could even make out, far to the north, where the upper city was within an interior wall. The keep loomed over all, flags fluttering with the Tumbar gate insignia.

After a while of gawping and feeling about as small as a person can feel, Kief spotted a man sitting by the side of the road in rags with his palms outstretched. The boy decided a beggar should know which way to go and so he trundled up and asked, "Where may I find the district of blacksmiths and metalworkers?" He tried to sound old and world-weary.

The beggar leaned forward, missing teeth, and with rotting breath, and gestured toward the small sack atop the barrow. He smiled expectantly. There was a small piece of salted meat peeking out. Kief obliged the man, watching him carefully, and then placed himself between the beggar and barrow. All around them uncaring city folk passed and continued about their days, their thoughts, and their tasks. Kief noted that in a village all would want to gawp, but not so in a city such as Rustgate.

The beggar, after much enjoying the dried meat, and surely seeing the countryside on the boy's visage, told Kief where to go in a drink-harshened Pallid accent, "Follow the throng and exit the square to the north and west, you'll see another wide road that will lead to a market, from there Irongully is plain to see." Kief thanked the man and continued on his way.

To the north and west, there was a long street where sounds of much bustle could be heard. Stalls of all kinds appeared along each side, and a second square opened up. Beyond that was another street, this one thinner, and smelling strongly of charcoal smoke. A sign swung from a steel rod high above the junction with the word Irongully stamped upon it in Braelian. The way was lined with hanging baskets of woven metal, all kinds of vines and plants dangled from them, and people moved hither and thither. It was a beautiful sight, and quite unlike anything in Pallid, or indeed in Mondar. There were many shops, all featuring different tools and smiths. The buildings seemed closer together here, some in odd shapes, sloping inward and leaning against one another. It seemed to Kief that most were made in differing styles and that this jumbled collection of architectural chaos was the work of hundreds of folk for a length of time few could know. Most of the artisans seemed ordinary, not arcane as it were. Men worked billows and were hammering glowing metal into every which shape.

Kief asked another local for advice as to who the best rune worker in Rustgate was. He knew that surely only the most learn'd would know anything of armour that could speak. He was pointed towards a grand shop matching the oldest architecture of Rustgate at the head of the road. At the front of it stood a group of folks in strange wooden garbs hammering at metal and using delicate instruments to apply etchings and inlays in a far more complex manner than the normal smiths and farriers. They also seemed more efficient and serious in their business, not uttering a word to one another as they worked. Beyond them was a large door of black wood that Kief did not recognize at the time as bastal. He steadied himself and pushed the barrow up to the workers.

Kief had always been an accomplished liar; a goodly skill acquired over years of subterfuge, the truth of his origins ever hidden beneath layer upon layer of untruth, and as he strode in, all manner of deceptions appeared upon his tongue.

He addressed the first metalworker who met his eye, a short woman with short black hair, and spoke. "Mam, might I enquire as to who the master of the shop is?"

To which the metalworker merely raised an eyebrow and shook her head.

Kief would not be put out and feeling a wave of strange anger in his belly he said, "Please, it is urgent. I have an item that they may be interested in. It ... it was found near Mondar, and I have been tasked with returning it, lest it creates a great danger."

The metalworker sighed and put down her wooden hammer and led the way toward the black door. Kief followed, lifting his barrow over the lip of the entranceway. Inside, there was an array of complicated machinery, spewing black smoke. Metal and wooden pieces stood in a strange lattice, all connecting to dials and valves. In the centre of the room stood a wide wooden table and sitting at it was a large, grey man wearing crystal eyeglasses, reading a stack of paper. On the table next to him was another wooden hammer and a jar of ink. He looked up and surveyed Keif, who surveyed him back, and that strange anger once again roiled in his belly. Kief was not prone to anger.

In times before this, he had prided himself on his ability to remain calm even in the most trying moments, and so this rage that boiled inside him took him by surprise. He felt, not wanted nor let, but felt all the same a hand go to his hip. His gut twisted as it grasped nothingness. The mace was gone from his side.

He felt all untruth slip away, as is often an uninvited symptom of surprise. The woman gestured toward the elder smith, said "Kanrick," and then departed out the front door.

Kanrick, the master of the smithy, looked up from his papers, "You were wise to come seeking advice, but you should know that I cannot cure you of the crane's curse. This is beyond any metalworker, and whatever you bring to sell in exchange will not help either."

"The crane?" Kief's mind cast back to the voice of the suit, to the cry it had made when he reached for the mace.

The smith gestured to the front door, and Kief saw that his weapon, once again smaller and slenderer, had fallen at the front door. He stooped to retrieve it and felt a rush of relief when he grasped it. "I am not here about... what is the curse of the crane?"

The smith put down his pen and settled his eyeglasses on Kief. He stared for a moment before saying, "You mean you don't know?"

"No?"

"If you are not here for the crane, then what is it that brings you?"

"I... well." The anger festered and warmed. Kief's blood quickened.

The smith's eyes fixed on the barrow and then flicked back to Kief, "Something of direr danger than a crane's claw, possessed by a boy who does not know the weapon he carries. Curious."

"*Curious?*" Kief's rage boiled to the brim, and he yelled, "Could you explain what in the fade you mean by that!? The horrors I have seen in the last few days! I come to you for aid, and you peruse me like an interesting book!"

The smith stood up sharply, "And it's not eaten yet." He sharply turned and disappeared through a door in the back.

"Where are you going?" Kief said, hefting the mace but feeling it oddly heavy as if it were being dragged back towards the doorway.

"This smithy has been built to guard itself against such things, boy" the smith called through from a back room, "so I suggest you cleanse your spirit before we continue this discussion." He reappeared at the small doorway holding a chicken by the legs, "It's no man, but considering you're young and clearly no killer, I suspect it will do."

"Suspect what?"

The smith held the crooning and struggling chicken down on the table and beckoned Kief to come toward him. Kief obliged, holding his mace, his knuckles turning white. An image of the smith's face smashed into gore and pulp flickered in Kief's mind.

"Kill the chicken."

"Excuse me?"

"Take that mace and kill this chicken."

Kief paused, panting. The chicken lay there under the grip of the smith. The anger within him boiled higher, a white-hot feeling in his chest and then with a cry he brought the mace down on the hen's neck. One side of the now sharply bladed weapon severed its gullet cleanly, and like a gust of strong wind, all the fury blew away. He dropped the weapon and fell to his knees. The smith put a bucket in front of him and Kief vomited. Yellow bile burned his throat and roughened the back of his teeth. Finally, gasping, he managed to regain his legs. The tension, the rage, all of it had evaporated.

"The crane's claw," the smith said, "is one of the many reasons rune workers such as myself are forbidden from the crafting of weapons." He put a caring hand on Kief's back. "It carries a curse that demands the spillage of blood, with increasing regularity. The weapon will change to suit its owner and will grant them great skill and reflexes, but if it is not fed it will drive you to madness. Do you understand?"

Kief nodded dumbly.

"Yours, it seems, will soon become a knife." The smith sighed, "There is not much I can do. The claw is already bonded with your spirit. Removing the weapon will undoubtedly kill you, and refraining from killing will send you into madness. May I suggest that you take on a role that will allow you to satisfy the violent tendencies that will brew inside you, like as a soldier, or a sell-sword?" The elderly smith bent and looked closely at the item on the floor, seeming somehow both admiring and filled with distaste, "This is the first time I've seen one, but we are all told of them at the refractory. Was it always red?"

"This isn't... I mean... I didn't come here for this," Kief said, letting out a shuddering breath.

"Yes, you did say that" Master Kanrick stretched his back, cracking it in several places. "Why indeed have you come?"

"This," Kief said. He wiped his mouth on one sleeve and, standing up, he pulled away the tarp of the barrow.

The metalworker's sudden intake of air was matched by a hiss of steam from the machinery behind him. His eyes widened, "What do we have here?"

"This is armour of Nul," Kief said. "It came to life and killed some men. I... was told to bring it here to you."

"To me specifically?"

"To show to a runesmith."

The smith looked on with a certain nervous hunger in his eyes, "This is indeed something worse than a crane's claw. A suit belonging to a Nul knight, and a crane's claw with one boy. This knight will no doubt seek the return of his armour, and might I suggest that you not be present when they arrive."

"The suit told me the knight was dead."

"The suit spoke to you?"

"It walked and spoke and killed."

"Perhaps the crane's madness has already taken hold of you." The old smith grinned slightly. "I'm sorry, boy, but this is not the place for this. No suit of Nul can walk of its own accord. Such spirit work is beyond comprehension. Rustgate belongs to the king and if I were found with items such as these, great danger could befall me. Though, if this is truly something of the Nul, summoning them would be a solution..."

At that moment, there came a knock at the door. The smith quickly threw the cloth over the barrow, and said, "You should go into the back with your claw and in a moment I will decide what to do with you."

That was something that Kief's father, Lord Mulrek Stroongarm used to say, *"Stay there, while I think on what to do with you."* It was normally followed by a swift lashing or some form of menial punishment.

Kief rounded a corner into a small kitchen and he thought of the grey chambers of the Stroongarm estate. His father of course had believed it his duty to shape his sons into proud and noble men that he could send out to govern his lands in his stead. A fate that, due to his own failings, was not to befall his three sons, two of whom now lay as ashes on a Hemmec hillside. Lord Stroongarm gave them lessons with much impatience, taking time from his duties as steward to school his young ones. He would tell them of such things as taxes and war and the noble houses, not that Kief had a care for the latter. Kief recalled his words as he took a seat in the unkempt backrooms of the smithy, between mops and brushes, on a bucket for a stool.

"There are a number of reasons for war: land, for instance." The Lord of Stroongarm once said, "When the Gutmen of Lektek, a band of ravaging Darbhein axemen invaded The West Ward at the end of the 12th cenurad, they did not do so simply for their own enjoyment. Their lands had a terrible drought, and so they sought a new place to raise their young. Other reasons for war can be ideological. When Killik the Smitten proclaimed his new god, *The Risen Man,* he led a bloody rebellion at Blae-Muk-Tur. Had he won, they would today be living without thought or honouring She Who Sleeps. What other reasons come to mind, Creng?"

Creng was his father's favourite. He was the only one allowed to receive sword lessons. The only one who was let to sit in at house meetings, and the only one taken to clan moots, though that was because the eldest son would soon have to command those duties himself, and Creng accepted this fate stoically, if with a tinge of smugness.

There came a loud rap of knuckles on wood, jogging Kief's mind back to the metalworker's shop. The old smith called back, "You can come out now, boy."

Kief peeked out timidly and eyed the master, who had placed his eyeglasses on the table. He stared at Kief with a stern, yet kind look. "I apologize, there was something to account for, product-wise. Nevertheless, I have considered your situation, and I believe that I can indeed be of some assistance. I think perhaps the Nul will be pleased with us taking the time to return their items, and so on the morrow I shall gather some men and some carriages, and we will ride west to Bastaun. The master there shall be better suited to this task, and on the way, we may concoct some manner for you to manage your new... condition. What say you to this course?"

Kief stared at him blankly for a moment and then gulped and nodded. The smith stood and patted the boy firmly on the back, telling him to leave the armour, and then to spend the evening in a local tavern, the famous Shann's Tavern, known for its glorious pies. The smith handed Kief three copper pents, on the request that he pay him back in labour when all of this had been straightened out.

Kief happily obliged, ate a pie, and slept in a warm bed. The night was comfortable, for his back and feet at least. He turned in his straw bunk and looked at the mace on his side table, at the arcane beauty of it, the delicate artwork, and the elegance of the grip and his eyes closed as he listened to the noises of a bustling tavern.

The following morning, he awoke early and returned to Irongully, only to be greeted once again with something that would make his stomach turn. To his great horror and dismay, the street was abuzz with stammering conversation and the type of milling about that people do when a great tragedy has befallen a community. There was a thin string of smoke coming up from the rune worker's workshop, and the area was cordoned off by a single guardsman. The fire appeared to have been quelled in the early hours, and the damage to the rest of the street appeared minimal, but something fell in Kief's stomach. He asked someone what had happened.

"Old Kenrick must've been working late last night," a woman in a leather apron said to him, "burned himself to a crisp."

"Mother almighty," Kief said, and he strode past her, quite unsure of his strategy for the next moments, but as in many junctures in his life, he walked into uncertainty with strength in his thoughts.

He ignored the questions behind him as to whether he'd known the master Kenrick and went straight to a guard by the bastal wood doorway, untruths spilling from him like wine from a cup, "Good ser, good ser, what in blazes has happened here?" he injected the perfect balance of superiority and frustration into his voice, hoping to send the man off kilter.

The tactic worked, and despite Kief's slight and bedraggled stature, he shot to attention and dumbly said, "A fire."

"I am squire to the lord knight, Emmanuel Physik. It was my duty to take his armour here for re-enamelling services. Tell me, did you find this item, or are your men thieves as well as incompetents?" The name Emmanuel Physik had been a part of one of his father's long and arduous lessons and was the name of a knight of some status and renown in northern Brael.

"I'm sorry young lord, but we have been through the workshop and found no suit of armour."

"Curses," Kief said, almost dropping the façade, but then on second thought. "What of a half-rusted barrow, did you spy one of those?"

The poor guardsman thought for a moment and then nodded. "I do believe there was one such item, in the back passages of the smithy. Would you like me to show you?"

Kief breezed past him, "Do not trouble yourself. I shall be in and out in a moment. Please continue at your duties."

The guard stepped aside, and Kief once again walked through the bastal wood door. He felt the tug at the mace again on passing the lintel, but he kept a grip on it. The central room was blackened and scorched, emanating from the area that had once housed the collection of machinery and pipes. The metal had ripped away in several directions and was scattered in soot across the room. Where the table had once been was a pile of charred wood, and in one spot there was a dip in the ash as if something cumbersome had been lying atop it and had been recently moved. *The body of the smith,* Kief thought grimly. He held his breath against the lingering smoke and continued into the back. Sure enough, there lay the barrow, still with the cloth atop it.

He breathed out heavily and lifted it, but to his dismay there appeared to be nothing beneath. An empty barrow. He stared into the darkness and rust of it for a moment, unsure of what do to. What was Kief's task now that the armour had disappeared?

But then, at that very moment, something difficult to explain happened.

A rune appeared, white in the air, hovering about half a foot out of the well of the barrow. The glow became brighter and more intense. Kief blinked, and as if it had been there all along, once again lay the pile of blackened armour. It seemed to sigh and settle into its space.

VII

A Scry

Something in the old man's eyes had unnerved Kraf-Krak. There was a hardness to his stare that reminded the captain of the masters of the Algonorium, a Kammarite school of sorts. The same masters who'd rejected his plea to continue his studies and learn such things as spirit speech. Doleful old busybodies, and the very reason Kraf-Krak now had to scrape a living doing things he would rather not do, in places he'd rather not go. Masters sitting on their thrones, surveying the grinning aye-men and toe-suckers. Resentment flared within the riverboat captain, so much so that he almost forgot what he was doing.

"Will that be thirteen plates, then?" the merchant, Themmeran, said. She was a thrifty and altogether untrustworthy woman. She had a northern Braelian accent and rich, lavish clothes, dyed a deep red. She also had a hooked nose and dark hair pulled back into a tail. She and Kraf-Krak were meeting in the back rooms of her shop. It was a bare space with a table, a safe, and no window. There were shelves lining the walls, but they lay empty, and through a flax curtain behind the captain came needles of light from a swinging copper gerlamp by the front door. The shop was a place he'd always disliked. He disliked Themmeran and her sharp ways, and he disliked the cold and empty nature of her shop. It was always empty and Themmeran always seemed displeased to see him, in the depths of her unassuming yet eerily sunken eyes. As far as mutual dislike went, they agreed, especially that night. The hour was later than when the riverboat captain usually came into Neuport, which had certainly affected Themmeran's mood. Yet, the captain had grown accustomed to dealing with folk such as her, and though it unsettled him he felt overall at ease, at least as much as one could. Folk can grow used to all kinds of things.

"Chemist's dozen, did I not say?"

"Indeed, you did," she held out a hand for Kraf-Krak to shake and he took it. Thirteen blue plates stashed in the bottom of candle crates. He had earlier purchased his usual stock of supplies from the dock men and more honest merchants near the shore and had then disappeared into the darkness of the upper town to get his hands on the plates.

They were of particular use to alchemists for anaesthetics, accelerants, catalysis, and chemical cauterization. They were also used by rune workers, for the blue rust could be melted with ordinary copper to make a fine and light alloy by the name of Alumineam, which had innumerable applications. Though, such people tended to buy the plates wholesale, had writs of ownership, and had reasonable means to acquire them. Kraf-Krak's customers, like this merchant, tended to lurk more so on the shady side of the street.

Kraf-Krak paid the woman and stood to leave, upon her promise that the plates would be carried to his boat shortly, but then he remembered the last request of his strange passenger: to find a suitable blanket for the two children. Had he not remembered, he would surely have died in the following moment, but as luck had it Kraf-Krak turned just quickly enough to see the shifty Themmeran holding a curved dagger.

The Kammarite was no stranger to a knife fight and knowing quickness to be the greatest of allies, his hand whipped out like a striking snake and grasped the merchant by the wrist. He leapt forward and shunted his knee into the base of her elbow, and with no effort at all, he broke it. Themmeran screamed and doubled over, clutching her now dangling hand. There came a commotion from beyond the door, some calls and stomping of boots. Kraf-Krak knew she always had two guards and also knew at that point that he was not going to acquire his plates, given the injured merchant's evident sales tactics. He snatched his bag of coin from the table and darted for the entrance.

One guard was already in the doorway, holding a hand axe, and the other could be heard just around the corner. Kraf-Krak whipped his arm over his head and, with as much force as he could muster, he tossed his newly acquired curved dagger at the man. It buried itself up to the knotted hilt in the guard's chest and he fell backwards with a jingle of chain maille. Kraf-Krak almost took a moment to admire the throw but was roused by the sound of more movement outside. He leapt through the doorway, and without looking to spot the other assailant, he sprinted toward the lower town, ducking into alleys and leaping over crates with an almighty clamour. It occurred to him that if Themmeran was bold enough to attempt to slay him, then surely the true prize was the Adder. It was one of the fastest ships in eastern Brael and the likes of Themmeran had often noted it in their docks. Perhaps the merchant had debtors or certain costs that required a quick payday, and Kraf-Krak was simply the first poor sap who'd crossed her path. He cast his mind back over the last few months to bring to mind any time he may have wronged her, but he could remember nothing. Business in its purest form it seemed.

When he made it to the dock and he saw the Adder swaying gently amongst the skiffers and other rivercraft he noted with a grin that the dock hands had just finished loading the supplies, another turn of Kraf-Krak's famous luck. He leapt aboard, yelling to his men to move off. One went to untie the rope, but she wasn't quick enough. Just as Kraf-Krak had feared, a group of Themmeran's men appeared at the end of the jetty and came charging toward them holding blades and clubs. The crewmember on shore pulled a little knife and hacked away the rope, following up by kicking hard against the boat and leaping aboard as it pushed off. Kraf-Krak pulled a rusty broadsword from somewhere below decks and he and several other members of his crew readied themselves.

It was at this moment that his elderly passenger stood up. He'd been watching the ensuing chaos calmly. He pushed the two children behind him and, saying a word that Kraf-Krak didn't recognize, he lifted his staff and then slammed it hard against the decking at his feet. The little girl cried out and the captain fancied he saw a small spark of light appear at the end of the old man's staff. The boat lurched forward as if some great hand gripped its rudder and rent it through the current as a child bobs a plaything, tipping the rope cutter and Kraf-Krak clean over. The Adder nimbly and unnaturally split water with its bow and sped away downstream. Grappy stood tall, muttering incomprehensible words into the breeze, his long beard flowing over his shoulder and his cloak flapping out into the darkness. Sounds of yelling and the plop of missiles in the water behind them quickly faded into nothingness. Within moments, Neuport disappeared, and the boat slowed to a regular pace. Grappy sank back down, panting.

Kraf-Krak took a step toward him, but Grappy raised a hand, his eyes shining. "If you intend on soliciting extra money again through unscrupulous means, could you consult me first? I can pay you extra if needs be." Kraf-Krak swallowed and looked the old man up and down. He looked about as frail as a man could look. Grappy breathed out heavily and arranged his cloak once again over his knees. The boy beside him seemed to set his little jaw, and Kraf felt a rush of cold through his bones. The captain nodded but was unable to make words out of his jumbled thoughts, so he returned to his post at the back of the boat, promising himself that he would find the old man a blanket somewhere below decks.

Grappy sat in silence for a time, as did Timmin and Saph. The exertion had pained him. He suddenly looked terribly sad and lost, and after a bobbing, aching while Saph seemed to take it upon herself to cheer him up. She put a hand on his and, looking up at him with her big doleful eyes, she said, "Grappy? Was Sen as wise as you?"

At that, Grappy looked down on his granddaughter and seemed to note something, "Much, much wiser. As I'm starting to suspect you will be as well... Where was I? Ahh yes, in the forests surrounding the ruin of Bastaun, Senhora was sleeping beneath a tree."

* * *

It loomed overhead, great weighty branches reaching wide and far into the crimson of the morning sky. Thick bows yawned in the wind, whispering deep and ancient secrets that only they who could hear them could know. It was one of the elder dreng trees, as tall as a fir but with white bark peeling like a beech. In the remoter corners of the land, where travelling merchants were few and far between, their bark was used as a cheap form of paper. The sun was beginning to rise over the hillside, like reaching red fingers as Sen's eyes opened. Staring up into the canopy, she could see jepesnapes bounding over the branches, chittering to one another, their tiny fingers gripping and releasing with every swing. Their feathery bodies flung through the air much like their winged ancestors had once surely flown. Sen sat up and looked about her. Rom was gone. The remains of his fire had burned to a solitary red ash with a single strand of rising smoke.

Sen took a chilly morning breath, though it was not as cold as one might expect. Images from the previous day came into her mind quickly and without pause. The fallen window of Mog's shop. The ribbons of light. She gasped and saw once again the last inkling of thought leaving the eyes of Fache. Tears rolled down her cheeks and landed on the leaf-strewn ground. Looking down, Senhora noticed that there was a shape like a kite carved into the ground covering the area she'd been sleeping in. Beneath the diamond, there was another symbol Sen didn't recognize, like a circle within a circle, with a cross in the very middle. She paused, unsure of what it meant. Gingerly, she picked up a leaf and tossed it over the line. When nothing happened, she relaxed and stood up, crossing it herself. The air felt strangely chillier on the other side of the shape, but other than that there seemed to be no ill effect.

Sen's entire body was aching, such was the distance they had fled. She stretched and groaned and again looked around. Rom, whom it would appear was now the only person in all the world she knew, was gone. Sen had nowhere to go. As she rubbed sleep from her eyes, her stomach began to gnaw with hunger, but without any food in sight, she again sat down, this time on an outstretched root. She listened to the bickering of the japesnapes for a time and thought about what had happened, and what she should do next. She thought about what that mayor had said about the

Darbhein, how they were betrayers, and at the horror in Fache's eyes at the thought.

Of course, many people had their theories. The king of Brael resented them, as did all those who towed his line, Mog had thought politics had called them back to their homeland, and others thought some arcane destruction had cleansed them from the earth. Sen thought about the face of old Gil'denon, cracking as Rom's hammer was driven into it again and again. She thought of the pain and fury in the smith's eyes at the death of old Fache. She thought deeply of Rom, of his quiet ways and the easiness of his posture, and like a striking match; she knew where he was.

He had returned to Bastaun.

Standing up, Sen saw a trail of disturbed undergrowth leading downhill toward the town, and so she followed. The forest looked different in the daylight, less ominous. Still, beauteous even. Quiet now she had left the chittering featherkin behind. Gentle pillars of light filtered through the green canopy, silent save the rustling of wind through the leaves. Not a sound, not a bird, not an owl-fox. Nothing.

Sen walked for a long while, following Rom's heavy footprints. He must have been turned around as she soon followed the trail to a familiar slope that came down onto the main road into Bastaun, a good way south of the town itself. By then, the redness had faded from the sky and a clear blue morning was beginning to show its teeth.

She pushed through scratching twigs and grasping vines and half-tripped as she came onto the road. She looked around but then started at the sight of some woman walking down the road toward her. As the stranger drew closer, Sen could see that she was quite thin, with an angular set of fingers grasping a long staff lightly, and over her shoulders hung a rough spun cloak with a hood. The woman's dark eyebrows went up in surprise, and she halted in her tracks, grinning foolishly some metres from Sen, who was dusting forest particulates from her stockings. The woman's clothes were plain, mainly browns and greens, and seemed rather hermit-like. However, there was something in her stance that told of a certain grandness, especially in her face which was as fair as it was wild.

* * *

Drelle, the stranger to Senhora, grinned all the wider. She was quite surprised to see a young woman clambering out of the bushes. Not much so by the act itself, having clambered through many bushes herself over the years, she was more perplexed as to why the birds hadn't bothered to forewarn her of this girl's approach. This led Drelle to conclude that the birds themselves found the girl equally confusing. Surprises were something that Drelle had always relished, since to her they were so uncommon. "Well, well, well," Drelle said, remembering to use the Braelian tongue. "They say mages never meet accidentally."

Sen jumped back. "Mages?" she said. There were twigs in her hair and moss littering her clothes.

Drelle's tumbling hair was almost black at that moment. "A turn of phrase an old woman used to tell me. She was a cracked-pot." Drelle grinned again and leaned on her staff.

"Ah. Well, unfortunately, I'm no mage," Sen said carefully. There was, so far, nothing fearsome about this woman, but the past day had taught her that one should be especially wary of fools. Lessons learned at the most trying of times are often the most valuable.

"And neither am I! Merely a talented conversationalist. Are you headed to Bastaun?"

Sen froze in place. Much like a rabbit. "I suppose I am, but the town has been…"

Drelle heard a warning on the wind, not just from Sen's words – from the trees, from the birds: a *great fire*. No, not a fire. What is like a fire, but is not a fire?

Drelle's eyes hardened. "What happened?"

"I don't know, the king's men broke a statue and… it's *destroyed.*" The word seemed to float out of her mouth, shuddering into the air and then collapsing into a thousand flakes of ash. "My… friend is there."

"Come," Drelle strode past her and started toward the town. Something unsettling had happened there, something that was likely beyond the comprehension of this child. Drelle, being as she was, intended to see it for herself.

They walked the empty road in silence. The birds and the trees and the wind all hung in quiet themselves. They, as much as Drelle, knew that seeing was better than telling, and so the unlikely pair continued along. Sen had a hundred questions spring to mind. She wanted to ask who this woman was, what she was doing here, and most importantly Sen desperately wanted to ask her for help. Yet, something made her hold her tongue. Much like a mood that had occasionally overcome Mog, most often in the early spring, Sen knew that it was no time for difficult questions.

Eventually, the trees at either side of the road thinned and opened to look down the hill on ancient Bastaun. It was much changed.

A swathe of the town, splitting at the centre and arching up Duny's Hill was reduced to rubble. Smouldering timbers littered the streets. Bricks and mortar and dust and ash coated everything and floated lazily from the sky, greyer than snow. On the other side of the town, the destruction was more sparing. In places, buildings seemed mostly intact. In others, walls had caved in, thatch was burned, slates tumbled, and there were great scars in the ground as if some colossal beast had torn through a crop of mushrooms.

Unheard to Sen, but clear to Drelle, was a low and deep moan. The rest of the forest watched on in stunned silence, but the cry of the bastal trees was unmistakable, groaning as boughs in a storm. They cried for the people, they cried for their home, and they cried for him they called *One Tooth*.

The road opened and Drelle and Senhora walked a slow decline, picking their way between great smouldering craters, and chunks of brickwork and metal scattered across the path. The smell of burning and sulphur, and flesh, wilted the nose. When Drelle and Sen reached the first houses; or the husks of what once were houses, they saw things more difficult to fathom. Strange runes hung in the air, shuddering and letting off steam. Fires burned to and fro. Bodies and limbs were scattered everywhere, blood pooling and growing sticky in the morning light.

Drelle had never been one for runes, but she was indeed a master of the wild and spirit speeches, and so she knew the significance of each one before them, floating aimlessly like will o' wisps of the swampland, or bees of the pasture. They seemed made of air, and they sidled along, unpredictably, making sharp changes in pace and direction. Some were large, some small. Some wandered into the remains of buildings, seeming to vanish into stone, which would then collapse into dust in their wake. Drelle looked once at Sen and then looked back to the heart of the town.

* * *

She raised her voice and began to sing a song in a language Sen had never heard before. Sen shivered. The destruction and oddities that floated in the heart of the town terrified her. Her knees began to tremble, and tears once again stung her eyes. All that she had known and loved for all her life was now reduced to crumbled nothingness, strangeness. Sen heard the song of Drelle, but it did not register a mite to her. She was looking down in horror and curiosity. She saw some of the bodies that lay before her, grotesque in their positioning, and she swallowed. Sen begged The Mother that Rom didn't share the same fate.

Drelle began to walk further into the town, her song forming streams and passageways in the ether. Runes in the air shuddered and moved away from her, and Sen followed, not knowing what else to do. Unnatural shapes were carved out of the buildings and ground alike. Much was still afire. As Sen looked from thing to thing, death to death, she tried to reconcile what she was seeing with the place she had once lived. She tried to look out spots: the weavers, the stables, Mog's bakery. In the chaos, she could find none of them. She looked up toward Duny's Hill and noticed that an enormous face of some Humaine man had been carved across it. From a distance, it had seemed random and chaotic, but from where she stood now it was clear. It was someone she didn't recognise, but she was disturbed by the fear on his face, and by his eyes, black as charcoal.

The main road, just before the square, was now but a gouge in the ground, the last cobbles and paving slabs split and clinging to the cliff edges. Sen's eyes traced the edge of it to find the site that had once belonged to her and Mog. Much of that part of town had been swallowed including the spot where the bakery once had leaned. There, a nothingness hung in the air. Where once Sen had lived all her days; baking pies, turning dough, and firing ovens; was nothing. The void filled the air, filled her lungs, took her insides until there was nothing but a cavern within her. Then, as her eyes scoured the scene, at the very centre of it all, in what remained of the square she saw Rom cradling a young boy by the fountain. It was the one thing there that seemed mostly intact, a thing Sen had barely taken notice of in her last life. Water bubbled from a crack in it, but its stonework was otherwise as it had always been. One of the boy's legs lay on the far side, the other was lost amongst the dust. Rom was shaking. At the sight, Sen took to her feet, ignoring the cries of Drelle behind her. She ran around the gaping crater, feeling the air go cold, then blistering, then cold again as she went. She ran across the main road toward Rom, little amongst it all.

Littler still, she nudged him and he stirred and looked up with red eyes. Some twenty metres beyond, down the muddied path upon which had trudged countless metalworkers was what remained of the refractory. A shattered mass of stone and brick, pipes and wood. Strands of smoke rose from cracks in it all, and the corpse of the refractory seemed to rise and fall like the halting breaths of some dying beast. Behind the ruin, the bastal trees stood motionless. Tens of them, no longer surrounded by high walls and encased at the rear of the ancient buildings. They ached toward the sky. All of it seemed to frame and surround the ash-covered face of Rom, who was trying so hard not to cry.

The air was abuzz with feint, vibrating energy, emanating from the ruins of refractory. A portion of the ancient site had exploded across the hillside. Great chunks of black stone and bastal wood peppered the remaining houses and the forest. Piles of ash tumbled between the fallen brickwork, and blood seeped from fallen bodies, some in armour, some not. Rom patted down the hair of the boy: *Selt*, Sen knew him as. A new apprentice as of the past spring. On the floor next to them lay his hammer, newly made. He liked pumpkin pies. He stared up into the sky, glassy-eyed.

Drelle called down to Sen, from the top of the road beyond the crater's crest. "Please, come back up here. It's not safe."

Sen said, "Rom. Are you alright?"

"None survived, none but us. We cannot stay here," he signed, his arms still around the boy. Then he made a sign she did not recognize. She frowned. He gestured around, putting his thoughts into simpler movements, *"Not all runes have finished their task."*

* * *

Drelle sighed at the sight of the two across the crater and once again lifted her voice. A warbling, melancholic song. Rom heard it and looked up, recognition in his eyes. This was spirit speech, runes of the air, runes of the soul.

Drelle could hear music all around her, from the life and movement within the destruction, and that song melded with her own. Forest and beast often sang together when they feared something together. Their fear twisted and became images and ideas. But then, the bastal trees overcame it all, drowning the voice of the forest. These trees spoke not in a language like most, but in thought, loud and muggy with age. Their speech was moving paintings, each brush stroke burning into Drelle's mind. She gasped. She had never spoken to a bastal tree before and the sheer power stunned her. She felt as a gnat on a giant's back. The trees feared not the refractory that lay in ruins. The buildings of men and Darbhein were mourned, but not feared. It was something else.

A song sprang into Drelle's mind, a song known by the trees. Not a song of the forest, a song of the Darbhein. A song sung by a smith as he folded metal by a forge. A song of warning, of fire and blood. *The Ghoul of Styrios*. A song that the trees had heard once upon a time.

A tale of fancy, old as time,
Ought to open with a rhyme.
The feather brood, their feelings late
Began to scribble at their fate.

The ghoul of Styrios was once a man:
Darbhein claws and Darbhein hands.
He longed to rule, yet lived a fool
and asked a mirrored, bloodied pool.

To send him one who could dain
To gift him power to ease his pain.

And from the depths of that murky pool,
Came a face of bane and might
It roared and glowed and wrecked and burned,
And settled in Darbhinian sight.

It said, "Ask what you need of me?"
The Darbhein paused but thought little,
And he chose the creature's spittle.

He said "Make me strong, I care not how
I wish to rule this land.
I wish to tower above Styrios
and let all see me for my might."

The creature grinned and agreed,
And drew the power from all the trees.
He sang a song of strength and height
That gave our fool an awful fright.

The fool fell to his knees,
beneath the weeping willow trees.
His feet burnt and bent and grew,
and his arms and legs and chest.

He became bricks and mortar, fog and ice.
A tower grew and sighed but thrice.
Shining white and climbing high,
His foolish rulership was nigh.

Drelle could smell it, feel it. She saw it in her mind's eye, just as the trees described it: a fade gate, a doorway to the Fogkeld. A red and sticky puddle became an ocean that rippled with a breeze that was the breath of a great creature heaving. Reflected in it was an ancient tower, rising into a blackened sky. From the water came claws and fingers, and then Drelle was there. She was looking not with her own eyes, but looking all the same, through roots, and branches, and wheedling bark bugs, down on the collapsed remains of the central chamber of the refractory, a place she had once stood and made snide remarks to an elderly runesmith many years before. On the ground, by the shattered column that had once been the face of Gil'denon lay the body of the smith, Fache, and from the puddle came something that filled Drelle's heart with ice. A great claw tugged at the seam at the edge of the thick red of the blood, like a finger pushing through a wet length of cloth, loosening and tearing.

Drelle, in fear, sang or near shrieked to the old bastal trees. They were slow to move and slower to speak, but they heard her plea. Rom and Sen looked up aghast as the bastal trees began to grow, higher and higher, and boundless roots, as thick as Rom's arms, exploded out of the earth around them and began to converge on the crumbled refractory. A light, a flame, appeared within. At first, Sen thought it must have come from some fallen stroke of thatch, or some burning wood within the rubble, but then it whipped out in a way quite unlike any fire should move and lashed out of the ruins at the bastal roots.

Sweat dripped down Drelle's forehead as she sang louder, higher and higher until the pitch was beyond Humaine. Her hair streamed behind her, seeming to grow lighter with every passing moment. A storm of sound surrounded Sen and Rom, and the ruins of the refractory. They huddled together, their heads low, their clothes whipped across their backs. The trees roared into the ruins of the refractory, and in response tongues of flame batted them back. The spellsinger and the trees fought a vicious battle with the flames for a stretch of time that could have been eternal or missed with a blinking eye. All became meaningless as these forces writhed before them, like stags rutting before ants. In the very centre, a clawed hand began to drag itself through the rubble, huge and wavering betwixt the roots of the bastal trees. They only saw it for a moment, but then Drelle screamed, and the mass of roots seethed into the gap, closing over the hand, and cutting away a shadowy finger.

At last, the battle ended, and the roots settled. They now covered the refractory and a piece of the town. From the wood then appeared huge, veined leaves and as Drelle sang, her voice quieter now, gentler, the leaves and thinner tendrils of roots began to take the bodies on the streets and wrapped them, pulling them into the earth. Slow, soft, and grand, and with more feeling than any funeral of men. Rom watched, a tear rolling down his cheek as the boy in his arms was pulled away from him and into the lattice of bastal wood. He made the sign of The Mother and stood up.

Drelle finished her song, and all was still. She was motionless for a long while looking out across the lattice of roots now braiding the lower half of the town. She then strode across the now wood-covered gap by the main square and past Rom and Sen and into what remained of the refractory. The vibrations and runes littering Bastaun were gone, the low hum was gone, and all the fires had died. Drelle walked up and over the noble bastal roots to what was once the central chamber of the refractory of Bastaun, now a tumbled eggshell. She picked up the finger, still cindering and alive. The bastal trees gifted her a length of bark and she placed the finger within, wrapping it. "It seems you didn't finish, Molag," she said with gravel in her mouth.

Drelle then turned away sharply. The bastal trees were still grumbling, low and subdued, begging to be alone. She gestured to Rom and Sen as she passed them, and they stood and followed, unsure of what it was they'd just witnessed.

* * *

All now was at peace, and the clean air seemed to sigh and slow to a breeze around them. Senhora looked back one last time at the space where Mog's shop had once stood and left the centre square, cutting between craters and rubble, and tree roots. Sen hoped that the trees had found Mog and that she would find peace with them, though her heart filled with glass at the thought. The three walked in silence until they reached the road. Drelle then turned to Rom. Her voice was brittle in the calm air, and she seemed mightily tired from her ordeal.

Sen looked up at her in awe, but Rom seemed wary.

"I came here in need of a rune worker, and it seems that I was too late to stop it from seizing its chance. I would ask you for your help." The road was calm, save the chittering of a small group of japesnapes somewhere beyond the treeline.

Rom made a questioning sign with his hand.

Drelle rolled her eyes and then responded with a flurry of her own hand symbols. Sen looked on as the two had a furious discussion, too quick for her to read. Something about *The Fade*, and about *souls*, and *armour*, and repeating, again and again, a symbol she didn't recognize. It was like *direction*, but not.

Rom seemed to want no part in whatever she was asking him, but she was insistent, eventually forgoing the hand speech and crying aloud, "If you don't help me make it, and the Baoleth breaches into our world, all we know shall die. Bastaun is but a trifle compared to the destruction it would wreak. Would you allow that? Could you allow yourself to be the cause, again?"

Rom looked as if a sword had been plunged into his heart. How could she have known, Sen thought. Had he told her?

Rom shook his head.

"Then you will help me?"

The smith nodded dumbly.

Sen, who'd been standing in silence, felt her mind grip upon another difficult question. As simple as a mixture forming into dough and rolling onto a tabletop. She thought of that Darbhein statue of old Gil'denon and then asked, "Is there a soul in every rune?"

Drelle turned to her and flashed well-used teeth. "I knew you were a mage. All this you will learn, and more, but for now there's little time. Do not worry. You are with me now and no harm shall come to you. The Mother has brought you two onto my most tumultuous of paths, and I believe she has made a wise decision. Come."

With that Drelle turned and strode into the woods. Sen and Rom looked at one another, and then dumbly followed.

* * *

After a long walk through glittering, green woodland, and past small streams that surely fed the Brenne, they found a low clearing and Drelle tossed her bag to Rom, a sack with a rough cord for one shoulder.

"Feed the girl," she said, and then she took a seat on a rock and started to sing in that strange warbling language. The song was subdued but steady, and it made the hairs on the back of Senhora's neck stand up. She felt almost at ease and almost herself, though a lump had made its way into her throat, and seemed set to stay there, mayhaps from that moment until her final moment. A final time she hoped she would not spend alone, as Mog had done, preparing a meal with no help at the ovens. Rom opened the bag and produced some bread and raspberries wrapped in a leaf. They sat and ate, watching Drelle as she made her music. It should have been alien, frightful, wrong to see a soulsinger, but it wasn't. The song soothed them, as did the green light of the many coloured leaves and petals in the clearing. From the earth, small thin roots poked their way upward, and leaves flicked out of seams. It was like what the bastal trees had done, but slower, more deliberate.

Rom looked concerned but said nothing. Sen looked at him, and again a difficult question arose within her, "Why don't rune workers work with weapons?"

Rom studied Sen, seeming puzzled for a moment, and then he began signing, taking great pains to make each movement obvious for her to understand, *"Runes for weapons, runes for warriors we do not. Make a roof to stop the rain, make nails strong, make tools, lamp that glows without heat. Weapons are forbidden."*

"But there are rune weapons. I've heard of them. That man asked for one," Sen said, aloud.

"We do not. Others, maybe, but in this land, we do not. Not those with honour, and who wish to keep their neck. We learn of them, but not how to make them. They enact a heavy toll. You are correct. Runes are made with souls. With lesser runes, we use pieces of our souls. They will grow back. For weapons, or more difficult things, we need whole souls, like those of animals or men. This is wrong, dangerous. Forbidden."

"What about armour?" she said, thinking of the sign that Drelle had made. She didn't know how she knew the sign for *armour*. It was similar to *protection* but with a combination of the sign for *body*.

"Neither armour," Rom signed, "Rings, documents, lamps, toys. All things except those of war. We do not make weapons."

"Are you and..." it suddenly occurred to Sen that she did not know their saviour's name.

"Drelle," Rom said, slowly, aloud. It was still strange to Sen every time he spoke.

"Are you and Drelle not making armour?"

Rom almost grinned at that, "No... we are finding armour. We make a..." and then he said aloud, and at the same time making that unfamiliar sign, "a scry."

At that moment, from within what was by then a domed room made of twisting branches and leaves, curled into a spiral at the top, Drelle called for Rom. It resembled an upturned wicker basket, but one large enough for one or two to crawl inside. He sighed and motioned for Sen to remain where she was and then entered the wooden room through a seam.

Sen heard Drelle say, "We need *behng, rodhir, olum, cavet,* and *trim.*"

***

Within the wicker room, which now had a strange wooden anvil at the centre, Rom looked on at Drelle who was holding a metal, circular object, inlaid with five stones of distinct colours, and a few lengths of blueish, wire-like metal legs poking out from underneath. Rom took the unfinished scry and placed it on the anvil, and then hefted Fache's old hammer. He took a few cumbersome breaths and then with the pointed back end, he scratched each rune into place above each ovulum. It took some time as, after each rune, he turned the hammer and struck with the flat end repeatedly, until he seemed satisfied. By the time he finished his work, his eyes had hardened and he seemed unsteady on his feet, and the scry began to glow. The many blue-metal legs, tendril-like, floated upward as spider string on a draft and, seemingly of their own accord, they twisted around one another, dancing until finally settling into a complex, knotted shape resembling a compass. Several tendrils became a pointer and quivered before resolutely bending and finding a direction.

It pointed east.

VIII

A Sea of Bluebells

Many leagues away, indeed to the east, Kief was again in the wood. The safety of their swaying growth surrounded him, and a quiet rain rolled down the thousand-weighted leaves. Birds and beasts alike sang and chittered into the breeze. Kief was pushing at his barrow, nervously looking about him from tree to tree, rock to rock, always expecting some phantom to appear, flame in hand to set him alight.

Something in that Irongully accident had spelt danger. No, it couldn't have been an accident. It couldn't be coincidence that his saviour would die mere hours before saving him. Without a second's thinking, Kief had walked quietly out of town, across the plains and returned as quickly as possible to the security of the wood.

This wood was not the same as the one in the Monterio Valley. It was at the eastern foot of the Copper Mountains. Kief intended to make his way with haste to Bastaun, staying off the road where he could. He knew that if he continued westward, keeping the mountains on his right-hand side, he would soon come upon a sign or a small village and learn the best route to the ancient forge of Bastaun.

As he walked, Kief found his thoughts straying homeward, but not to Mondar. To the north, to the Stroongarm ancestral clan grounds where now another lord surely resided. He thought of his father, striding across open fields, still muddy and waterlogged from the spring rains, the ground sucking at their boots with each step. With one hand on the pommel of his longsword, the lord had turned to the boys and asked, "At the battle of the Grey Lake, why did the Pallidar lose to King Wendtec?"

Kief's older brother, Creng, said, "Their allies did not arrive in time."

"Their allies did not arrive at all," his lord father corrected gently. "Their leaders would not make the accommodations the allies sought, and so in that instance, matters of steel were settled by the ownership of westland dockyards."

Creng looked much like Kief, but he was older, with lighter colouring to his hair. He said, "The Arbourian city was also the capital, giving it to the Mcinteh would have all but meant abdication of the throne of Pallid."

"Very good, Creng," his father said, his beard glinting as copper in the light. He then looked down on Kief and asked, "And what became of the sixteenth Pallid King?"

Kief looked out across the hillside. Below them, on the other side of a stretch of land was the cottage belonging to the Barley family, until recently headed by the late Renjin Barley, who'd died the previous summer of the delpox.

There was a coldness to the air, creeping across the lowlands and painting a whiteness over the sky that was even and spread from horizon to horizon. The plains sighed sprinklings of ground frost over the mud, and Keif sighed as well. He was lost in thought and so didn't answer his father.

"Kief?" Lord Mulrek Stroongarm said, irate.

"Who?"

"King Herred, what became of him following the battle of the Grey Lake?"

"He drowned?"

Creng laughed, and Kief's father scowled, "No he did not drown. He was hung outside the castle walls of Arbour, the very city he refused to give to the Mcinteh, the very city that indeed was promised to them by Wendtec. The same city they reside over to this day."

That mid-morning they were to meet with Riktor, the eldest son of the late Renjin Barley. A loutish and untrustworthy young man who'd been accused of theft of produce, among a litany of other things he'd supposedly done and said after drinking too much with the menfolk in the village, many of whom had petitioned Kief's father to investigate the matter. The lands around Ahrmguard were a grassy plateau in the sweeping lowlands of the northern kingdoms. The soldiers of the region wore large swords, and their armour was often decorated with knotted patterns.

"The most important reason for conflict," Mulrek adopted that familiar tone of sombre tutelage, with a hint of forbearing and shortness, "is ownership. They who do not wish to lose what they have. They who want more than they have."

The lord and the two lordlings descended the low hillside and hopped a fence near the cottage. The Barleys were in charge of shepherding upon the grazing grounds to the east, though at that moment shearing was ongoing, which was a task assigned to another family, so the Barleys could take some respite to see to their own affairs. This had been the run of the Ahrmguard estate for many generations. The three, with Kief's father at the front, marched up to the little cottage.

He'd barely rapped the wood of the door when it was flung open to show a large and sturdy-looking boy, nearly a man, with a pink face and round, worried eyes. "Lord Stroongarm," he said, the words tumbling out of him like ale from a barrel. "I'm sorry. I had always intended to refill the stocks when I had the money. My wife is with child, and we needed the coin, and whatever you heard about the fight with the Emmerten brothers had nothing to do with me. I was simply trying to calm things and ended up caught in the middle."

"If you'd needed the money, you could simply have asked it of me," Lord Stroongarm said, stepping toward him with an air of menace. He showed his teeth and said, "If I allow such betrayals to go unpunished then all under me shall attempt to take what I have, will they not?"

The boy, despite his largeness, and the obvious strength in his arms, shrunk back from Kief's father. "Please my lord,

I... how can I make it up to you? Please just allow my family to—"

At that, Mulrek raised a hand, and the boy's mouth closed. It had been a long time since the Herred and Wendec conflict. In Kief's age, the northerners were allied to the Braelian king in their civil war against Redheim. Kief's father would disappear for years at a time to fight in their wars, always coming back seeming to have left a little piece of himself on whatever ground he'd trod. Always changed, always thinner, always more frightening. He wouldn't talk of the battles he'd seen, but merely of ancient and almost forgotten conquests from the great annals filling his library. "A lover of history can't stand the present," his grandmother Sandy would say. This made Kief's father unpredictable, quick to anger. Kief and his brother watched on in silence, almost as afraid as the boy in the cottage.

"Do you know what being lord entails, boy?" Mulrek said, taking another slow and deliberate step. "I do not simply rule these lands; I am their keeper. The king has charged me with protecting them, with the rule of law, and with the punishment of offences. These are not *my* lands. I am merely their caretaker. My duty here is to clap you in irons and ensure you pay your debt either with labour or blood."

Riktor was cowering now, enwormed. Kief's father took one more step, his sheathed weapon in grip, and then said quietly, "But, my duty above the king, above even my family, is to the good folks of these lands. You will not tell anyone that I let this go unpunished. You can keep your coin and ensure nothing of this sort happens again."

Riktor nodded quickly and fell to one knee. "You will have my service always m'lord."

* * *

In the forest at the eastern foot of the Copper Mountains, many years later, Kief came out into a wide clearing, still pushing his barrow. Expanding over the dew-dripping grass was a wide patch of wild bluebells. They roared upward as a brilliant sea of colour, starkly different to the greyness of the day, a greyness that should have set Kief at ease. A greyness that should have reminded him of home, yet on that day it felt encroaching, foreboding, telling of coming storms.

Almost to match Kief's mind, in the midst of the bluebells lay the rotting carcass of a great deer. There were three gashes in its side and flies buzzed about it, crawling in and out its rotting flesh. A bear protecting its territory most likely, though Kief wouldn't have guessed that at that juncture. He knew little of bears for they stayed mostly among the peaks. The only thing he knew was that you should always face one and back away slowly until you leave their earth. Kief, of course, did not wish to become like that deer and so he turned away from it and continued into the thicket, but then something strange happened. As he walked, two white lights appeared through the tarp. He pulled it back to show the great black helmet staring up at him, the eyes lit. A gauntlet gripped the side of the barrow, and the suit said, *"We are followed."*

Kief's head whipped around, and in that instant, an arrow came out of the gloom and thwacked hard into a tree behind him. Kief hefted his mace, which had become sharper and slenderer still. He felt that watery hatred grow inside his belly: the festering, wild hunger. Casting around, he spotted nothing. Only the gentle patter of the last of the morning dew falling from the canopy to the dead leaves below. He could still hear the buzzing from the carcass in the bed of bluebells.

A voice called out, echoing through the trees, seeming to come from all around, "You dunno what that mace is do you, boy?" It was a southern voice, farmy. A voice that had seen harsh weather and harsh nights. Humour and menace.

"What do you want?" Kief called out. His mind drifted back to the scorch mark in the workshop.

"I saw the mess you made in that tavern," the voice said, again seeming all around, from tree to tree, but this time closer.

"As did I," came another voice from above.

"Who are you?" He thought of a man's head smashed on a wall, old Belroy cowering in the corner.

"We are humble scouts, but I think our lord would be rather interested to hear what we've found. Why don't we help each other?"

A man stepped out of a shadow made by slant light on the wood-growth. He had a large burlap sack over one shoulder that seemed to carry something long and slender, as well as a quiver of arrows over the other. In one hand he held a yew longbow loosely. It was nothing impressive, old and lined, but it seemed well used, much like everything else on the man. His clothes were old leathers, peeling in places.

He had two knives on his belt. His face was gaunt, unshaven, dirtied by a long time of travelling. His hair was dark brown, though it was hard to tell if it was from grime or not.

"Might I suggest you drop the mace and step back?"

To his left, hopping nimbly down from a tree came another man holding a small hand axe. This man was stockier, copper-haired, bearded. He had a jitteriness to him that made him seem like coiled rope, ready to whip forth, or away at the blinking of an eye. His voice was equally woody, "Little Renfrew died well, did he? Looked like someone choked the life out of him, though mayhaps it was the crane that did that. You simply deprived him of air."

Kief thought back to the man who had called himself reasonable. The dull ring of the mace striking. Kief felt fear then. It drained the blood from his face.

"Now don't do nothing foolish," the archer said, but at that, Kief leapt back, took a handle of the wheelbarrow and flew into the forest.

He burst from a bush, and not knowing the direction he was taking, he fled across the hard ground and between knotted tree trunks. To his left, he felt the thrum of arrows, thwacking twice into the ground. He veered to the right, hearing the footfalls of his pursuers. In his mind, he begged the forest to open and swallow him, to hide him and protect him, but it would seem the forest had other thoughts on the matter. The barrow caught on a root and boy and suit flew through the air to land heavily in a low shrub. Pieces of metal scattered across a trodden path and wind was knocked clean from Kief's lungs.

The two pursuers slowed and sidled up to Kief, who was now on hands and knees, gasping for air.

"That was foolish," the archer said, as he put his bow over one shoulder and drew his dagger.

Kief, in a rush of sudden and terrible rage, pulled the mace, but the axeman was quicker. He trod hard on Kief's wrist, pinning it to the ground and then knocked the weapon away. He struck Kief hard on the back of the head and said, "Hold still now, boy."

The archer walked around, surveying the suit, which was lying in pieces on the path and the forest floor. He picked up the helmet with gloved hands and looked deep into its eyes. Kief silently begged it to light up, to awaken. A tear rolled down his nose, and yet the living armour was still. "So, you wore this when you killed our shield brothers, did you?"

Kief said nothing, and the axeman leant more heavily on his wrist. There was a slight cracking sound and Kief saw white, "You wore this, and it gave you uncanny strength? Curious." He turned to the archer and said, "Why don't you try it, Gallar?"

The archer, Gallar, grinned and said, "I think not. Cursed items such as these are best left to learn'd folks."

He stepped to the fallen barrow and propped it back up, placing the helmet inside. He then went piece by piece, putting the remainder of the suit back in the barrow.

When he was finished, he turned to the still-pinned Kief and said, "So you've been doubly cursed? S'pose this sword belongs to you as well?" He pulled down a corner of the bag over his shoulder to reveal the handle of the great rune knight's sword, the one that had been leaning against the low fence outside The Lone Horseman. Kief's eyes widened and the archer continued, "We were entrusted to discover what'd become of Lord Caspian's Liegemen, and what had become of the taxes. I have to say, we were astounded to learn of their heinous murder. Though, through some amount of force, we did successfully get hold of the taxes."

"*Some* may be an understatement," the axeman said. Again, Kief felt a rush of hot anger. He thought of Tess and even of Belroy, and of all those many villagers that came and went in that tavern. He thought of them lying to these men and paying their price.

"And so, the trail led us to you, and of course to all those who would commit the treasonous act of harbouring you." The archer scratched his chin. "Possessor of illegal weaponry, and killer of the king's men at a time of war."

"Tuttle, tut," the axeman said, "but one thing I would like to know is, where in the blend's deep abyss did you come upon this cursed armour?"

Kief half-grinned and said, "It walked up the road and introduced itself."

The look on the axeman's face changed and he again struck Kief in the back of the head. Kief tasted blood and tried to wriggle free, but the clamp on his wrist was sturdy, and another blow from the axeman was enough to still him.

"I suppose our personal curiosity matters little, though I'm sure Lord Caspian would greatly appreciate the gift, as well as a runt to could make example of. You know it's quite rare to find any crime at all in the months following a quartering."

Gallar stepped over and kicked the mace further away. Then he took a rope from his bag and tied Kief's hands with it. He put another loop around Kief's neck and tightened the two knots. He held the other end like a leash and heaved the boy to his stammering feet. The axeman finally, with another length of rope, looped it around the mace and tightened it with a flick of the wrist so he would not have to touch it.

"I believe the curse can only pass over the corpse of the owner," the archer said.

"I do not wish to test your theory." He lifted the mace by the rope and then bound it hard to Kief's back, wrapping the rope around his torso four times and tightening it as much as he could. Kief felt a rush of relief when it first touched him, but then the bladed sides cut into his back. He felt blood dribble down his spine.

They turned about and went back the way Kief had come, again passing the deer's bloated corpse. The archer held Kief's leash, and the axeman pushed the barrow. Little did they realize, not being the sorts who had ever worn armour, that a piece had been forgotten. A single pauldron had rolled down a slope into a bush and there it lay in silence.

Kief glumly walked in the way that one who is resigned to their fate does. Any occasional pauses or sounds were met with swift kickery, sending him sprawling. The day wore on in trundling silence, and when they crossed back into the familiar valley in which Kief had lived much of his life, his heart sank. They were returning him to Monterio.

After a time of silence, Gallar said, "How about a story? D'you like a story, young Kief of Mondar Village?" Kief made no response and so the archer continued, "The way I 'erd it, the claws were first carved into twenty longbows." He prodded a gloved finger into the mace, which cut Kief and he stumbled, grunting. "The claws were given to a central unit of archers: the bowmen of Dos-Lommar, from the Kammar desert. A wild and unruly group at the best of times, but in battle, they were the most organized and efficient killing force known to the south. They've always prized ranged weapons down there, and so when these bows were crafted by the Kammar rune workers, they were given to only the most gifted archers. They were at war in some Braelian dark forest, so dark it was that nobody could see their arm in front of 'em. The archers fired and fired, hearing screams from all around but they couldn't rightly see what had become of the rest of the men in their army. Two thousand soldiers from Brael had routed almost all of the Kammarrite forces in a slaughter for the ages."

Kief could feel the archer grinning behind him, "Now, this was a good two hundred years ago. The crane's claws gave these already gifted archers unnatural strength and speed. As their own army routed, the blood rage overtook 'em and they fired volley upon volley into the charging mass. The army would charge, and the archers would cut them down like wheat to the scythe. After many hours and much-spent labour, the archers had killed a hundred men apiece, emptying their quivers to a man. The enemy lay slain, and the Kammar archers celebrated their victory. The Darbhein among them did the dances of their ancestors, and the Humaine drank their fill.

"In their blood lust, they had praised their bows, but in their revels, they cast them aside. The bows grew spiteful at their masters, and the dark and terrible magic within them caused them to come alive. The bows turned into great monsters of branch and wood and metal, and they leapt at the archers, twisting them apart and killing them in the most vile, spilling manner. The rage of the crane's claw would not be sated, and though they destroyed their men, still they hungered for more. They spread themselves across the field, taking the forms of scores of different weapons. When the crows and the looters descended, as they do at every battle, folk unknowingly took the crane's claws. They allowed them to take their souls and so the cursed weapons spread across the land, causing grief and havoc wherever they were found. The one on your back is a prime example. The man you killed took his in a moment of dishonourable bloodshed, and it seems you have followed suit. Isn't that right, boy?"

Rage flared up in Kief and his shoulders bristled. He could feel the cut of the mace on his back. He longed to hold it, to bring it down on the heads of his captors. Feel the spattering lift and fall and tense of his arms in the swing. He turned, but the sudden movement was met by another kick that sent him reeling into the undergrowth.

They walked for many more hours, Kief in bitter, fuming silence. His captors chitchatted about how they would spend their reward: which brothels they would visit, which drinks they would drink, and which food they would sample. Soon, they came to a familiar fork in the road with a wooden sign. One direction to Mondar Village, and the other to Monterio Castle. They went leftward, toward the seat of Lord Caspian. Kief had walked by it on occasion over the years. It was a small castle, but one situated for its lord to have certain importance to the Braelian Empire. It was a border keep, and so Lord Caspian was afforded a decent-sized army, and many luxuries befitting his station: horses, hounds, and subjects. When they arrived, the lower town of Monterio was abuzz with soldiers going to and fro, taking supplies from wagons, and training indentured infantrymen. In fact, it was unusually busy.

What Kief didn't know on that day was that the greater Redheim army was en route, with the usurper, Lord Kellar, cousin of the king of Brael at its head.

At the gate to the keep, Kief was passed to two grim men in plate armour who dragged him across the drawbridge. Gallar and the axeman turned towards a large door with the suit and barrow and disappeared. Kief was struck around the head by a gloved hand, causing his ears to ring, and in a daze, he was taken down a spiral staircase that grew dimmer and darker the lower they went. At its base, there was a long corridor. There were hollow-eyed men and women in rags staring out from their iron-barred cells. Kief was thrown into the farthest, darkest one.

One knight said, "Here you will await judgment."

The mace was taken from his back and placed in a small cage hanging from the roof, just out of reach. Without another word the knight left Kief, locking the door behind him. The cell was small and dark and dripping, and in one shadowy corner, a man was manacled to a wall.

As fate would have it, this was the very man that Kief needed to meet.

IX

A Castle

Grappy looked down to see his two grandchildren dozing at his feet. He sighed, his age showing on his features. He'd been talking for a long stretch of dark river, as it grew wider and wider, evermore complex currents turning back on themselves and spinning in eddies split by the stones below. Grappy had never felt confident talking to children. A story he could tell, indeed he'd told this story many times. In inns and beside fireplaces, over crushed pillows, and swaying on the backs of carts. In fact, this may have been the only time he'd ever told this story without a drink in one hand. Grappy removed his cloak and put it over the grandchildren and then got to his feet. He took a few unsteady steps, hunching over his staff. He crossed the deck to a small run of stairs and stepped down to the hold, where the drinking water was stored. He lifted a barrel's lid and took a long sip from a wooden ladle. It was cold and sweet, the same spring water used to make blue alchemical rust, he mused. After a moment of hearty sipping, he looked up to see a silent Kraf-Krak standing over him, slightly up the stairway, his eyes shining in the darkness.

Kraf-Krak cleared his throat and said quietly, "Now, I want you to know that I appreciate your assistance back there. I see you have spent time at the Algonorium."

Grappy's grip on his staff tightened. He said nothing, sipping again.

Kraf-Krak breathed out heavily through his nose, "I believe it best if you tell me exactly who you are and where you intend to go."

"I go to the sea."

"You present a danger to my crew. Please satisfy my curiosity so we may continue this journey in peace."

Grappy noted the sword on the captain's hip and the look in his eyes. There was an eloquence to the boat captain that Grappy recognized, a honeying of words familiar to all those who'd spent time at the Algonorium, but there was also a threat. One that could be tasted in the air, like finder's smoke.

"My name is Gaelar Stroongarm," Grappy said as if he hadn't spoken his name in a long while. "I did indeed spend time in Kammar as a boy, and I am indeed what you think I am. We are, however, no fugitives. The crown does not want me or mine." He sipped again, "I am simply taking my two heirs to my home. We were separated for many years, mostly due to my own misgivings, my seeking..." he trailed off.

Kraf-Krak's gaze softened, and Grappy took a slow seat on a stack of flour casks next to the water barrel. "I see your braids and I know you're wiser than your station. You know I mean it when I tell you that the eastern winds, whom I know well, told me that my grandchildren and the rest of my son's family were in danger. I hurried to their aid, but I arrived too late. As they say about men living alongside swords." Almost a grin. "I retrieved my grandchildren and chose to leave hurriedly, escaping tragic and tormented sights. Know that I would never endanger you or your crew, and only wish to take these children somewhere safe and warm."

Kraf-Krak studied Grappy's face for a spell, seeing the lines around his eyes, the leathery skin of his brow, and the long grey of his beard, until he finally spoke. "I will take you to the sea, Gaelar Stroongarm. I appreciate your candour, and I pity your children." He turned back up the steps and disappeared.

Grappy smiled wistfully, listening to the slop of the water in the barrels alongside him. He sat for a long while, feeling the creaking of the wood of the Adder, the gentle movement of river water beneath, and the flap of the sails high above. He was also tired but knew he could not sleep that night. Verily, he wondered if he would ever sleep again.

After a time, he stood and walked up the wooden steps and back to the children, wondering all the while if it was his bones or the steps that creaked so. When he came near, he saw they were awake and were speaking in hushed tones.

"Awake so soon?" Gaelar Stroongarm said.

"Saph dreamed of the man," Timmin said.

"You will never see that man. You will live in peace and safety, and nothing will..."

"I want to see him," Saph said, her voice pinched.

"As do I," Timmin's jaw was set in a way that was all too familiar to Grappy. He took his seat again alongside them.

"We're going to avenge Pappy," Saph said.

Grappy pushed his silver hair back from his eyes. "Children, it's not so simple as revenge. Your father... foresaw it. He didn't know what day it would be, but he'd already agreed to the price. I wish it weren't this way, but it is. I wish I could explain to you... but there are some things that..." he trailed. "I'll have to tell you more as you grow. All faults are to be laid at my door, in truth. I had a talent for giving him foolish notions, and your mother..." Grappy's face took on a gaunt, pained look. His eyes went to the abyss. "You must live out your lives and learn from our misdoings."

Saph and Timmin looked at one another for a moment, and then Timmin said "What if we don't want to?"

"In this world what one wants isn't always what one needs or deserves, and neither is it often what one gets, to which my own father could attest."

The two children's faces took on another look. A look that told Grappy that this wasn't to be the end of the discussion. He said, "This journey is coming close to its destination. Don't you want to know what became of the great hero Kief Stroongarm in his cell, or of the great mage and spellsinger Drelle of Coldharbr?

The children did not respond, but Grappy settled himself again and began to speak, "Sen and Drelle argued often as they walked. It was usually the fault of Drelle, who seemed to delight in ignoring anything that wasn't plant or animal."

**

"What did you say your name was, again?" Drelle snapped. As was growing ever more apparent to Sen, Drelle's wildness simmered away, ever-present, and ever beneath the skin.

"Senhora," Sen exclaimed, having already said her name countless times on their hike, following the direction of the scry.

"Ahh: the messenger, well p'raps you'd stick to the delivery of information rather than the gleaning of it."

"I thought you said I was to learn."

"I say a lot of things."

Behind them, Rom was walking in silence, resolve and exhaustion set onto his aged forehead.

"So, you're a liar," Sen said, matter of factly.

"I am no liar," Drelle narrowed her eyes. "Fine, I will teach you something." She stopped on the beaten road and stretched her back, "Do you know the term, operative phrasing? It is a form of verbal manipulation."

"I'm not interested in manipulation. I want to know how to ask a tree how old it is."

"Before you may converse with wild things, you should first master the art of conversing with your own kind. Operative phrasing is when we refer to the *way* that something is said. If one part of the phrase contains the thing you want from the conversation, even if it is in the negative, the idea will weigh more heavily in your target's mind. For instance, tell me the difference between saying; 'Do you want me to go with you?' and saying, 'Are you sure you want to go alone?'"

Sen paused for a mite. That was a tricky one. Mog, for all her skill at speechcraft, had never asked her something like that, although Mog hadn't been moon-driven as this witch of the wood appeared to be. "You're saying the same thing in a different way?"

"I am, but what's the *difference*."

"Um..." Sen thought about the phrase, not as a whole but in its parts. Then it struck her. "One says, 'go with you,' and the other says 'go alone.'"

"And what does that tell you about what the speaker wants?"

Sen considered for a moment, "One wants to go, and the other doesn't. It's simple."

"It is simple, and it's the foundation of speechcraft. Now go bother Rom. I have something to do."

"What do you have to do?"

It was a fine day. Summer was upon Brael. To their left, northward, as had been the way for many hours, rose the copper mountains, their great slumbering spines tracing the sky. The forest had lessened as they followed the river eastward. It had been an easy journey, the group only stopping once to make camp, whereupon Drelle had done some secretive thing in some bush and had returned with a cloth full of nuts and berries that seemed too fresh and large to have been hand-picked from wild shrubbery.

When the sun reached the midpoint of the sky on the second day, they had fully left the forest surrounding Bastaun, the Den Woods. Their path continued onwards, crossing the Baelrod plains coated in long grass, ever bending and rippling in the wind that flowed down the mountains. To the south, they could see faint white dots of sheep and an upright figure of some herdsman with a crooked staff, but he was too far for them to figure anything beyond that. Soon, the plains rolled lower into a short slope and far enough away they spied another wood, at which point the manic nature of Drelle seemed to lessen. She grew pensive and seemed every few moments to look down at the scry, sigh, and then back toward the wood.

Drelle did not see the need to inform her companions of this, but she knew that particular forest to be rude and disdainful and that it was highly unlikely to do anything for her. It was small-minded and uncouth, and so she resented having to walk through it again. Seeing, however, that it would soon become a necessity, she let out a low whistle that echoed across the grasslands unnaturally.

"What was that?" Sen said, still at Drelle's heels.

"It was none of your mother-be-damned business," Drelle said.

"You called something," Sen said, which was an accurate guess, as indeed Drelle had called something. She knew that Pecham should be a few miles out still. It would have taken him two days to fly to Kammar and another two to return. However, letting him know she needed him may well have sped him along on his way.

"What did you call?" Sen said.

Rom rolled his eyes.

"I called a cripplingly rude crow, who has the timekeeping skills of a Pallidar lanceman."

Rom snorted, but that only raised more questions for Sen, "What is a Pallidar lanceman?"

"Mother, mother, mother. Will you cease? I've answered more questions than someone of your station deserves. It's just one after the other with you. Don't you know it's rude to speak to your betters in this manner?"

"It's rude to lie."

"I'm not lying."

"Then why did you call a crow?"

"Pecham is an old friend of mine, and before we cross into that forest there, I would greatly appreciate having him to keep an eye on things."

"Why?"

"Because I am wise, and you are not."

"Why?"

"Because the mother deemed it so. She deemed that you would be a pinch of mouth-frothing spittle and that I would be a famous spellsinger."

"What's a spellsinger?"

"Stop." Drelle stopped in her paces, "One more question out of you and I will ask the earth to swallow you whole."

"Could you do that?"

Drelle seemed about fit to explode. She opened her mouth to say something that she was certain to live to regret when they were interrupted by urgent cawing above. A black crow circled once and then landed on a stump by the pathside.

"*Ahh, Pecham. For once you're not late,*" Drelle said to the crow, which to Sen and Rom appeared like she was murmuring in a wholly strange and indecipherable language. The crow cawed back at her and Drelle's hand whipped out to grab at its neck, but it hopped away, seeming to laugh at her. What followed could only be described as an intensive argument between a mangy crow and a middle-aged woman, at the end of which Drelle threw her hands up into the air in frustration.

She then turned to Rom and said, "There's an army marching on Monterio."

Rom looked concerned but said nothing.

"Which... is the direction that we are heading. Perhaps we can take the long way. Though, who knows if they will cross near where we may find the suit."

Rom made some hand signs, *"I thought you wanted to follow the scry?"*

"Of course, I want to follow the scry. I simply don't want to be anywhere near a battle."

Rom nodded and then pointed to the scry. *"We follow."*

Drelle seethed but relented. The scry led them, with crow whirling overhead, across further miles of grassy plains and then into that other forest, of dark and foreboding feel. Gnarled roots raised out of the ground every which way, crossing paths and clearings. Drelle seemed visibly uncomfortable in this wood, and so they walked in silence. Branches shifted overhead and leaves rustled. Not a bird sang, or cricket stirred. The spellsinger led them steadily, keeping one eye trained on the scry which, after a while of walking, suddenly and quite sharply shifted to the left.

"That's odd," Drelle said. She turned herself and disappeared into the undergrowth for a moment. Sen and Rom looked on bemused. After three beats of scrabbling about they heard her exclaim, "AH-HA." Drelle exploded out of the bushes holding something flat, metal, and black. It was a pauldron, a shoulder guard covered in dirt and moss, ash and runes.

Rom's eyes widened and he stepped toward her. Sen hadn't seen him draw it, but old Fache's hammer was in his hand. He made some hand signs quickly and without pause, seeming in some peculiar way to incorporate the hammer into the rapid movements. Sen couldn't quite make all of it out, owing to the hammer, but he evidently thought it was a terrible idea that Drelle was holding the scrap of metal in her bare hand.

"Relax, Rom. This is what we are seeking. Though how but one piece of it came to be in this forest is purely up to speculation. I suspect foul play on the part of that tree there," she said, pointing at a nearby tree, and if it were possible for a tree to comically feign ignorance, it would have done so. Drelle narrowed her eyes and then wiped the dirt off the delicate runework on the pauldron.

Rom looked horrified, *"Do you know how this was made?"* he signed.

"It's better you not know, dear Rom," Drelle said.

Rom's eyes took on an insistent look, *"You will tell me, or this is where we part ways."*

Drelle sighed, knowing that she may soon need him again. "I suppose I would've had to tell you sooner or later." She paused, seeming unsure of where to begin, "One of the last great Darbhein rune workers instilled his own spirit into this armour and gifted it to the knight, Molag Nul. To slay that which I have already told you."

Rom took a step back, holding his hammer up as if to strike at some invisible foe, *"When?"*

"To slay what?" Sen said.

Drelle sighed again, "Around fifty years ago, not long before they disappeared. It was one of the final acts of the Darbhein, in an attempt to right a wrong that I still do not fully understand. I have been given the task to find the suit and return it to Kuh-Dul."

Rom's hand started shaking, and he signed, *"This is unheard of. This is dangerous in a way that you cannot fathom."*

"Oh, I fathom it, Rom and that is the very reason it must be returned with absolute haste to the masters at Kammar." She wrapped the pauldron in a strip of cloth from her bag and sang a little song under her breath. She then drew a string around it from somewhere in the folds of her cloak, creating a strange and unusual knot that seemed to twist and tighten itself into a labyrinth of symbols and hemp, showing no clear way to undo it, save with a knife. Rom seemed to relax slightly, but he did not put his hammer back into his belt.

"*I do not wish to be involved with this,*" Rom signed. Sen looked at him and then looked at Drelle.

"You are involved, Rom. If not you then who, pray-tell, will be able to help me when we find it in its entirety. It is dangerous, as you say, and only one such as yourself will be able to protect us from it."

"*And what of her?*" he gestured to Sen.

"I'm coming."

"I am… uncomfortable with her presence," Drelle said, looking down at Sen, "but the mother has placed us together and I am not one to deny her."

Rom let out a shaky breath, "*She's just a girl.*"

"She's more than that. Aren't you, messenger?"

"I want to stay with you."

"And so you will."

And with that, as was Drelle's way, she finished the conversation by striding off, crossing a nearby clearing littered with bluebells, and buzzing with rotflies. After a moment or two of pause and consideration, both Senhora and Rom followed suit.

* * *

That night, Sen dreamed of Mog. They were pulling in old Chester's donkey around the back of the shop. It was well known for being a surly and uncooperative beast. Mog was telling Sen to hold the rope while Chester was trying to undo the straps on the bags of flour, bottles of milk, and other pie-making supplies. The squat little delivery man lifted each item one by one to the ground as Sen held the reins and whispered calming words to the donkey. Mog was laughing, and then they were inside, Chester was gone, and they were pushing at dough on the countertop. Mog's laugh was like honey dribbling down a slab of warm bread. Her rosy cheeks were full, and they shook with every chuckle.

She told Sen to grab a cup of milk. Sen obliged, going into the back. She felt warm and safe, and she was looking forward to telling Mog about her lessons that week, on spinning wheels and spindles. It was a craft that Sen loathed in practice, but it was Ghef, the tailor's son who'd been giving the lesson. A jolly and modest young man with wise eyes and smart hair. He liked pumpkin pies. Sen poured milk into a cup, and looked down into its frothy whiteness, swirling again and again. Then, from within, something strange and unnatural appeared. Something spinning and liquid, black, bubbling, and filling the cup. The thick blackness exploded over the top. Sen tried to stop the pouring, but it wouldn't stop, black sticky bile flowed down her arm, thick onto the floor. Sen screamed and turned around to see a smouldering crater, a black mass where the shop had been, surrounded by fire and death.

She woke with a start.

Drelle was sitting on the grass watching her in the morning darkness. Sen looked back, tears in her eyes. Drelle said, "Up ye get. No sense sleeping on a nightmare."

Sen sat up and took a few shaky breaths and then looked again at the spellsinger. She was cross-legged and was absent-mindedly fiddling with a blade of grass, and something in her gaze made Sen stifle the tears already stinging her cheeks. Drelle caught her eye and then looked purposely to the fire. Sen sniffed and obliged, setting to blowing at the remaining cinders, still feeling Drelle's quiet gaze on her. Drelle was seeing something that she was yet to decide on, yet to name, or tell, and so she watched on in silence.

After a time of huffing and panting, the fire awoke, and Sen turned to making breakfast. The sun was starting to show, glittering through the roped trunks. She put three thick oatcakes stuffed with dried fruit and nuts on a flat rock and warmed them. Drelle had produced them the previous night. She said the dark forest had no gifts for them, so old food would have to do. At the smell, Rom finally awoke and sat up, groaning quietly. Judging by his mood when he came to the fire and began to eat, he too had dreamed that night.

With the sun rising through the canopy, they continued on their trek. Drelle was always ahead, following the point of the scry. Soon the forest lessened once again, and they crossed the river Brenne on a thin wooden footbridge which seemed almost forgotten about, covered in weeds and vines. They walked further along a woody path, up a slope to a ridge, and soon looked down on a wide valley. At the far end lay a castle, with a small town at its heel. To their eyes, it was a warren of pebbles, littered with ant trails. The architecture was unmistakably Humaine. It lacked grace but it was sturdy, weathered. Drelle led them off the path and they took a wide circle, walking low among the thin birch trees and undergrowth that forested the slope. Soon they reached the valley's far side.

Monterio's town spread densely for a stretch before lessening to single houses and farmsteads on the outskirts. At the heart of the castle was its stout, angular keep, fortified with wooden battlements. It sat atop a rocky hillock, surrounded by deep trenches. Distantly, they could see many people, many spears, many carts, running and preparing with fervour. Across the valley floor were dotted yet more houses and farms, with people busying themselves with one frantic task or another. None paid any heed to the three flitting along the hillside. Drelle looked down at the scry, and indeed its needle pointed, shuddering slightly, at Monterio Castle. Yet the lady of Coldharbr was not convinced. She let out another low whistle calling the haggard crow to her arm.

"Pecham, take this," she said in the Braelian tongue, to which Pecham cocked his head in confusion. The spellsinger cursed and then said something else in her strange language of wind and undertones. The crow almost seemed to smile and lifted one clawed foot to accept the scry. Drelle then produced another piece of string and tied the item twice around his foot, turning to Sen and saying, "Word of wisdom, do not trust a crow to carry something for long."

Pecham cawed and hopped on one leg, seeming to test the weight of his new baggage, and then he flapped his wings twice, grazing Drelle's mouth with a feather as he took off. Drelle hacked and spat on the ground and said something under her breath as the bird disappeared into the sky.

By this time, the sun was beginning to close its lidded eye. Drelle led them further up the small slope, which was dotted with glacial erratics and gorse bushes, every so often breaking their line of sight to the castle. They soon scrabbled up a final incline to a vantage point which showed the entire valley in brilliance, from the sun-kissed hilltops to the cobble town. Rom took a seat on a large rock and Sen sat beside him. They watched the crow circle the castle once and then wheel back toward them, a black shape twisting and turning on the wind. There were many other birds in the sky, crows and ravens, wood pigeons, and smaller wrens and starlings. All circled anxiously, feeling the stir on the ground below, and as Pecham flew on he seemed almost lost in their midst, only to appear once again above to caw a few times, before landing with a skeeter on the grassy slope beside Sen. He looked up at the girl and cawed once. Drelle whistled, more quietly this time, and the bird took one last look at Sen before hopping to the spellsinger, whereupon she spoke to him in her strange language and undid the string on the scry. He made quiet chirping sounds as she did so.

Drelle sighed and gave Pecham a nut, which he took gleefully and hopped off behind a rock with it.

"What did you learn?" Sen said.

Drelle's hair seemed to go pale at that moment. "The suit is within the walls."

Rom made a hand sign that Sen did not recognize.

"It is not lost," Drelle snapped, seeming to grow confident. "This bundle of straw that they call a fortification holds fools and cowards who likely do not know what it is they hold."

Rom kept looking at her with that stony gaze of his, not motioning at all with his hands.

"This castle is on a lay line, Rom. We cannot waste any more moments."

Rom made the sign for *questioning* and *us*.

Sen said, "So our suit is within the walls, how do we get to it?"

"I have a friend who would gladly oblige." Drelle reached into the folds of her brown cloak and after a moment of digging around, she pulled out something small, black, and furry.

"A mouse?" signed Rom.

Sen started to laugh.

"He knows his craft," Drelle said.

"The mouse?" Sen said, now laughing deep in her stomach. All of the stress and uncertainty of the past few days filled her guts and roiled up through her throat. She doubled over, tears streaming down her face. An unamused Drelle looked down on her. Rom raised an eyebrow, as did the mouse.

"He will infiltrate the castle," Drelle said flatly, "and give us some entry potentials, and locate the knight." The mouse seemed to nod, and it looked up at Rom with sharp, intelligent eyes.

Rom grinned, *"How will a mouse know a knight it has never met?"* he signed.

"He is a spirit speaker. The mouse will ask the air to speak for him, which will allow him to locate centres of polymancatic rhythms," Drelle gave Rom a withering look, "Are you capable of such feats?"

The humour drained from Rom, and he shook his head.

"It's a wonder the mouse doesn't look at you and say, *'It's a man.'*"

Drelle stroked the little mouse on the forehead and then whispered something into his ear. Sen stopped laughing and watched as Drelle placed him gently on the ground and then the black form of fluff and fire scampered away.

X

A Cell

Grappy scratched a thin line into the wood of his staff with a thumbnail. The boat rocked beneath him. Saph was staring into the middle distance.

"I expect you've never seen the fervour of folks preparing for a siege. Men and women and children strong enough to hold a tool, sawing, splitting, and carrying. Their bodies aching, their minds pinched. Weapons are stacked outside barracks' and gatehouses, arrows are cut, and stones and other missiles are placed on battlements. Every effort is spent in hoping to survive, in hoping to repel those who will soon be looking to roar into your home, destroying and burning all in sight..."

* * *

The walls of the castle were sheer, tall with battlements and ever-growing wooden frameworks. Slits for archers were cut into the woodwork and ballistae were tuned and readied under birch canopies. The soldiers and townsfolk alike moved with urgency, fear spurning them on, but with grimness holding their hearts. They rushed to melt spent candle stubs into huge vats, harden arrows in small fires, sharpen stakes, and account for grain and water.

Such was their fervour that Kief was all but forgotten, as was the suit. Caspian of Monterio, who'd surely been informed of the boy and the armour, was a shrewd man, so it would seem he'd decided that the dangers and potential boons the two represented would be better dealt with at a later and calmer date. He stood in the central chambers of the castle keep, surrounded by his liegemen, preparing orders and battle plans. They moved wooden whittlings on map boards and discussed bodies and numbers as if they didn't represent lives, but game pieces.

In his cell, Kief sat in the corner, not much wanting to look at his fellow cellmate who lay in the shadows at the other end of the room. Kief was cold, damp and afraid, but all the same, he felt the pull of the crane deep in his belly. It had its own anger, which melded with Kief's. Roiling and rending, awaiting, ankle-deep in river water, within the boy's very being. A fury unlike anything else. A struggling thing with limitless strength in a vice of limitless grip. For many hours he lent on that feeling, pushed at it, taking slow breaths of dank dungeon air. He did not look at his cellmate. He did not speak. He did not wish to entice whichever monster was manacled to the far wall or give any guard reason to cuff him again.

As was his way, he came to think of warmer places and warmer times. He thought of old Sandy telling stories by the fireplace. When the body is shackled, the mind looks to escape. The Sandy of his mind scratched her leathery chin as she tried to think of a story to tell; a story that would give the young something to learn. Sandy rarely spoke of the foundation stories, but in times of strife, it is common to look for solace in the past, in the mythical. Kief recalled the tale of Mesuda the Lonely; a tale known by all but told a thousand ways.

This is the way Sandy told it.

In the beginning, beasts roamed the field. There was no fade, no ether, no thought. There was balance, beasts, and cool winds, yet alas there was no thought. Not even a whisper. Then one day, a day like any other, the wise Mother Mesuda crawled from the earth, as tall as mountains and wise as stars. Her scales and teeth were made of fire and iron and within her was one thing that had never been known: thought.

Mesuda wandered and lived, dragging her great copper tail behind her, wondering at who, where, and why she was. She caught thoughtless beasts to feast on them, and she watched water trickle from mountains to grow into long rivers. She sang bellowing songs to the stars and with every footfall the world shook. She knew not where she came from, or why she had come to be. The only thing she truly knew was that she was lonely.

Mesuda's voice shook the heavens, yet her loneliness was only echoed back by the endless sky. The beasts of the field brayed and mewled and yet loneliness would not creep from her soul. This was when Mesuda decided that she would have children. She laid a thousand eggs of blood and ash and breathed life into them. They became the first legion of Darbhein: The Hevamir.

They stood tall as men, were wise and noble, and above all they thought. They carved cities from stone and shaped rivers from the earth. They lived as one, at peace and with thought. Mesuda watched over them, finally together, and finally without loneliness. There was no disease, no suffering, and no death. They were happy for a time, for a time that did not know time, content to build and write and create all manner of things that have since been lost to ages. But, for all their luxuries and security, and the joy that they brought their Mother, the Hevamir too were lonely. They saw the animals of the field and saw that they lived, gave birth, died, and were reborn. They saw the brutality of it and the simple joy of it, like murmurings on the wind. They saw that these creatures' lives had meaning where theirs did not, even though they lived without thought.

There came a day when Permethiar, the wisest and most passionate of the thousand Hevamir, came to his mother, proud and tall. She could not help but love him as she looked upon him, remembering him crawling from his egg of blood and ash, thick with the mucous of life. He said, "Mother, the loneliness is gnawing. We have done all there is to do and lived all there is to live. Would you grant us one wish?"

Mesuda, remembering her own loneliness in ages gone past, looked down on him, her great form blocking the sky. She said, "What is it my son?" the sound of her voice was a cascade of fire and lightning and thought.

Permethiar shook at the sound and said, "I would ask that we be granted the power to sire our own children. To watch them grow, become wise, and teach them things, and live our lives anew through their eyes. Great and wise Mother, grant us this one wish, and never again will we ask anything of you."

The Mother paused and considered. She had not thought this was possible. She had not taught her children to be lonely as she was. She had not created them to wonder and to question her, and yet here was her wisest son asking for the gift of life. "I must think on this my son," she said carefully. "Give me three days and I will offer my answer." For three is a sacred number.

Permethiar returned to his brothers and sisters and told them her response, and so they sat at the base of Mesuda's mountain perch and waited. When the three days were spent, The Mother's great amber eyes opened and she told Permethiar that his wish would be granted, but that all things of life and death came at a cost. In her infinite wisdom and knowledge of all things, she told him that there would have to be an exchange. Life for life, death for death. She said, "If you wish to have meaning, as the beasts of the fields do, as I do, then you must trade something. The Darbhein must give up their immortality, they must give up me, and then I will allow three mothers to be chosen. They will have children who will usher in a new age. You will live with these children and guide them in all things. Allow them thought, and allow them blood, and this wish shall be granted."

Permethiar fell to his knees and said, "Mother thank you, this is all we have desired for untold lifetimes, to bring new thought unto the world. We will give you up Mother and know that, though you are watching us, we will never ask anything more of you."

The Mother smiled and said, "You may have what it is you wish."

She chose three Darbhein mothers: Mamu, Sena, and Kel. With an almighty song that shook the earth, she took immortality from the Hevamir. They would live and die like beasts of the field, but in their thought, they would find meaning and purpose. She then breathed the fires of swift, slow, and watchful thought into the mothers. They each laid a hundred eggs and from the shells crawled the first men. The Muthudites from Mamu, the Seneele from Sena, and the Kelten from Kel. The Mother then cried a terrible cry, for she was soon to be as lonely as before, but she would do anything to gift joy to her children. She breathed unto herself, and the air enveloped her. Her mind leapt across the sky as stars and her body lay down in the mountains. Her spines became copper peaks, and from her great eyes, tears flowed across the world. The Grey Lake was born as she wept, and the rivers cleansed the land.

Mesuda the Lonely was finally at peace.

The Darbhein raised the new Humaine children, guiding them and watching them grow. The Humaine bred with one another, and untold generations of them toiled in the land, living, weeping, and loving. They spread to the land of Kammar, in the south, to the green rolling hills of Brael, and to the northern kingdoms of Pallid. The remaining Darbhein found that they could birth more of their kind with one another and so generations of them passed as well. Though their lives were longer and harder than those of the Humaine, they were no longer lonely, and so the world began anew.

* * *

Grappy's grandchildren, of course, had heard the tale before – but never with such gusto, never with such ambience as the chittering of night things, and the swaying of black water all around them. Timmin looked at his sister, and saw a shining light in her eyes, as if worlds were passing through her thoughts.

Then, Grappy grew sombre, "When my father told me of his days in the Monterio dungeon, he spoke hesitantly, and with few details. He told me of how he would spend his days and nights imagining his late grandmother, Sandy, spinning tales. He said he was fearful of his cellmate. He told me of the burning of the crane's curse, but most of all he said that this was the darkest time of his life. He said that beyond it, things grew and formed, and in the years that followed he became more the person he not only wished to be but whom he was destined to be. If one were to believe in such things."

* * *

The roof of the prison cell was made of thick and heavy grey stone, covered in the moss found in dark places, and dripping with fetid water. Along one side were metal bars and a rusted gate, with a port hole for food to be passed, as it was twice a day. Since he saw nothing of the sun, it could not be said when in the day the food arrived. Kief couldn't help but gaze with a terrible longing at the small cage suspended by a chain high above, housing his crane's claw. Not having it pained him in a deep and unsettling manner that set his flesh crawling and his belly afire. For the first night, he sat in silence, thinking of Sandy and warmer days, of fields and rivers and beasts. A hundred screams prickled his inner thoughts.

On the second day, his unwanted companion broke the silence. "Prickle-prackle, spittle-spackle, young manling."

Kief looked up and it seemed that all the torchlight from the corridor flickered at once and lit the man chained to the wall. He was scratching at something in the stonework, and his visage was shown for but a moment. He was in rags, but his scales shone a dull green. He had a row of yellowed spines atop his head and a great and powerful jaw full of razor teeth. His eyes glittered in the darkness.

Kief started back, crying out. "You are Darbhein?"

To which the lizard man laughed, his manacles jingling. "You see me as I was," he snorted. "Missed the boat, Darbhenian no longer," his voice crackled with hidden flames and hissed with stolen air. The light flickered again and, in his place, appeared an old man – manacled and wearing rags. With a fingernail he scraped some brown fungus from the wall and ate it, chewing the morsel thoughtfully.

"Would you like some godfood?" the stranger said.

"What is godfood?" Kief said, shaking with fear, but like a fire deep within him, his rage began to grow.

"This," he scraped more of the fungus from the wall, and with another flicker of the torchlight, he was a lizard once again. At the end of a long claw was a wet morsel that he held out to Kief.

"No, I will be fine. Thank you." A part of him wished to take the godfood, to take it all from this tortured wretch, and to dash his scaled head against the cobblestones.

The Darbhein whispered something to the morsel and then again fed it to himself. "Now, how does a soul like yours come to see a soul like mine?"

Kief said nothing, grinding his teeth, watching the thin and pitiable creature.

"I think it may have something to do with the soul in the cage above us," the Darbhein gestured to the crane's claw and again Kief felt the deep spark of rage. "But I sense you do not wish to speak of it, manling."

And it was true, Kief did not. The chains hissed as the creature turned over until it faced the wall. Kief lay back down, and they remained in their cell in silence for a long while. A day, perhaps longer. To Kief, time was beginning to lose meaning, and to the Darbhein, it had lost meaning entirely.

On the third day, Kief arose from his wooden bed and walked across the cell, keeping out of reach of the Darbhein. The anger was paining him and was becoming more difficult to contain. The lizard watched him, the light flickering his visage between reptile and man. Kief was afraid, but soon, as was his way, curiosity got the better of him.

"If you are Darbhein, are all Darbhein now men?" he asked.

The reptile chuckled, "The first question you ask is not my name, but the fate of my people. Is that rude or friendly?" He scraped more mould from the wall and chewed upon it.

Kief sat back down, "Then what is your name?"

"My name is Remyl. You are the first to look upon me and see me as I am, so I will tell you what you wish to know, but in return, I would ask of you one service."

Kief froze, wondering what the service could be. He was afraid, but not of the wretch. He was afraid of the thoughts coursing through his heart. He asked, "What service could I do you?"

"I would have you hear my tale and tell it. That is all I would ask."

Kief considered this for a moment, but then, knowing that there were few tales that could hurt flesh, he agreed. Remyl settled himself, crossing his spiny legs, and he said, "Unlike man, we exist in three planes. To most, I appear nought but manflesh, like you." A shadow crossed him and there appeared once more the old and haggard man in chains. "I was left behind. Every time anyone with thought does anything, whether Humaine or Darbhein, there are reflections in the fog and eth kelds. The ether and the fade. Evil acts grow fade creatures, and good acts weaken them. But with us it is more, the connection is deeper. We live in all three at once. And so, long ago, when the rupture became itself and we lost our grip on this world, some of my kind went into the fade, and some went into the ether." He again scraped one long claw along the wall and licked it up with a long and yellow tongue.

"I had a horse, a great and noble horse. She was cowardly at times but loyal, nudging always gently with her muzzle. I also had a dog. A brave, playful, and insightful creature. Mine was a simple life, away from folk of all creeds and broods. It had been that way since I was young. My mother raised me in the wood, as her mother had done her and so it had been as far back as memory and tooth allow. The only time we would venture into a place of folk, a township, would be on the days before Wintermorn as we knew we could not hunt or harvest enough during the long cold season.

"It was in that small and isolated town, far from our forest home, that my mother met my father, spending one night together before she left. I learned much of the world through books in the wintertime. I knew most of my kind had broodgangs, many parents, and many young. Darbhein had always seen the wisdom in the collective. Unique, it seemed that I was born to her alone and raised by her alone. We only knew our quiet life, as had many ancestors of mine.

"The first of my folk to live as hermits is beyond memory. Why he chose to hide in the forest all his life, we did not know, and it did not matter. When I came of age my mother, who had lived for many manling lifetimes before I was even hatched, fell sick and died. I grieved for her, laid her to rest in the forest, and continued living as I had been taught.

"I hunted and wove and sang to the forest, but then it was that a day came to bring change to me and mine. A serpent with slipping tongue found way into my stables as I was out gathering herbs. My horse, Kemir, was bitten and she cried out, sallying brave Mohnk the hound, leaping to her rescue. Mohnk killed the invader but was himself bitten on the leg. I arrived alas to find the three dying on my stable floor. I knew the snake, the Ashtail, as my mother had called them. I also knew which herb was needed to heal the wound. I ran into my home, the small and hidden ancestral home of what you may almost call my broodgang. I looked at the herbs I had and to my dismay I had but one rebete petal in the box. The Ashtail is a rare snake and so I hadn't thought to prepare myself properly. That was my crime. I ran to my fallen friends and was faced with an impossible choice. My horse, Kemir, my great friend and travelling aide, my connection to the outside world, or sweet Mohnk, the brave hero who'd risked his very life for Kemir. I stood before them and wept, yet I knew I must use the petal in that very moment. Without thought I chose Mohnk.

"I chewed the flower into a poultice and put it into his wound. I know not why I chose him and not Kemir and yet I did and after I was finished I carried him into the house and returned to lie with Kemir. It took her until the moon rose to finally slip from this world and I wrapped her body in a blanket. That was the only true wrong I ever committed. I allowed my friend to die, and to die slowly. But as I had also saved a life, the great weighing scales of Mesuda balanced in a way unfathomed. I believe, though I cannot prove it, that this was the very moment that my kind were drawn into the Ethkeld and to the Fogkeld."

Kief had read that word before. *Fogkeld*. The fade, as most folks called it. A place of myth where it was said that terrible fiends and monsters lived, punishing the wicked and pouring fear into the hearts of the honest. It was said that the Nul knights hunted fade beasts, separate from all kingdoms and peoples. Had he not seen the things he had seen, Kief would not have believed them real. The fire in his belly roared into his throat, a pain unlike any other, a burning of the spirit, but aware or unaware, the Darbhein continued his tale.

"Once my dog was healed and my horse was buried, I took two family treasures that were saved for such occasions, and a bundle of hides. Mohnk and I walked to town with the hopes of buying a new horse. This was the first time I had come into the town alone and instead of the usual three days ride, it took me closer to a trihad. When I did arrive, I did not know anything was different. I saw no other of my kind in the town, as there usually was, but at first, I thought nothing of it. People were running around calling names. Supposedly two Humaine women had gone missing alongside the Darbhein, and rumours began to connect unconnected events. They blamed my broodfolk for their disappearance.

"A merchant I spoke to told me that he'd always known that the Darbhein weren't to be trusted and that he'd always despised them. To which I was taken aback. I was Darbhein. Why should he tell me such grim hidden thoughts and resentments? I looked behind him at the shop counter and saw on it a looking glass. I had the look of a young manling, much like yourself. I couldn't understand it, and so I thought it a mere trick of the light. I asked the shopkeeper to sell me a horse and offered a ruby ring as payment. It was an elegant lady's ring, and he immediately grew suspicious and asked me where I had gotten it. I said it was a family treasure, which was the truth, and yet he called me liar. He beat me and called upon the Humaine guards. I was clapped in iron and was told that my punishment would be worse than death. I would live out my days in a stone cell with no light or companionship, lonely as Mesuda before our birth."

Kief didn't know at what point he had risen to his feet. He had been transfixed by the Darbhein's story, listening, his blood running quicker and hotter. He hated this weak and mould-addicted creature. He hated the lies in its story, and he hated its skin. There was a dull clattering sound behind him. Something fell from within the swinging cage above and landed on the ground at his feet. The handle of the crane's claw was much the same, but where the four prongs of the mace had once been, was a glinting, pointed blade. The claw had finally grown into a dagger. Kief bent and picked it up and at that moment a terrible longing filled his soul. He gripped the dagger and looked down on the Darbhein.

Remyl said, "Grant me peace, soul-woven, and I hope it grants you the same."

Kief screamed and threw himself across the cell, falling upon the frail old creature. The knife descended again and again. Streaks of blood whirled into the air and up the walls.

Kief screamed and cut until the final breath left the Darbhein, and the spell was broken.

Act III

A Task

XI

A Mouse

"A journey is a funny thing. Be it a jaunt to the sea, a homecoming, a merchant's sojourn, or even the travels of soldiers, every moment is felt, larger than itself and oft in discomfort. Every forced step, stern word, or whipped churl. But then before you know it, your journey is complete. You've arrived, the lord has called upon you and your fellow footmen to make camp and then you set about your next task. You may have controlled your feet and hands as you walked, but more so than not, a soldier does not control their destination or ought much else."

The sun was growing on the horizon, a low crimson, as the boat's cook, an oak of a man, strolled across the deck and offered a cauldron of stew. Somewhat precariously on top of it, he'd stacked wooden bowls and spoons, as well as a little sack. Grappy smiled and nodded, and the cook put down his cauldron. Then came running the cook's lythe and anxious assistant, mortified that her colleague should carry everything himself. She snatched the spoons and set to doling out steaming portions of a pungent, if watery, river fish stew. She also produced a tough bread roll from the sack for each of them.

Grappy accepted his bowl and, once the pair had moved on, continued to speak, "When a king adjourns his court he is declaring that the journey taken by speech and mind has reached its conclusion, though those gifted in diplomacy will know that the end of a day's sessions are far from the true conclusion of any matter. Words themselves journey from paper to rune to tongue to ear, and then they take another journey within. A journey is an intangible movement between two points, though even in ending it is hard to name a journey so. To say it has been a journey is the most curious of falsehoods, so say the thirteen masters of Kammar. It is hard to say when one journey ends and when one embarks upon another."

* * *

As the Redheim army's journey reached its momentary destination by boot, wheel, whip, and thought, tired men began unravelling tents and feeding themselves. They wore red, to commemorate their old king and his new lord son who continued his war. Their king had claimed a line through an eldest son who was scorned many generations before, though the real truth of that matter will never be known to the common folk. What is known is that Redheim was formed when a royal cousin declared himself king at the end of a fruitless battle to claim Pallid land. He declared that the current ruler was a fool and that their loss was a punishment from Mesuda who rests. The blood on his tunic became the banner of his new kingdom and so generations of futile war began.

In the Monterio Valley, the Redheim army at once set up cordons and blockades on all the roads, cutting off supplies to the castle. Raiding parties moved across the land from house to house, farm to farm, taking what they could over the course of many hours, and a sprawling camp was set up on the plains on the eastern side of the castle, long out of arrow shot.

In these camp grounds, lords and lordlings donned armour and set to assault preparations, which in some ways mirror defence preparations: food is needed, ranks of men are made, and defences are erected around pickets. When a large force makes camp, particularly on the eve of battle, the force itself is encircled by men-at-arms and knights who will hem in the churls and peasant forces who would likely run for the hills given half a chance. Churl forces are made of prisoners, or men and women forced from villages on long marches to battlegrounds. They of course often outnumber the voluntary force, but lifetimes of cajoling and station holding make them subservient. With vacant faces and terrified minds, brimming with horrific thought, they do as they are bid.

That first night, Sen, Drelle, and Rom watched on long through the darkness as the wind caught scents of burning thatch, and they knew that distantly below them untold crimes were unfolding at the tips of spears. They saw soldiers gather supplies, clamp shut the gullets of roads, and set to starve the great stone castle of all contact, and all hope.

On the second day Sen, Drelle, and Rom awoke on the covered hillside. Safe and untroubled due to their obtuse positioning away from any field or house. It was not the tallest place by far yet was still up a mile or so of difficult terrain. Around mid-morning, they watched as a red-clad group of horsemen rode into the besieged town.

Sen must've looked concerned at the sudden movement of soldiers. "They cannot see us, do not fear." Drelle said, "I cannot be snuck up upon. Well, aside from by the likes of you." And with that, she grinned.

"Why not me?" Sen said.

Drelle looked at her, emerald eyes boring deep into her soul. "You have an aptitude towards forest speech, it seems."

"Forest speech?"

"There are those of us who can speak to the forest, those who can speak to the sky, and those who can speak to the sea."

Below, the small group of red-clad horsemen turned towards the heart of the town and rose up a stiffly rising cart path. The lower town of Monterio had been emptied and now sat as a dusky no man's land between castle and army. The riders picked their way through the empty town wearing shining armour and holding crimson banners that fluttered in a heady wind that flattened grass across the valley. It was a distant onlooking, but the horsemen seemed flustered, and their mounts agitated. At their centre, separate from the red flags, was one of white colouring. Drelle explained that this flag meant that they sought to parlay.

The rest of the Redheim camp seemed to hover in anticipation, the only continuous movement being three separate groups who were rapidly carrying logs and rope, seeming to busy themselves crafting strange and heaving structures. Behind Drelle and Sen, who were perched on one of the large rocks that broke up the hillside, sat Rom staring glumly at his feet. As they'd neared the castle his usual quietness had thickened into a vile mood that neither food nor friendly cajoling from Drelle and Sen could cure. This was a mood that Sen had never seen in a man. There was something animalistic in it, and it unnerved her.

The small unit of Redheim horsemen made their way along the main town road, watched nervously by archers on the castle walls, the tips of their bows catching the early morning sunlight and looking almost like a field of grass, unbothered and unbowed by the wind. As the group of horsemen neared the portcullis, a horn sounded and a man in golden armour appeared above the gatehouse.

"Could they find us if they have a mage in their army?" Sen asked.

To which Drelle didn't turn, and growled, "If there is I will be sorely disappointed, and I may be forced to kill them."

The riders closed in on the gate and halted. A thin man, cladded in furs and fine fabrics, spurred his horse forward and seemed to call out to the man atop the gates, the shrewd Lord Caspian himself. The distance was too great to make out their words, but they could see how agitated the riders were becoming as the meeting went on.

"What do you think they're talking about?" Sen said.

"They'll both ask the other to surrender, they'll snap yardsticks until they can accurately guess the length of each other's manhood, and then they'll force their slaves to kill one another across this small town, leaving a scar that will take decades to physically heal and centuries to mentally heal."

To that Sen had no response.

The horsemen below abruptly about turned and then rode back across the deserted town. The man in gold on the castle walls disappeared and the scene seemed to sigh.

* * *

Deep within those same castle walls a Fenn mouse, who went by the name of Darmok, scurried along a kitchen counter. For a day and a half, he'd made his way through the town with the subtle skill common to his kind, until finally finding a thin grate through which to enter the castle itself. He paused and sniffed the air, smelling bread, sweat, a burning fireplace, and fear in the hearts of the cooks. He could also smell cold air through a crack in the brickwork and could feel in his fur the low hum of deep soulwork beneath his feet. He turned and ran, skittering through the small gap, and continued into the darkness. He had no safety of family or friends, and aside from the truth of his senses he had no knowledge of his surroundings. For these reasons, Darmok was courageous to quest into the bowels of this beast. He'd made a promise long ago to always do what he could for the good of the world, trusting that Drelle would only call upon him for the most important of tasks.

Through the wall, he came to a dusty crawl space that opened out into an old airway that most castles carve into their under floors, lest the underground pressure and air become too thin. Other mice had been there, well-fed ones. Darmok continued until he was able to turn left and then went into a descending, small, and well-trod tunnel leading to a network of crawlspaces and cobwebbed corners throughout the castle. He could smell iron on the air, and fear, and bone soup, but he paid those things no mind. He could feel the hum in his fur, but it was faint and difficult to track and so, as he was trained, he spoke a thought and the wind shifted in the narrow passageway. Feeling its direction on his fur, he turned again and came out through a crack in a wall at the top of a spiral set of stairs. He quickly descended, hopping from one to the other, deeper and deeper, sticking to the edge of the wall so as to hide in the shading. He soon made it so deep he could scarcely smell the other mice and knew that even they did not often venture this far into the dungeons.

At the base of the stairs, there was a long corridor. It was darker there, lit only by torchlights that were few and far between. He heard guards up ahead, playing cards and laughing over warm ales. One of them smelled of dog, like a dog in pain, with small traces of hair and blood on the tip of his boot. With a hop and a slide, Darmok ran along the line of the wall, quickly went under the table, past leather boots and spilled droplets of ale, breaking cover at the final moment to disappear into a side corridor. Here he smelled different blood. Fresh blood, not normal blood, a form of blood that he had only scented once before, in a laboratory in Kuh-Dul.

Above the blood, in the blood, and through the blood, he could feel the runework as it touched flesh. He could feel the breeze of its soul workings on his fur and so he scurried forth to speak to the one who could only be the rune knight of Nul. He could feel the power of him, and the pain in him, both of that moment and of many that had come before. Darmok could feel the cries of pain coming from the bird in the rune knight's hand. The mouse scurried behind the knight and saw him standing over a corpse, one still warm and bubbling, and smelling of something foul and peculiar, something ancient which made the rodent bristle. The black mouse began tapping at the bars, but the knight was deep in thought and so he did not hear. Darmok called out in wind speech. Though, *called* is perhaps the wrong word. He did not speak in a way that others do but, in his way, he called out. Still, the knight did not hear. No true knight of Nul should have been unable to hear him.

To a mouse, all men look alike, and so Darmok had little knowledge of the age of the knight or of the look of him, aside from the smell of the blood covering his arms. He called out once more, but there came no turning head and no reply. Perplexed, Darmok instead decided to follow the other great power in the walls – the man suit. He ran through more dark places, cobwebs, and crawl holes until he finally came upon a small gap in the roof of what must have been a hidden lock room, an armoury. He could hear guards outside running to and fro and he saw weapons on walls and racks. On a table against one wall lay a pile of dark and tarnished armour. The brave mouse scurried down and came to a stop by the helmet. He could feel the glistering soulwork within and sniffed at it.

The helmet seemed to stare back and in a moment that felt like a cascade of thought and time, it spoke. In a low and echoing voice, it said, *"Greetings Fenn mouse. My master once tended to your cousins."*

The mouse jumped back, horrified, but having seen magics before he gathered himself and took a step towards the suit and spoke. Again, *spoke* is the wrong word, for mice do not speak as menfolk do, certainly not Fenn mice. Darmok sent a thought drifting on the wind to the helmet, an image, a mere idea. He asked the helmet why it could speak, and why it and the knight had been left in this way.

The helmet considered this for a moment, and it said, *"I am a task. I slay the Baoleth and protect Kief of Mondar."*

The mouse sent another thought, the image of the boy standing over the corpse in the dank cell far above. *"You do not protect him."*

To that, the armour glowed faintly and said, *"The crane guards him also, even from me."*

The mouse had smelled the crane, yet hadn't known its name, and conveyed this to the helmet. He then said, or thought, *"A soulsinger of Kammar has come to rescue you. Would you come with us?"*

The helmet again considered this and said, *"If Kief of Mondar Village may come as well."*

Darmok conveyed that he would speak with Drelle on the matter. He also conveyed that he would return with the solution to the suit's predicament. The suit thanked the mouse and then Darmok scurried back up to the hole high on the wall, once again leaving the strange armour in darkness.

* * *

On the sheltered hillside, Sen watched on as Pecham flew down and conversed with Drelle for a tense minute. Moments before, any Braelian guard atop the western wall of the castle would have been surprised to see a mouse and a crow deep in conversation, whereupon the two had nodded to one another and then scampered and flew their separate ways. As it was, the soldiers were too preoccupied with keeping their eyes on the invading army to notice.

"Under the western castle wall there is a grate, out-letting heavy rain. Meet Darmok there," the haggard crow said, with an air of seriousness that was rare for him.

"Was he well?" Drelle said.

"Too smart mouse. Darmok does not be caught."

Sen strained to hear as mage and crow sat and discussed all that Darmok had seen, and after a few moments, Drelle thanked him and offered an oatcake. Pecham took it and hopped off to another rock. Drelle then turned to Rom and said, "I have found them, both suit and knight. Though, it seems this knight is not the same as the one I seek. It matters not, we shall recover them nonetheless."

Rom nodded slowly, and then signed, *"I will not go down there, and neither will the girl."*

Drelle signed back in agreement and also signed that Rom's black mood would do nothing to aid their cause. *"The quicker our task is completed the sooner we can leave."*

Rom protested, saying that he was in no black mood, to which Drelle said that every grumble that came from him spelt mannish despair, to which Rom said that perhaps she should close her ears to it then.

Drelle then said aloud, "How pray tell does one close their ears?"

Sen hadn't understood much of what had been spoken between the two, so quick had been their hand speech, and she suspected that had been their intent. The harsh wind grew in strength, seeming to punctuate the mood of her two companions. They had spoken of a grate that Drelle had to go to, and of the battle that would soon begin, and of how they would need to complete their task before the tensions boiled over.

As the two met eye to eye on the hillside there came a sound, a *crack* like wooden lightning. Those structures that the men had been working a day and a night to build were finally finished. Three trebuchets stood lined up on the outskirts of the town. Huge, triangular frames of wood with a weighted arm that could, with great accuracy, toss enormous rocks across great distances. The missiles of Redheim, as was often their tactic, began at once, dipped in tar, and set alight. They roared red and streaking across the sky, followed by trails of black smoke. They almost seemed beautiful to Sen before they rained down their fiery horror on the walls. The sound echoed across the valley, and smoke and pain rose from the castle walls. The machine crews set to reload their weapons. A border castle such as this was a prize worth collecting. It meant a foothold in Braelian lands, strength in supply routes, and control over the river Yonn and all the riches that such a river could supply.

Drelle and Rom turned and too watched on as the streaks of fire rained down on the castle. After three hits, Drelle turned back to Rom and said, "You must make a gam."

Rom raised an eyebrow. *"A gam?"*

"I need it to speak my words clear and true." She reached into her bag and drew out a thin strip of metal, and a thin piece of wood. She also produced a knife and handed the three to Rom.

The weary metalworker agreed and, taking the items, he descended to a wind-guarded spot behind a boulder. Sen stayed by Drelle. She knew what a gam was: a children's toy or a common birthing day gift with words from a loved one. A trinket that was commonly sold up and down the country, made by every paltry metalworker. Little boxes with a small, engraved filament inside holding a few moments of speech, to be released with a button. To be used once and then reset with a new filament. What Sen could not fathom was, "What do you need a gam for?"

"I need to break a spell, messenger, and I'm hoping that I can do it without ever setting foot within those castle walls."

Sen puzzled this over but seeing that Drelle contrived to offer no further explanation she descended the rock and decided instead to watch Rom at his work.

The barrage continued long into the night. Great arks of fire crossed the sky and battered the castle, crumbling battlements and cracking mortar. Drelle didn't sleep, watching it closely, her heart in her throat – especially at one moment when it seemed that Brael were fit to sally out against the trebuchets. A gate behind the castle slid open and riders came out, a score of them sporting blackened armour and pole arms, but Redheim archers swiftly cut them down before they could get close to the siege engines, leaving riderless horses tramping away and fearful screams echoing up the valley. Sen had started to rise at the sounds but with a flash of angry eyes, Drelle made her stay behind the boulder, so as not to see such blood and carnage. After that, all Caspian could do was await Redheim's assault as fire rained upon his home. Drelle fretted and drummed fingers on her legs watching it, shuddering with each hit, afraid for her mouse. If brave Darmok was slain, the loss would be unbearable and their chance at completing their task would be dashed.

When morning came, Rom gave the completed gam to Sen. It was small and beautifully rounded, with a sturdy shell and accurate, well-crafted runework. Sen marvelled at it. It was finer than those seen in common shops, even though it had been made on a hillside from barely anything at all. She turned it over in her hand and saw the wooden underside, polished smooth. She then passed it to Drelle who thanked Rom in a way that made it seem almost like an apology. Drelle held the button on its crown and whispered some words into it. It glowed faintly and then she called on Pecham.

"Lose this and I will wring your neck," she said – to which Pecham laughed. He took the gam and flew off. Drelle then turned to Rom and said, "Take care of her, I will return tomorrow. If I do not, your task is complete, and you are set to go wherever you will. Might I suggest Rustgate. They always have a need for skilled metalworkers there."

Rom nodded. Drelle then turned to Sen and said, "Do as Rom says. If you don't see me again, journey to Kammar when you have the wisdom and age that allows you to do so with safety. Tell them I sent you."

Sen agreed and without another word, Drelle began to hike down the rocky hillside toward the village.

* * *

Pecham flew in a wide arc, looking down on the castle. Soldiers were huddled closely behind those parts of the walls unbroken by the barrage. Archers looked tired and haggard, and horses moved around fearfully. In a stable, a soldier was calling a dog to him, but the dog seemed scared and unwilling. The man shouted for it to come, but it would not. On the wall, came the call of Darmok, and Pecham landed, skittering on one foot next to him. No one paid them any mind. Pecham handed the mouse the gam and the mouse conveyed thoughts of gratefulness to Pecham, complimenting him on his flying ability. Pecham laughed heartily and flew off. Darmok took the gam and went back the way he had come. He moved silently through tunnel and crawlspace, down spiral stairs, and into heady darkness until finally coming upon the armoury. He crawled through a gap under the door and then climbed the table to stand next to the helmet. In two paws he clutched the gam.

"Greetings, Fenn mouse," the suit said in its low voice.

Darmok greeted him in thought and then held up the gam. He pressed the single button on its crown. The gam whirred oddly for a moment and then a clear, if metallic, voice rang out; the voice of Drelle.

It said, *"Dear Gromhir, I am here to tell you that you no longer need to be worn and that your task is your own."* And then Drelle's voice said a few words that her master had taught her, words of Darbhein origin, but Humaine invention. *"Geas avak tumhil."*

The mouse looked on at the great helmet as the crackling voice faded and the pent energy that made its runes function evaporated into the air. The mouse stared long and hard into the chasm of the shadowed eye sockets until finally there came a low groan. A gauntlet seized the helmet, Darmok leapt back fearfully, and another gauntlet seized the breastplate and, piece by piece, it reassembled itself, groaning and roaring until finally, it stood, missing one pauldron. In the corridor, two guards came running at the sounds.

"WHAT IS MY TASK?" the suit roared to the mouse, to which the mouse scurried back, terrified. Pecham had warned nothing of the terrible anger within the suit. It

stood tall, shining in the darkness, steam erupting from every crevice.

Darmok was a wise mouse and so he did the wisest thing. He gathered all the air he could into his fur and then with a tremendous shake of his body he used his power and told the suit that its task was to *follow*. The mouse scrambled under the door and moments later, the suit barrelled through it, wood splintering and metal bending asunder. Two guards in the corridor shrieked and half-lowered their halberds. The suit lifted its greatsword and charged, running one guard through and lifting him clean off his feet. He then flicked the blade out as though through butter and descended on the second who screamed and turned to run. The mouse cried a victory cry and leapt forth down the corridor.

XII

An Escape

Grappy looked down at his stew, feeling in his hands that it had grown cold. The cook and assistant had long since moved on to feed the other folk aboard. The two children had finished their plates and were bickering over the cloak wrapping their knees. It was large enough for them both, but it is the way of siblings to bicker.

Along the deck drifted sweet smoke, finder's leaf, from one of the riggers. He was a pale silhouette in the fog and Grappy inhaled the flowing scent, enjoying it. Grappy's son, Pauel, like himself, and indeed like his own father Kief, had been quite fond of the finder's leaf. A dried herb that was common in cities and drinking places of the southern kingdoms. Grappy liked it on occasion, but not in the same way his son had. It calmed the body and quieted the mind, which was peace when seldom used, but a habit of it slowed the reflexes and dampened the spirit. He recalled tendrils drifting from under doorways and sticking to hairs in their little seaside cottage. Lidded eyes of a sullen boy prodding at his meal.

Grappy took a cold spoonful of stew and chewed at a piece of shellfish. A little while after Pauel had been born, they settled in the coastal duchy of Creybridge to allow for the child to grow, but Grappy continued with his searches and his travels, his work. Every time he returned, Pauel was taller and more distant. More smelling of the sweet red leaf.

It was something they all had: a lusting for movement, a restlessness, an intensity. The difficulties that afflicted Grappy held his son all the same, worse so, for he was never taught of elder wisdom and of the commanding of the mind.

Grappy, at Pauel's mother Meeph's request, chastised his son for his low behaviour and for seeking solace where none could be found. Pauel hated him for countless stray words and sharp moods, and there came a time when Grappy had no idea what to do with the boy. He and Meeph decided that if only they could get him away from that town, with its salt and spray and idle tongues, they could loosen him, and give him perspective.

Regret clung like salt to Grappy's grey beard. The morning could be seen in the flecks of colour that had begun to appear on the horizon. The old man took another spoonful of cold fish stew, looking up and out across the water. The river was steadily widening, the boat churning along through the waves as the water became choppier and the river yearned to intermingle with the sea. He could hear gulls and could make out more vessels further downstream. He smelled the air and heard the murmurs of the water below. He told himself that the mistakes he had made with Pauel would not be repeated with Saph and Timmin. Even, as he'd first laid eyes on them, at the beginning of what had turned into a long and storied night, he'd had this thought in his mind. He would not fail them as he had their father.

Almost seeming to spring from Grappy's mind, Kraf-Krak appeared again, striding down the deck, giving a shock to the crewman still smoking the finder's leaf. The man started and dropped his pipe with a little plop into the water. It flowed away with the river and the sailor cursed. Kraf-Krak shot the man a daggered stare and continued toward the Stroongarm three. With an eyeless grin, the captain told them that their destination was close, some two or three hours depending on the wind. Grappy thanked him and as the Kammarite returned to the tiller, he took the last portion of his stew in one quick gulp. The children looked up at him expectantly, seeming worried that the end of this journey might spell the end of the story.

Grappy said, "Kief's father, my grandfather: Mulrek the betrayer, was a curious man. His history was told in vague terms to me by my father, and I later learned more from Pallidar histories at Kuh-Dul. My grandfather saw what he perceived to be an opportunity to end the Redheim war and he took it, caring not for the victor's name, and knowing that he may soon die as well. Of southern Pallid, many clans were sworn to Brael, as a part of what was known as the Grey Lake Concord, which had on the whole ensured peace between the two kingdoms for three generations, since even the days of the Darbhein. The line of clan holds along the northern side of the copper peaks were called The Hemmec, the sworn men, and the Braelian empire had a similar collection of fiefs below the mountains, including those of Rustgate and Baelrod. They were in turn known as the Bremmec. Both lines of keeps and lands were sworn to the other king, and as such the Pallid Hemmec found themselves, for generations, inextricably tangled with the Braelian civil war. Many of The Hemmec saw themselves as closer to Brael than they did Pallid, and the trade and stability this brought was seen as a great and noble boon. The Stroongarm clan was no different. As Hemmec, they had deep ties to Brael, which I believe was what informed my grandfather's fateful decision.

"He and his men came to a hillside on the eve of a king's battle and chose to ride into the flanks of the losing side, no matter their banner. Both sides were of their own folk, so he said. When the Braelian king learned that what was to be his greatest battle, had become his greatest defeat, at the hands of a lesser lord of the sworn Pallid knights no less, he was enraged. He demanded the king of Pallid bring justice to those who would break the concord of the Grey Lake and so it was done. My grandfather, as the story goes, went to the Redheim court to ask for safe haven for his folk, knowing the sureness of the Braelian king's wroth. However, Lord Mulrek Stroongarm was denied. The king of Redheim, with a gesture, had one of his guards slay Stroongarm where he stood, for a traitor has no rights in Brael.

"The king's men, alongside a sizable Pallid force, swept into Ahrmguard, killing and burning all. This was shortly after my own father, Kief, had left his home on a journey to become a scribe at the Jeffet Oratory on the southern coastlands. This was a journey that would not see its completion. Such guilt Kief felt; such terrible and haunting guilt that not even the sturdiest of warriors could contain. Yet he did for years, playing at his lute, smoking his leaf, and serving his drinks. Not a single tear was cried for Sandy or his mother or his two brothers.

"Indeed, after fate had set him on his course, and he stood over the man he had slain in that dank cell, he thought back over the length of his life and considered how it all had led him unwillingly to this place and time."

* * *

With the pounding at the walls and the men of Monterio Castle readying themselves to fight for life and limb, Kief was ignored and untended. He stood over the body of the old man for a long while, at first basking in the glory of his actions, but soon tasting something bitter. He looked down at the tattered, bloodied remains of the old Darbhein. He fell to his knees and wretched and cried, until stinging-eyed, nothing remained within him. Grieving his mistake he put the slain man's arms over himself, closed his eyes with filth-streaked fingers, and laid a blanket over his head. He then paced for what could have been many hours or few. Long he felt the rumblings of distant missiles hitting the walls, until finally, on the second day, a guard seemed to remember to bring him a meal.

At the sight of the murder, the guardsman opened the cage and drew his sword. Kief held his dagger aloft, almost in a trance, unaware that it clung to his palm. The guard ordered him to drop it, and when Kief would not, the guard swung for his neck. Kief, with alarming swiftness, ducked the blade and then took a step into the man's guard, and with the crane's pommel, he beat the fellow square on the nose. The blade seemed to scream for blood, wind straining around the metal, begging to slice at the guard's exposed throat, but Kief whirled past him into the corridor. Not yet did he need another kill. He kicked the guard into the cell and shut the door behind him. As he turned to go, Kief almost saw something in the pool of Darbhein blood. A shadow with crimson eyes and a crimson tongue, hooked teeth, and a gaping maw.

Thinking it some trick of the light, Kief darted up the stairs to find two more guardsmen who, seeing who he was, and seeing him drenched in blood, drew their weapons and threw themselves at him. As a twig on a stream, he bent and turned and swayed about their blades. His knife tasted blood as he removed the fingers of one guard's hand. The man screamed and bent to catch his falling digits, and away Kief flew down the corridor. The guards shouted after him, but in their armour they were slow. Kief turned a corner and, taking two steps at a time, made the spiral stairs his. He heard a deep clatter of a trebuchet's missile. Mortar and dust arose and on he went. At the top of the stairs, he ducked another small group of guards, fled through a near-empty canteen, and found himself in a wide courtyard. On one side was a row of stables and feeding troughs, and behind them were the tall exterior walls. Atop those walls, he saw men scrambling to positions, and he heard horns rising above the cries of many men.

More guards appeared at the gateway on the far side of the courtyard and so Kief winked into the stables. Some number of horses were panicking and whinnying, straining against their stall doors, nipping at one another's bobbing heads. Their blood seemed hot to Kief, bubbling, tasty meals for the hungry claw in his hand. The soldiers outside seemed that way too. A sick and dreadful hunger filled Kief and he smiled. Men roared in the near distance and there was a clatter of steel outside. Kief's rage grew. He began to shake with it and turned to run into it, into the shrieks and the madness of battle. But then, from what felt like many miles away to his tumbling mind, there came a whimper.

Kief whirled around, and in the corner of an empty stall cowered a hound. A sleek and bewildered hunting hound, her grey fur matted with dried old blood. He fell to his knees and the feeling, whatever it was, went away. The dog whined and cowered deeper into the corner. Outside, the beating of steel and the screams of battle grew louder. Inside the small stable, Kief felt only pity for the dog. It must have been mightily loud for her. Kief spoke kind words and held out a hand, finally touching the dog's muzzle. She settled a little, so Kief sat beside her and leaned against the wall. She was flinching in time with clamour against the castle. Once again himself, he could think of nothing but comforting this injured hound. It mattered not that there were rows of red-clad men racing for the walls, forming bridges over the dug moat and lifting their ladders to the walls. Kief was a mountain and from him burns bubbled, formed arteries and rivers to swell, ever falling, ever running to the sea.

Who could hurt a little dog so?

* * *

Spittle flew from Grappy's mouth as he painted the scene, and all around him crewmembers seemed to lean in to listen. The Adder's sway with the current punctuated his words. "It was at that time there came a twin rumble. Two of three flaming missiles struck the western wall, frontage fell away and the stonework crumbled and cracked in the middle. Then, with a colossal cheer and pounding of drums, the men of Redheim brought on a metal-tipped ram, which some claim had runic markings of great power, but that is just a part of the tapestry of The Battle of Monterio Castle." Grappy looked around at his audience, "One must always remember that tapestry is wool and that history is written to be amusing.

"Picture this: you and a score of men and women are in a unit led by a grizzled knight in a red tabard. You poke at cook fires and your belly rumbles, but you don't wish to eat for you are sick to your innards. You sweat and shake and listen to the crack of trebuchets somewhere beyond the picket. Someone rides through and yells an order to your commander, and he forces you to your feet. You don't want to, but it is understood that this knight will kill you himself if you do not. You pick up your shield and axe and follow in line, anxiety in every vein. You join a larger group, all in line, and without any ado, a horn sounds and the horde gathers speed. There are some with ladders, and some with bows, and others like you have shields, held above their heads. The horde first cheers, but in the tension it becomes a scream. The ants in your stomach bore upward into your chest and you cry alongside them all, sprinting at those walls. Heat, noise, and sensation blend into chaos. You run through a burning town, and your commander shrieks at the men to lift the ladders. Somehow you grasp one and up it goes. All around you arrows fall, folk beside you, whom you know very well, yet you cannot recognize are hit. Some scream as they die, others don't.

"Other missiles fall; wax, rocks; and still you help the ladder upward and hold it steady. Men begin to climb, but for every three that ascend, one falls into a mounting, churning pile of corpses in the ditch. Your turn comes, somehow no arrow has hit you, no rock. Smoke swills into a red sky, and you grasp the rungs, awkwardly, holding your axe and shield. You begin to climb. The man in front of you stops halfway and makes a choking noise, blood froths from him and wets your forehead. He falls, winging you, but you hold on as the ladder sways. Already many are climbing below you so up you must go. The stone face of the wall looms black and mighty, and you climb evermore. Other ladders are raised alongside you, and similar scenes occur on them. Finally, you see the top, the precipice, and there are men, billhooks, green cloth. Their faces are contorted in twisted ways that fill you with loath. You leap at them, with little else to do, cresting the battlements. You catch a blow on your shield and bring your axe down on a man's arm. It is just meat after all, and not. He shrieks and steps back and you take the chance to stand on firm stonework. You see the burning and bloodied interior of the castle for the first time before something tears your stomach. It sears. You look down and see a child in ill-fitting garb, grasping the spear that fills you. You split his forehead with your axe, and you die together on the wall.

Grappy took a breath, "The green-clad Braelian defenders shot man after man with arrows and thrown rocks. Those enemies who made it to the walls and up the ladders did so with the fervour of folk who had just witnessed the terrible and pointless deaths of many close ones. Desperation such as that comes only when folk need such horror and death to have meaning. Though, as with all battles, only one side could win and so only they could have meaning. Only one could take home tales of defending, or taking, bringing glory and peace to their mother lands.

"Redheim sent wave upon wave, wearing down their foe over many long hours, and by the time the ram was raised, hundreds lay festering, filled with arrows, and gurgling their last blood into that dug moat."

Grappy paused and looked at the children, and then he looked downriver, at the distant boats, and further to the feint blue line that was the sea. "Caspian of Monterio had no such luxury in numbers as the men of Redheim. His men were few, and so had to fight long and hard, unable to ration their strength. His physik bays soon filled to the gullet and

THE SUIT OF NUL - A NIGHT ON A RIVERBOAT

his archer's supply ran empty. Despair filled the hearts of his men.

"Inside the stables, Kief held the dog to his chest. Tears rolled down his face and matted the fur of the hound. Do not think my father a coward, or a weakling. He was neither. In fact, aside from what fate had presented him, he had begun as something plain and ordinary. Let it never be said that ordinary folk cannot step forth when the time calls for it. Ordinary folk have great power and great worth, and if you know this then you must also know that the actions of Kief's father, my grandfather, the so-called traitor Mulrek Stroongarm, were justified and noble.

"However, Kief did not sit idly in the stables for the many hours that the battle would last. In the time it takes to well-knead bread dough, he decided that the time had come for him to stand and see where he could go. Fate is a peculiar beast, and had he not told it to me in this way himself I would never have believed this the truth."

* * *

The noise seemed to lessen, almost still. Kief carried the dog outside the stables, poking his head out first to see what went on outside. The courtyard had filled with wounded, and above on the walls, he saw the Braelians finish some straggling boy on the walls. Blood drenched the tall stonework and the wailing and screaming began once again, further along at another wall. He stood dumbfounded, watching haggard groups running or limping, or carrying those limp, depositing them in heaps every which way.

None paid him any notice at all. But then there came another sound, one that rattled Kief to his centre. Again, he was standing in the black pool of water, stretching in all directions for all distance and time. The water rippled and he heard a bellow.

The Suit of Nul roared its low and tragic roar. A small group of guards at the entranceway to the courtyard turned and then came the great blade. The suit cut down three men in one long swipe and kicked another soundly into a nearby wall. They must have thought it some knight of Redheim, as more rallied to attack it, but as a child with carved toys, the suit cast them aside. It then looked at Kief and the ink blackness of its eye slits swallowed him tooth to foot.

"KIEF OF MONDAR VILLAGE!" The armour's voice was cavernous, as deep as the Stretch of Yell. It sprinted toward him across the lake of nothing. *"OUR TASK IS TO FOLLOW THAT MOUSE."*

The world rippled about them, the suit turned on its heel, and Kief looked down to see that indeed there was a black mouse, bounding across the courtyard. It went down a sideway betwixt some smouldering woodwork, followed by the suit, and not knowing what else to do, Kief followed. They were led on a winding route. Mouse, then suit, then boy and dog. Two guards turned a corner on them, and more were behind in pursuit. The suit swung its greatsword and took a deep wedge out of one man's shoulder, and in the same movement slammed the pommel into the next man's chin. The suit's impetus was unyielding. It broke through

THE SUIT OF NUL - A NIGHT ON A RIVERBOAT | 213

another group of guards, hotly followed by Kief and his wayward hound.

Then from beyond the walls came a great cheer as the ram of Redheim completed its task. "To the west wall, to the west, they come!" followed the cries of Braelian lieutenants and captains.

The suit and boy and mouse and dog charged through the mass of bewildered men, who were unsure of which to defend from, the black knight or the encroaching army. Like a great plough through the earth, the unlikely group carved a route into another courtyard and went down a side passage until nearing a wide, stone well. The mouse did not slow, and it leapt straight into the well. It was closely followed by the suit and then hesitantly by the boy and dog, who turned and saw pursuers nearing them before finally casting caution aside, and vaulting feet first into the darkness.

The water was cold and deep and immediately dragged them under.

* * *

It was near enough this time that Drelle was making her way through the lower town unseen, for she had many ways to hide herself. She could smell the blood and hear the fervour of beasts all around. Foxes feared and hungered, and flesh-eating birds rejoiced at the meal they would soon enjoy. She drifted downhill, away from the castle and continued out to the eastern road. Pecham circled above and told her which ways to avoid soldiers, but she could tell that he too planned to wet his beak on carrion. She cursed the world, cursed men, and cursed their evil appetites. The town could have been pretty in the right light, without the orchestra of battle, the pickling corpses, and the rising smoke.

She went east, then south, then back on herself, spreading as moss in a doorway as a group of Redheim soldiers passed. There came a great cheer that echoed across the valley, as the western wall fell. Soon, Drelle came upon a low grate, below an embankment that marked the town's outer limit. Above it was an old mill, its clothless frame unmoving. Pecham cawed his approval when Drelle touched the grate, and she began to sing a song.

This was a difficult song to sing. The thrumm she could normally pluck with ease failed her, lost in the noise. It was not simply the clamour, it was more. She looked up the valley and saw the way the patchwork of field and grassland disappeared into the forest. She pondered that the forest may have once been much closer to Monterio Castle, that its construction had meant the cutting of trees. She knew there would be a lay line here, as there is in many valleys, so close, near where she stood. Her voice warbled in her throat, and she could almost not finish her song. She thought of the fiery finger in her pocket, and of the one it belonged to.

Her voice hardened, and her melody grew. From the ground sprouted thin roots which braided the grate, finding purchase in every seam, nestling into the rust and flaws in the metal. She sang louder still, and the roots multiplied, they gripped at the grate, and with a colossal effort, they ripped it asunder. Once inside, she called upon the roots to rise once more, to fill the hole and to hide her entry. They did as she asked, knowing that she did this for them as well.

**

The water was power. It dragged them downward, scraping Kief's back against rocks, and sending bolts of pain through his body. It seemed to continue for miles and just when Kief's lungs were set to burst, the under-river spat them out into a low and dank cave. The water became a thin trickle. Much of it seemed to disappear into cracks and seams in the earth. The dog hacked and coughed, and the mouse leapt free from some crevice in the suit's shoulder and shook itself. The suit began to glow from its chest and the space around them lit up a pale blue. They were in a long passage that continued in a gradual incline upward into further darkness.

"You can walk again?" said Kief to the suit.

"Be calm," said Darmok to the hound.

The Suit of Molag Nul and the terrified hound both voiced their agreement in their ways. The hound ran up to Kief and began to lick his face. Her fear was replaced with joy and gratefulness. The scents and sounds of the battle were gone. They had survived, and Kief could not help but smile. He was frozen, sopping cold, and heartily harrowed. Yet they lived, and he was free.

The suit was now clean, shining as if freshly polished and oiled, glistering in the light from its chest. They sat for a while catching their breath. The suit stood vigil and the mouse licked at his fur. It was then that Darmok made a strange sound that to Kief seemed quite unlike a sound a mouse should make, and then they heard watery footsteps further down the stony passage.

Out of the darkness walked a red-haired woman, wearing a brown cloak and a woollen robe. She held a wooden staff and her eyes glittered in the suit's glow. "I am mightily pleased to finally make your acquaintance, Gromhir," she said.

XIII

A Hillside

The river widened, the edges slanting out first into beaches and then on the port side into man-made boundaries and wooden shunting that rose to a high sea wall. Those on the Adder soon began to see all manner of vessels bobbing with the current: fishermen in their skiffs, bargemen, and transporters, even one or two covered paddle craft likened to those used by seal hunters on the Pallid northern coast. There were aching sounds of gulls and floatwood all around. They shipped oars and brought the Adder to a slow, joining a long queue of boats. The display seemed unusual to Kraf-Krak, and he developed a brooding mood, staring off one side into the mass of wooden masts. People were sitting on decks, eating and talking amongst themselves, their voices blending with the creaking of their boats and the scuffing of the water below. The crew resigned themselves to the same as they inched along. They took seats and talked and fiddled, and seemed to tense as a whole. A little while later they passed two port authority riverboats with the red sails of their station, hemming them in at either side. Kraf-Krak let out a long sigh into the cold morning air as they passed. The light was rising more and more as time wore on, and it soon tinted the scene a bare blue.

There was a rising tension the closer they came to the port. If Grappy craned his neck, he could just about see it through the mass of sails and rigging covering the widening river mouth. It was a wide and well-used bay, with wooden cranes and all manner of person on shore. Beyond the port, there was a mass of warships bearing capital insignias and the green colours of Brael, all in a line blocking the river mouth. Where saltwater and river water mixed, the light caught it strangely, the colours distinctly separate, like fish oil in a puddle, roiling beneath the flotilla.

Grappy watched with interest as Kraf-Krak called out to another vessel just ahead of them. A man leaned back and shouted a reply. Unable to hear, Grappy and the children looked on in puzzlement. Kraf-Krak finished his conversation and wrung his hands.

"When will we arrive, Grappy?" Saph said. The noise and hubbub was clearly bothering her in a way that seemed not to have infected her brother. Timmin was leaning over the starboard side taking it all in with broad fascination.

"Soon enough, little one," Grappy said, putting a hand on her shoulder. "Our port is this one, and then it'll be a short carriage ride home."

"Do you have a boat, Grappy?" she said, eyeing a fishercraft some yards to their right. There were two men on board having a heated discussion that somehow related to a net of fish atop their deck.

"I do, but it's currently in use by a friend of mine, otherwise I may have taken it to collect you."

"Is it big?" Timmin said, turning around. The light caught the sandy brown of his hair, and he seemed to have a grin about him. Mornings treated Timmin well.

"Small, but with these bones it's a little large for me to handle, my lad. Mayhaps you would have better luck."

It was then that Kraf-Krak, along with a couple of his crewmembers, came along the deck, their jaws set. One man had his hand on a rigger's knife on his belt.

"Is there no way you could put us ashore back stream a touch?" Grappy said, "I would rather walk than wait."

"See those two vessels we just passed?" he gestured back to the port authority boats with the scarlet sails. "They're there to stop folk from turning back. Happens sometimes. The boat ahead said they're searching, mayhaps looking for something in particular."

"Or someone," the rigger said.

"Well, then we have nothing to fear," Grappy said. He smiled a winning smile. "For now, we wait."

Kraf-Krak raised an eyebrow but said no more. He gestured for the crew to go about their work, but Kraf-Krak and the one who may have been his first mate took a seat on the steps leading to the tiller above, keeping one eye on the Stroongarms. Grappy put an arm around Saph and said, "You know, it's good when you ask questions. You should do it more."

"What sort of questions should I ask?"

"Questions exactly like that one," he grinned. "Take Senhora. She knew how to wonder, ask, and find. All great and valuable talents that served her well in life. When I first met her, she was like a coastal wave, breaking upon you with a question, and then the currents underneath would roll backwards, and she'd return with another. A wave lifts its energy and then crashes it down, only to lift it again anew. This is the way of things.

"When I grew up, at least for my youngest years, I lived at Kuh-Dul, the capital city of the Kammar Isles. They call it so after the twin rocks that the city lies between. Hulking boulders of red rock, carved by sand, or wind, or even by Mesuda herself if you believe in flights of fancy. If you stand at one and call out, the landscape has a funny way of shaping the sound to always arrive at the other side as 'Kuh'. On the Dul side, the same happens but with the sound 'Dul.' Many of the southern islands have similar landscapes, with heavy walls of sandstone that make sounds call and carry in unusual ways. This is why their naming is often reflective of this – two sounds with a link of land between. Like our friend Kraf-Krak there."

Across the deck, Kraf-Krak looked up and smiled, and then turned back to the mate he'd been speaking with. They both appeared to agree on something, and the crewman walked off. Kraf-Krak remained where he was, listening to Grappy's tale.

Grappy smiled back, and continued, "I was schooled there, which I mostly did not enjoy, so in my younger years

I would instead disappear into the crowds of the upper city and find my way into the hills. It's a vibrant and exciting place, grander than any city of Brael, and full of unusual folk, but I wasn't much for people. Even today I am not much for people. So, this day I went to Kuh, and was studying the inscribing on the rock. It tells some aged, cracked-pot theory that the world will one day be shattered by terrible winds, and in the final moments of time, the two rocks will roll down and collide together in the centre of the city. I thought it drivel.

"I'd met Senhora for the first time, at least in memory, earlier that morning as she returned from a long journey that had kept her free of Kammar for many years. We had been introduced by my parents, and as they stood in conversation I slipped away. She must've seen me somehow, or some creature had told her, and so she'd followed me to the great rock. I was mightily shocked to hear her voice behind me as I inspected the scribings. She said, 'What do you think of the Meeting of Kuh and Dul?', which was the somewhat unimaginative name for the tale.

"I turned around and I quivered in her presence. I said, 'I don't think it could happen.'

"'Why?' she said, grinning. She was as tall as she was talented, her dark hair braided into the learn'd braids, like Kraf-Krak's braids, but where he has three she had five. A mark of great respect in those regions.

"I said, 'The rocks, they are offset, and the line of the hill – that must've been obvious even as they concocted this tale. The rocks would not roll into the city, they would only go slightly down the slope and stop in the grass banks. The momentum would surely not be enough, plus Dul isn't even rounded, it's flat on three sides so it would slide even less.'

"'Do you think the storytellers were fools?' Senhora said.

"I paused at that, sensing the trap, but of course, the defiance of youth took my humours and I said, 'Yes, they were fools and now they're deceased fools.'

"She chucked and said, 'Do you think your mother a fool?'

"I had no response to that. I have always had a talent for losing my tongue at choice moments.

"'Who do you think sent me to follow you? It was rather sloppy of you just strolling about with that on,' she gestured at my scarf, a light blue one my Ma had made me that summer to keep the dust from my face. I again said nothing and Senhora said, 'You may not like it, but older folk know the ways of the world better than you. You'd best listen to their advice.'

"She looked out across the city, sprawling across the grassy valley. The grass of Kammar is not like ours in Brael. It's tall, sharp, and wide. It's not uncommon for people to cut flutes from it and play melancholic tunes at festivals and the like. She continued, 'I didn't like it either, especially those first lessons – but what you learn now is the foundation for greater things.'

"She let out a low whistle and with it, called down a hawk. The Senhora hawk. The natural runework on its beak faintly danced in the light, and the golden spread of its wings caught the wind as it circled and then landed on her wrist. I do not doubt that Senhora found keeping her namesake as a familiar amusing. Some say we have mimicked the runework of the animals, others say they mimicked us. I say it is coincidence.

"Even at that age, I knew my father's tale well, and so I knew that she was clever, trying to show me something subtle. So, I laughed and said anyone can whistle for a pet. She showed me her teeth and whistled again. The ground beneath my feet began to rumble. It grew wet, earthen water sprang forth over my boots and the hillside, then came thin roots, with white flowers growing on them.

"'Do you know what became of the Darbhein?' Senhora said, her words echoing across the scene with a shuddering timbre.

"I shook my head, though it was a question that I had long mulled, and one that I mull still. More than mull; I breathe, eat, and defecate that question. That question is mine.

"She said, 'They asked questions without speaking, and did not listen to the answers. They turned a blind eye as one of their own fiddled in matters beyond his comprehension, and for that, they were stricken from this world.'

"'How?' I burned with it, with the mystery, and with the suffering of my world since their departure, 'How did they disappear?'

"'Only Mesuda knows that' Sen said with a little smile.

"It is not in the answering that lies the story, it is in the asking. That is what Senhora taught me. A story is a promise, and if that promise is kept the story becomes a great one. Now, knowing that she would soon become one of Kammar's many masters, it may be perplexing to imagine her as a thin waif of a girl, wrapped in blankets up a rocky hillside."

* * *

Looking down semi-distantly on Monterio Castle, Sen and Rom could still hear the clash of steel, the screams, and the dull thuds of falling bodies. As the battle raged, the two remained where they were. The warfare below them was something that they watched with detached fascination. It is hard to fathom such carnage from such a distance, and so one's mind compartmentalizes the reality and the viewing. Not ignoring the terrific sounds and the lasting echoes across the valley, but knowing it has nought to do with you and so not fearing it. Even at the great cheer as the west wall fell, they felt little as they watched the men, specks to them, surge toward the breach and continue their fighting within the walls as the sun fell to a red whisker.

They knew not what occurred inside those walls, or what had befallen Drelle, or indeed her mouse. They simply did what they could, and that night all they could do was sit and wait. It was a crisp night, with a chill in the air, but not a breeze to lift the chill through their cloaks. Sen was leaning against Rom, with a larger rock to their back to shelter them. Rom was warm, and though she could tell that his joints were likely aching from all this sitting outdoors, he did not show it, other than occasionally shifting with a quiet groan. She mused that Mog had been much like that.

She would not show when she was in pain, or when she was tired, or if any ailment had befallen her. Sen decided, looking up at Rom's bearded chin, that the folk at the foot of the copper mountains all were sturdy as metal, and as beautiful when tempered.

Sen felt a terrible sense of loss then. She thought of the children in Bastaun as they had once been, all jostling and laughing with whichever lesson they had to learn on the village circuit. She thought of the feeling of the warm ovens at her back and the sound of the rain on the shutters as they took orders, pinning them with wooden pegs to string above the counter. She thought of Mog lashing red-faced boys with her tricky tongue. The laughs, and the safety. Sen thought of sitting by the well with her friend Jessep Fentshcook, the youngest of the three weaver children. The two of them used to look down it and howl into the water. The reflection showing her glinting eyes and brown hair, and his freckles and copper hair. She thought of peace and quiet, and in the Valley of Monterio, she felt tiny.

Below, the sounds of war continued and Rom did not notice Sen's melancholy. After a time of watching and waiting, a question came to Sen, a question that she mused was surely one of the most common and asked questions known to Humaine kind, and yet one seldom answered. She asked Rom of the future.

"Where will you go, Rom?" Sen said. She wanted to ask, 'What do we do if Drelle dies? Why did we even accompany her? What is the meaning of the events of the last few days?

Why us? What do we do about it all?' But she did not. She asked him of himself, and what he would do.

"I have family in the South Ward." As he signed it, Rom's great head looked down at her. She noticed that his eyes had a glistening quality as if he was sitting downwind of a campfire, though they had made no fire that night. *"I suppose I may go to them. You can come if you wish?"*

He gave her a look that, on one hand, brought her comfort, his fingers closing around her and keeping her from the world, but at that same time that comfort could never be sustained. There were too many questions that could not be answered in a little village smithy.

"What about Kammar?" Sen said, straightening up, "Drelle said I could learn there with the masters."

Rom sighed again. There was a pause, not just in him, but in the battle below, as if all hung in a precarious balance, and none wished to be the one to shatter it. The second dragged on into minutes, all the valley bated its breath, and then a horn sounded. They saw the torches of the Redheim soldiers below turnabout and, like sparks from a blade they disappeared from the castle walls and make their way back to their camp. The night's assault, it seemed, was finished.

Finally, Rom held up his hands so she could see by the moonlight, *"It is unwise to stake too much at the feet of those you've never met. Fache often said the masters of Kammar were not to be trusted. He said they were grand puppeteers, pulling great strings across all the world. They know too much and too little at once and though they aim to serve all, they forget themselves and serve their own needs first. Knowledge and power corrupt. This is why at Bastaun we had the charcoal law."*

Sen was getting used to hand speech, it flowed smoothly into her mind, as easily understood as if it were tongue-spoken words. "The charcoal law?" she asked, still speaking aloud.

Now, there was a question. The charcoal law was something that had governed every moment of life in Bastaun, and as an extension had governed much of her life as well. Had she stayed there perhaps she would have sworn by it and taken up a bowe of bastwood as her hammer. A question of a life unlived.

Rom lifted his hands again, *"Do not speak, lest your words turn to runes. Do not share secrets. Do not fight, lest your soul be corrupted, and your work tainted. Make no sharp thing or part-thing, or take a life for your work."*

Sen had known these laws without knowing their names. She remembered the silent and fidgeting queues outside of Mog's bakery. She recalled how they could joke and bicker and do all things that people did, only in silence, or as near to silent as people could be. She remembered Mog chit-chatting with merchants and passers-through whenever she had the chance. Sen remembered the strength in Mog's hands and the colour of her hair, and her eyes.

Sometimes the children used to say that the rules of silence had been conjured up by a sly old Darbhein as a joke once upon a time, because the smiths were irritating to him, and he wanted peace and quiet. As with all folk tales, there was a nugget of truth, but that is a tale for another time.

Sen sat back and considered what Rom had said. The thought of a place to go and find a new life had been a salve to her, something to numb the pain of the death of Mog, her mother in all ways but one. However, what Rom had said was true, and it was wise of him to say it. Sen needed caution if she was to make it in the world, and she turned the thought over in her mind like a coin. Even with Rom and Drelle, Sen was alone, more alone than she had ever been. She would soon need to decide what she would do, where she would go, and live with the consequences.

Sen thought of Drelle, how she was like Mog in temperament and humour. Drelle was certainly madder than Mog, and fiercer, or was she just as fierce but in another way? Sen's eyes drifted down to the castle, lit by fires and torchlight still. She could almost make out small groups of men inching out of the torn hole to carry the bodies of their kinsmen inside. She thought of Drelle in there somewhere, somehow retrieving a suit of armour.

And so sprung forth another question, "This suit, what is it really?"

"*I know it belongs to a Nul knight,*" Rom answered simply. Any irritation he'd had at answering her endless questions was gone that night. Perhaps he had come to realize what she had realized. She was alone and she would need to make her own mind up on what way to be in this world.

"What is a Nul knight?" She, of course, had heard the name before, crossing the lips of bards and storytellers, but she had never spoken frankly with anyone on the subject. "Do you think any fight in the battle down there?"

"They are not ordinary knights. Nul knights live by their own laws, like our Charcoal Law. They use magics forbidden to any other than themselves to guard our realm from the fade."

Sen looked him in the eye, and he turned, making himself more comfortable, as is the habit of many a storyteller. There's always an anticipation when a story begins, and from one as honest as Rom it would surely be interesting.

He began, his hands moving steadily, resolutely. *"I saw a Nul knight once when I was small. A Darbhein Nul knight. Me and Relc and a few of the other weans were there, Moggy too. She was..."* He sighed. *"She would have made a great smith. Didn't want it though. Liked chatting too much, she said. So, this big Nul knight was in Bastaun, and it was all abuzz. He had meetings with the head smith at the time. Kelvin. Now the amusing thing is that a young and foolhardy Fache pinched the knight's sword. The Darbhein had removed it to enter the refractory and left it leaning on the wall outside, not expecting any to dare to touch such a blade. Fache took it and ran afoul with it, playing at warrior and slashing and swiping wildly behind the grain store, where his father worked. I remember the glee, but also the shock when he swung too wide. The blade slipped from his grasp and flew across the way, almost impaling little Jennef, a girl from the village. It cut her arm and she screamed.*

As Rom was telling, Sen felt a chill on the back of her neck. It was a peculiar sensation, a bristling of the hairs, a warm chill, a warning. She turned and saw nothing. Just the hillside and the night. Rom noticed no such thing. He continued, *"All came running, including the knight who took up the blade and cursed Fache. He was clad in black and there was a fire* in his one eye. The other was horribly scarred as if he had been struck by a bear. He screamed at the young Fache, lifting him by the scruff of his shirt. 'This is Fell iron, made to cast beasts of the Fogkeld back to their den. Not for the cutting of girls,' he said.

"I never saw Fache so frightened. The Darbhein bared his teeth and said, 'Brood children who cannot be tamed must be devoured.' Fache near wet himself and the knight dropped him. The fearsome Darbhein then put the blade in his mouth and with those reptilian jaws, he bit a chunk clean out of the centre. He spat it at Fache and then sheathed what remained of the sword and strode off. I never understood how a weapon made to kill monsters could be bitten by mortal teeth. I asked Fache about the shard once, many years later, when he was then the forge master. He told me he kept it safe, as a reminder of both good metalwork and noble intent."

The chill was weedles in her ear, a nail on her spine. She stood up bolt and quested about, while Rom looked at her quizzingly. All the world around Senhora seemed to be making a sound, a low humming, a vibration. *The World Thrumm.* This was the first time she'd felt it, and it terrified her. All of creation seemed to shudder. Rom heard none of it but seeing the look on Sen's face, he put a hand on his hammer. Sen strained to hear and caught almost a whisper on the breeze. An owl was wheeling above, picking for a night meal.

It said something to Sen.

She could hear its cries, the pure and clean screech of a tawny owl. It seemed so familiar, and yet so unfamiliar. The owl recognized her, and she recognized it, and for a moment there was nothing but the two of them hanging in the shuddering world. The owl said two words, but Sen knew not what they were. Sen shivered, and the owl cried out again. This time the words were as clear as cut glass, *"It comes,"* the owl said, and then it flew away into the night. Sen sat back down suddenly. *"It comes,"* the owl whispered again into the black.

"What comes?" she said to the sky.

Rom put a hand on her shoulder and turned her, *"With whom do you speak?"* he signed.

"It comes," Sen said, her eyes stung by salt.

XIV

A Realm of Fog

The Adder edged closer to port, boat by boat – a stream of floating traffic building behind them. The captain grew ever more nervous, as did the rest of his crew. Saph and Timmin too felt the unease that roiled across the noisy riverbanks. They felt the cold that appears at first light and huddled closer together. They heard gulls and wind and the sounds of the docks, and yet they could not help but absorb the ease of Grappy. He seemed unconcerned and uninterested in all around him, only in his tale. His eyes glazed over, and he lifted his arms with a dancer's artistry, flicking his wrists and rolling his fingers as he spoke. "The origin of the fade is, as some say, the same as the origin of the Nul knights. Of the Hevamir: the first legion, they who made and broke the world, it has long been said that many were good, and many were evil, but it has also been said that of their number most were somewhere in between. Perhaps good and evil are so polar, that middling folk end up simply pulled to whichever side first lays a hand on them.

"As the tale is told, a long and terrible war was fought between two sides of the newly reborn Hevamir: the first war. The war that would one day be ended by Gil'denon One Tooth. After they were made mortal, and since never before had those with thought crossed the doors of the grave, when those first Darbhein died in battle a new place was born for their thought to go. Since the poles of the conflict were so stark, the thought of either side could not go to the same place. Thus, the Ethkeld and the Fogkeld were created not with purpose, but by accident. As the millennia stretched out and common folk sought to bear morality in the tales they taught their children, one became a symbol of punishment for wicked sorts and the other became a gift for the righteous. Generals would tell their soldiers that they would be rewarded with paradise and that the enemy would be Fogkelded. Mothers told it to their tykes and priests spewed the same on the streets, standing atop wooden stages.

"Legends tell of Darbhein mages who could use magics to banish their foes to the Fogkeld, though none speak of such banishment to the Ethkeld. The ether is thought of as heaven, and so none sought to punish the weak, or monstrous, by sending them there. Scholars, the kind not often read, have been known to equate this to the serpent and the egg. Which came first, morality or banishment? Indeed, legends speak of metal specially crafted to enact such banishment and to prevent punished spirits from returning. These mages have long guarded the gates to the Fogkeld and have kept their ways secret, only sharing them with those initiated into their order. They came to be known as The Nul and they have stood long and proud in their secret places of iron and rune. They initiate those whom they deem worthy and guard their confidences as a bee guards her queen.

"Now, the Fogkeld is described as a place of towers and castles, cities and forests – a reflection of the middle plane, crafted entirely of mist. Imprisoned souls are deprived of all senses aside from cold and hunger and the decaying semblance of their memories. Souls are maddened in the Fogkeld and their spirits drift apart into dark clouds wanting nought but vengeance for their plight. At lay lines on this mortal plane the fog drifts and the eldest and most fearsome of those drifted, or Fogkelded, beings claw their way from the abyss and bring their torment to the living realm. The Nul are gatekeepers and wardens, both guarding and banishing. The true nature of their work is unknown to man and king alike. They are rarely seen but when they are they must always be given passage and supplies, such is the writ of ancient law. It is said that freed fade creatures will wreak bloody havoc if they can find a way to return, and so when a Nul knight is seen he must be helped. Many believe the Nul exist only in faery stories. In plays and shows, they are harbingers of doom. When one appears, it is a signal to the audience that the play is to end in tragedy. Not many can claim to have seen such a knight but those who have say they are grim and frightening folk, wearing plate armour and carrying great blades of black steel. Such was the visage of the Suit of Molag Nul.

As Drelle stared upon it in the damp of the caves beneath Monterio castle, she could not help but feel her pulse quicken. The armour regarded her with chilling stillness. She knew not if it had responded to its true name. It seemed cold and empty, and yet moments before it had moved. She looked down at the rest of the ensemble: a boy, the one whom Darmok had surely mistaken for the Nul knight, the suit, and most surprisingly of all a hound. The boy seemed bedraggled. The dog seemed injured. As one they staggered to their feet, and in the boy's hand was something Drelle knew well: a crane's claw.

"Who are you?" Kief said, the tone and fear in his voice sending a shudder up the back of the dog next to him. Her hackles rose, and a growl grew in her throat.

"Who is anyone other than a fleeting series of sensations folding into one another?" Drelle said with a smile.

Leaning on its sword, the suit said, *"You are the envoy of Kammar, sent to aid me in my task?"* The delicate runework across its breastplate shone a pale blue in the darkness.

"I am." Drelle wanted to say more, but looking down on Kief she wondered if she should, fearing to fray his already tangled mind. "You must come with me."

"To find a battleground?" the suit's voice echoed from the wet stone walls.

* * *

Kief looked from suit to mage and said, "You are from Kammar?" He had heard tales of the masters of Kammar. Their status was common knowledge to all folk from the towns of Pallid and Brael. He had even known people who'd been sent to Kammar to study at the master's college of Kuh-

THE SUIT OF NUL - A NIGHT ON A RIVERBOAT

Dul, known to some as the Algonorium. He knew that they possessed powers and wisdom that no others had and that they spread across the world doing all manner of task. It was known that they all owed every allegiance to their secluded masters.

* * *

"I am," she said, studying him curiously. There was something striking about this scene: the suit, this boy, and the sodden dog at his heel, and in that moment Drelle almost forgot herself, almost forgot the battle raging above them, out of sight and earshot.

* * *

Kief Stroongarm shivered in his wet clothes, clinging to his flesh. He tasted the cold air of the underground waterway and marvelled at this woman emerging from the darkness. He marvelled at the light cast by the suit and thought of the mouse that they had followed. He thought of his dagger and the events of the past few days. In the depths of him rumbled a storm. A tempest, whirling and spinning. The torment and upset, the cold of the water at his feet, the scent of burning flesh somewhere beyond the cavern. His pulse quickened and a deep longing stirred in his chest. He longed for home. A home that no longer was, or never was. Not a roadside tavern, not a clan hall. His hand began to shake, and the dog by his side whined and turned to him. He looked down at his dagger and saw that he was pointing it at the mage.

"Who are you?" Kief said finally.

Drelle looked down on him, and pity stirred in her gullet. She looked at the dog and the dog looked back. Her gaze then returned to Kief, and her voice softened. "My name is Drelle, and I am here to help. Please put away your dagger."

Kief's eyes flickered on his blade and in the damp and dark of the cave he found that he could not put it down. It seemed to whisper in the blackness and once again rage stirred in his chest.

* * *

Drelle could feel it in the air, the unspoken question at the very heart of the blade, and without thinking she stepped toward Kief. The suit came forth to block her path, but Drelle missed not a step, slowly and carefully picking her way around the armour, which seemed to sense her intent and let her pass, the gleaming hounskull turned to regard her as she did. The dog shivered, and Drelle could almost see the string that bound them. A silver line of soul crossing from boy to knife to suit to dog. The academic in her found it remarkable, and yet she knew if something was not done it could spell disaster. She told the dog that she would help, and calm spread through its body. It stepped back and Drelle seized Kief's hand, the hand holding the dagger. He shuddered at her touch but did not recoil. Drelle looked him in the eye and then began to sing. The song she sang was not an old and learned song, such as those she used to speak with trees. This was a song she wrote at that very moment.

THE SUIT OF NUL - A NIGHT ON A RIVERBOAT | 239

* * *

Kief felt a warmth grow in his chest. It spread through his limbs and into his hands. The runes across the suit glowed ever brighter, and once again Kief found himself standing on the flat black lake. The music surrounded him. It came faster and faster, and all the pain and hurt of his life flowed out of him into the sounds.

The music took him, and he fell backward into water.

When Kief came to, they were in the woods. For a moment he lay there, seeing the sun filtering through layer upon layer of green leaves, their veins darker than their flesh, and making little noise as they swayed in the breeze. He could hear no sound of battle, no horns, clashes, or screams. The dog was licking his face.

"Ragtail, leave him," came a woman's voice.

Ragtail, Kief thought. A name a dog would give to a dog. To his right, a huge old man with a matted beard looked down at him. He wore a blacksmith's felt clothing, clogs, and had a hammer on his belt.

The smith made some hand sign that Kief did not recognize and then a girl said, "He tells you to stand."

She had long brown hair, ungroomed and unkempt. She looked road-weary, and there was something oddly cheerful about her.

Kief got to his feet, his clothing still damp and his muscles sore across his back and chest. They were in a clearing, ringed on all sides by birch trees, their wood peeling and white. There was long grass and daisies, and a single fallen trunk in the centre, covered by moss and vines. The mage, Drelle, was humming to the woods on the far side, her hands gripping a staff that seemed almost to be twisting and turning unnaturally in her hands. At the very centre of the clearing stood the suit. It was clean and dark and glistened in the sun. There was an almost dreamlike quality to the scene, something fey and otherworldly in the clear light and in the dew dripping from the grass. It was then that Kief felt a sharp pain on the side of his head, and touching it there was a welt, surely from when he had fallen in the cave. Kief looked about him, thinking to see Monterio looming somewhere nearby, but he saw only trees. He felt a pang and thought of his dagger. Where was it? His hands went to his belt and then he cast about looking for it.

The blacksmith made an angry sign and the girl, who was still regarding him with a certain amusement, cut through the tense air and said, "Your knight has it."

She then pointed to the suit, who was holding the knife in one black gauntlet, between finger and thumb, staring out at them from somewhere within the inky darkness of its helmet.

Kief breathed out a shaky breath. Seeing the Suit of Molag Nul once again alive and moving after all the time he'd walked it in that barrow was strange. He felt connected to it. No longer so afraid of it, and at that thought something within him stirred.

"Stand tall, Kief of Mondar Village," the suit said. *"It comes."*
"What comes?"
"Our task."

The suit flipped the dagger over and passed it to him. He felt the tension ease in his chest when he touched it, but there was something different in that touching. Whatever the mage had done had softened the edges of the feeling. The desperation that he had almost grown used to in holding the weapon was gone, replaced by a strange numbness.

* * *

Grappy grew grave, and the bobbing of the Adder beneath him almost stilled to a stop. He looked at Kraf-Krak, and then back to the two children, paying no heed to the anxiety on in their faces. The battle of Monterio castle was pyrrhic in its doing. Though Redheim broke through the wall and fought long and hard in the breach – many hundreds piling up against the sturdy Braelian defence – they failed. To their great amazement, the Braelian soldiers at Monterio Castle held firm and pushed back the wave both atop the wall and within the breach, and a retreat was called to tend wounded and bury dead. What none there could fathom was that those preceding days of carnage had weakened the barrier betwixt the kelds.

"The knights of Nul are adept at knowing when a fade beast is to cross into our realm. The portents are lay lines and blood, among other things. Lay and blood were at Monterio Castle that day in abundance, and this is why Drelle was so afraid, but even she at that time could not guess as to what was to soon occur within those walls. That knowledge would come to her, Senhora, and my father later, and they would all be burdened with much guilt at being unable to prevent it.

Mere hours after Redheim called their retreat, the Braelian troops were burning their dead and lamenting their suffering when, as the tale is told by the minstrels of the former Redhirrim courts, a grinning beast crawled limb by limb from a bloody puddle in the bowels of the keep – the Baoleth. Its body was smoke, and its claws were fire. It seized upon the first men it saw in that dungeon with glee, whispering strange words and striking as lightning does the tallest tree. Tendrils rent skin from flesh and slipped into the noses and mouths of fleeing and screaming soldiers, only to burst free in bloody spatterings, bending and torturing and relishing its feast. What I may tell you is that it is most likely that the Darbhein blood in Kief's cell was where the beast had first crawled into this world. It would have hissed and basked in the suffering around it and flitted from shadow to shadow across the castle, silently and viciously eating its fill while Drelle and the rest hid in the caverns below. It would have been fast, and merciless. A cloud of smoke one moment, and a beast with claws and a face of blood and scale another. Yet not a scream, not a noise, not a warning, was heard by any Redheim soldier, or by Rom and Sen.

"It is said that the following morning, when the warriors of Redheim resumed their attack, they found the fortress devoid of all life. Blood smeared the walls and filled gutters, bodies lay in unnatural positions, and horror was found at every turn. Flesh littered the courtyards and crows pecked at the eyes of severed heads. Monterio Castle was declared cursed, the Redheim siege weapons were dismantled and used to block the entrances, and to this day none have dared to step foot within again."

**

Hidden in the waterways below Monterio, Drelle knew what was coming, and knew that their only hope would be to choose a battleground without shadow and with life aplenty with which to battle death itself. She chose a spot in the forest and opted to call the beast to her with its lost finger, mocking it – for Fogkelded souls have little but pride to motivate them. And so it was this that Kief awoke to. Drelle prepared the battleground, and the rest readied their weapons. Drelle knew that the enemy was devious and so knew she could not send Sen or any of those weaker in the party away, lest they be used as a bargaining tool. She knew they must fight it, and with their combined strength they must banish it.

In the forest clearing, Drelle took out the fiery finger, unwrapped it, and began to sing. This song was sharp and shrill, and any of those with a propensity toward soul singing would know it to be a challenge. When she finished, she passed the finger to the suit, which opened its visor and dropped it inside.

"What comes?" Kief asked, his voice beginning to shake.

Senhora, who was for once without a question on her lips, lifted a stick that she had come upon on the forest floor. Her knuckles went white, and her face took on a pinched, fearful expression. Drelle had explained to Sen that soon a fade creature would come upon them, as Kief had ridden the iron shoulders of the suit on their hike to this forest, and only now was the fear that came alongside that truth beginning to set in. Beside her Rom hefted his hammer. Drelle looked back at them, guilt stirring within her. They seemed a pathetic motley.

"A beast of the fade," Drelle said. "You shall need to have your wits about you and be ready to move when I say." She turned to the suit, "Complete your task, and I shall guard the rest."

The forest around them seemed to halt in anticipation, the birds were silent, the insects fled, and even the silver birch trees seemed to distil a fearful mood.

To say they heard or saw the creature's approach would be a dire misinterpreting of this tale. They felt more than saw it come. The lines of the fade rippled the air, and through the trees, darkness encroached upon them. A throbbing, thrumming darkness sunk into the shaded parts of the forest beyond their clearing and rumbled through the heartbeat of the wood. Drelle raised her staff and began to sing a low and rumbling song. The suit lifted its sword in readiness, and the rest quivered. The humming grew and grew, near drowning Drelle's voice, and just as it seemed she would burst from exhaustion, there came another sound, a hissing, unnatural voice.

"The crab scuttles and turns to dust, its shell strewn on the beach. A meal for thee, a meal fit for a king, and fed to him by a knight."

Senhora shuddered as the sounds echoed through the trees. Smoke appeared at their feet and poured from the treeline. Kief raised his dagger and took a step in front of Senhora and the hound, not fancying either of their chances and feeling some instinct within him to face a foe with bravery. Rom came to his side holding Fache's hammer. In front of him stood Drelle, still casting shrill and piercing tones into the mists. In front of her stood the knight. Then, like a lick of flame, came a long black tendril. It flicked out at the suit from somewhere beyond the treeline, but the living armour – fast as a striking snake – parried it with its black blade, cutting away the end, which dispersed upward as smoke.

"It jolts, it molts, it guards the gates."

More smoke poured into the clearing betwixt the white trees and Drelle raised her staff higher. The air began to hum, and some invisible force pushed back at the black vapour in a wavering circle around them, but the smoke would not stop. Pinpricks of black tendrils pushed into the sphere of clean air that Drelle held, chaos whirling beyond. It was disturbing, yet beautiful, as it went all around wheeling and spinning, its formlessness finding purchase. Ahead of them, the suit bellowed and leapt forward, toward something they couldn't quite see.

"With finality," whispered the voice, and at that moment smoke plunged into Drelle's sphere. She let out a yelp, and her song abruptly stopped, the smoke was hot and thick, and in a moment, it surrounded them in swirling darkness.

Drelle leapt back and took a hold of the dog's scruff, then grabbed Kief under the arm holding her staff.

Blackness prevailed.

Distantly, Kief could hear sounds of clashing steel and the hollow roars of the suit. He could almost make out flickering silhouettes of a knight cutting away at a black cloud somewhere beyond. Kief could feel Drelle's arm around him and could feel the hound at his feet. It smelled of burning, but not of woodsmoke; of molten stone, sulphur, and otherness.

He knew not where the girl or that man, Senhora and Rom, had gone. All sensation was lost to him. After a time of nothing and nowhere, the fog seemed to clear, and they found that they were standing on worn cobblestones. Grey fog swirled into towering pillars of smoke that drifted on unfelt wind. Drelle slowly unclenched her grip on Kief and stepped back. Ragtail growled low in her throat, baring her teeth.

"Where are we?" Kief said, but even as he said it, he knew the answer. His voice whispered and repeated and echoed out in all directions, returning and shifting. The Keld of Fog. The prison of doomed spirits. Drelle looked at him with fear in her eyes but she said nothing. She quested about, as did Kief. There were strange sounds, whispers that seemed to drift past them, words too muted and fleeting to make out. The suit was gone, the clearing was gone, Sen and Rom were gone. Then, they again felt more than saw something that rattled their bones to the marrow. Dark shapes lumbered toward them out of the smoke on all sides, making halting, strange steps. Their edges were adrift, much like all else around them, but in the centre, they were man-shaped. They had eyes of pale white, and when they drew near their faces seemed stricken with grins wider than mouths should go.

Drelle barked a word that made the dog recoil, but it made little sense to Kief. The figures paused, still grinning, and more came behind them. One turned to another and in a strange voice that was low and murmuring, he said something, and the others began to laugh. Echoing laughter, like many more voices than could possibly belong to those before them. Drelle barked again, lifting her staff. She shook it and splinters of wood fell away. She shook it again and the wood fell as dust, drifting off into the murk until underneath, a thin and sharp wooden blade remained. She pointed it at the lead shadow, who grinned and put his hand to his smoking hip. He drew his own foggy blade and they all laughed again.

"What are they?" Kief said, his voice once again absorbed by the smog.

"The damned," Drelle said. "We must survive until Gromhir has completed his task. Only then may we return – if we may return at all."

The shadow lurched forward and swung a glancing blow at Drelle, and in a movement that completely surprised Kief for its grace, the mage bent around the flowing sword and whipped her wooden blade up the smoke of the creature's body. It screamed a terrible scream in a hundred lost voices and its form dispersed into nothingness. The rest of the shadowy consort shrieked and drawing their ghostly blades they too hurled themselves at Drelle, but she was as a leaf on the wind, bending and curving and cutting at them. One came toward Kief, but the hound bit at its leg, tendrils of smoke coming away in her mouth. Kief lashed his dagger across its face, and the creature reeled away.

* * *

In the clearing, the suit snapped around and saw that the fog had taken its allies but the black helmet betrayed no fear. The runes on its body began to glow and with the great black blade, it carved away a tendril of smoke that came toward it. A parry and a slash, and another piece of smog drifted away into nothing.

"*What ist thee?*" said the whispering voice of the Baoleth.
"*I am a task.*"

The suit leapt forward, to the source of the voice, plunging into the tree line. There, deep within swirling mists, stood a shadowy figure. As the suit's sword cut away at the tendrils of smoke, fire spurted out and the trees around them lit up. The creature reeled and whipped out at the suit, but it parried easily. Then, faster than the eye could see, came another shadowy tendril that caught the suit full in the back, and sent armour and sword soaring through the air. It landed heavily through a thin tree that splintered in all directions. The suit roared, and using its sword to get to its feet it whirled back toward the Baoleth, its impetus greater than its bulk and weight should allow. As it cut the smoke, it dispersed, along with hissing and echoing laughter. The suit's helmet began to glow from within, and the great rune of the Darbhein hand on its forehead glowed a bright white. A pillar of celestial light cut through enough of the smoke, burning it away into nothingness, until finally amid the haze, a dark figure stood alone. Its scaled face and cold eyes stared back at the suit until the pillar of light near crossed it. The Baoleth swept its shadowy form to the side, narrowly avoiding the arcane fire. It drew something from the murky fog of its belt, a hand axe, smouldering and smoking.

"*I have not known the taste of steel in many long years,*" the Baoleth hissed.

* * *

Voices drifted through the mists asking questions. Sen heard them, but the moment they passed her ears, she forgot what they said. She tried to make sense of all she saw. The mists surrounded them, spinning and whirling, strangely beautiful in a way, but also numbing. It was not hot or cold but in fact it lacked all sensation. One could stand still and close their eyes and forget that they even existed in the mists of the Fogkeld. The feeling was seductive. The desire to fall back and drift away into nothingness. Senhora almost forgot all feeling, all thought, and all burdens, but then with a jolt, she remembered: she was lost. She was standing in the same place, but she felt as if she had wandered for miles blindfolded. Her memories and knowledge started drifting from her just as the smoke around them drifted. Occasionally, the drifts revealed towering stonework, smooth and uncannily made with no brick or mortar. She saw walls and ground and dead trees. Only then, as she gathered her wits, did she notice that Rom still held her shoulder in one hand and Fache's white hammer in the other.

***

Smoke span past Rom's eyes, and he was back in the forge of Bastaun. Smoke and heat stung his face. He saw the young ones working the great bellows, he heard the clinking of metalwork and the humming of new runes. He still held Sen. He could still feel her shoulder in his hand, but he did not see her, and his feeling of holding too began to drift from him. A shadowy figure strode toward where he stood, by the great stone face of Gil'denon, One Tooth. It was Fache, larger and grander than he was before. He bore down on Rom, who quivered at the sight.

"Always a fool. Quick to anger, slow to learn," he said in his rasping voice, awash with malice. "Not a soul would have chosen you to take my place, and thanks to you, not a soul can."

"I'm sorry, I didn't know what to do," Rom said aloud. His voice felt weak and trembling. He looked up at the great stone reptile face, and with a colossal sound that rattled through Rom's mind, it cracked.

"You were foolish and weak and un-tempered. A poor excuse for a smith." Fache dominated the room, powerful and fuming, and Rom shrunk before him.

"I loved you," Rom said weakly.

The face of Fache changed. The anger within him roared into a white fire, his eyes ablaze, "YOU KILLED ME, ROM. YOU KILLED US ALL WITH YOUR SPITE AND YOUR WEAKNESS! YOU KILLED ALL YOU HELD DEAR AND FOR WHAT!? A LITTLE GIRL?!"

* * *

Sen took a step back. A shadow was bearing down on Rom, fixing him with its glare. Its white eyes were pinched within the storm of black smoke that blew all around them. It was not Humaine or Darbhein – it was something other. Some great and forgotten creature, resembling almost an ox but not. It had rows of carnivorous teeth, grinning and dripping. It stood on squat hind legs and at the front seethed huge knuckled arms. It put a clawed hand to Rom's throat and lifted him, but he did not struggle. Sen screamed and threw herself at it, batting it with her stick, but the branch simply passed through, twisting and sliding in the smoke. She whacked again and then the stick became Mog's favourite rolling pin, and she was warm.

Sen hit at the dough, making a slapping sound against the countertop in childish frustration. She was younger than she was, and could not get it to roll flat. It kept breaking and sticking to the counter. Mog put a hand on her shoulder and said, "More flour, and don't treat other people's things with disrespect."

"Who first made dough, Mog?" Sen said, turning to her. The kindly face smiled sadly.

She said, "I think that is a question none will ever know the answer to."

Sen sighed and took a handful of flour from the sack below the counter and sprinkled it onto the dough. Mog's grip tightened on her shoulder and Sen whipped around. Mog looked shocked. A ribbon of light whipped through the low window and across her body. The upper half of the woman slid away and landed heavily on the ground, a slab of meat.

* * *

Kief carved away a shadow man and another came forward to take its place. In front of him, Drelle was knocked back and a shadow bore down on her. It drove its blade into her side, and she screamed. Kief ran at her and lifted his dagger once again, but in his hand, he was surprised to find a quill-tipped pen. He was in a hall, a writing room; a study. Books were piled high, and filtering through the window he could hear his mother's song as she watered the plants.

The Fisherman and the Pear. A lilting tune Kief knew well, a forgotten memory. The fisherman's wife bought the pear at the market from an exotic merchant, who had in turn brought it by carriage from lands afar. The song had a sad melody, rolling up and down like the waves under the fisherman's boat. The fisherman sailed out one day and caught a selkie in his net: a beautiful woman of the sea, who lived in the clothes of a seal. The fisherman did not know what to do with her, so he offered her the pear.

Kief's mother ceased her singing.

Kief could not remember the end of the tale. He looked down at his writings, a poor scratching, copied from one of his father's books. The room smelled of dust, and the late summer sunshine warmed his back. Then came a shrill noise, like the caw of a crow. Kief looked around. There it was again, louder this time. Then, louder still, a *scream*. He rushed through the doorway to the entrance of the Stroongarm house, an ornate room with feathered pillars and fresh rushes scattered with sand on the floor. He could smell smoke. Someone screamed and then tumbled headlong down the stairs. It was Sandy, battered and broken.

A man appeared beside her with a sword, his face obscured. In silence, he slid the blade slowly into Sandy's belly and then called back up the stairs. "Here's another one." He looked down on Kief, "Time to meet the king's justice, boy."

* * *

Rom had always remembered Fache as a gentle man, slow to anger, quick to laugh, but that day blood dribbled from the master metalworker's mouth and from the gaping wound on his neck. Rage boiled in his eyes, and he made a manic sound, lifting Rom high with one great arm as fire grew all about them, burning and broiling his flesh. The skin on his forearms crackled and yellow tongues licked the air. Far below, in the reflection in the glass of the window to Mog's shop, Sen could see it. Rom was shrouded in fire. The grey smith gritted his teeth and lifted the hammer in his hand. It was heavier than all the metal of Redheim. Fache vomited blood on Rom. It fell as smoke, steaming and burning into the air. All around was afire.

Bastaun burned, Rom burned, all and everything. Rom's arm was as lead, but he forced it up and then brought it down on the head of Fache. It clanged like steel, and Fache stumbled back. Rom turned the hammer, and with a fluid and resolute movement, he carved a rune into the forehead of his old master. The rune of truth. A most dangerous and uncontrollable rune. He turned the hammer and brought it down again and again, grinding his jaw until his teeth shattered in his mouth. He poured his soul into the rune, and like a passing storm, the fog parted and the powers that gripped them all flickered out of life. The shadow beast that held Rom sank its black claws into his neck, tearing his throat, drinking the last of the smith's lifeblood, but it mattered not. Rom's soul was already burned into its forehead. He had spent all his life on that rune. The beast made the sound of a thousand braying animals, flinging the smith's body away like a dusty coat. Sen stood there, in nothing. She clutched her twig aghast and watched as Rom's broken corpse disappeared into the mists. As it flew the final sight that Sen would ever have of the noble smith, her saviour, and the last true Bastaun master was seared into her mind.

Behind her came a yell and a bloodied Drelle sprinted toward her out of the smoke, carrying a wooden sword. She struck at the huge shadow beast, the slayer of Rom, the truth rune still glowing on its forehead. A strange and rippling rune, a near-perfect circle flattened on one side. Three dots in the centre, one with a slash. Sen would recall the look of that rune for the rest of her days. Surging behind Drelle came a hound, and then Kief, as his own nightmare dispersed. The shadow men followed and again surrounded them, laughing. Drelle whipped at them with her blade, but they would not stop.

* * *

The armour of Nul cried, "No" with its tragic voice, swinging its blade. It cut through smoke and tree alike, destroying all that came between it and the Baoleth. Its movement was poetry, stark and brutal, yet perfect in each way.

* * *

Within the Fogkeld, Drelle would cut away a shadow man, and another, twisting and whirling, only to be cut herself, blood flicking away from her and becoming smoke in the air, Kief to her right darted his knife wildly, but with none of the skill that possessed the mage. Sen darted and dodged, ducking and holding onto the hem of Drelle's cloak, lest she be lost again. The dog howled and barked and bit at feet and legs, but the moment they would slay one creature, another would appear in the mists. They knew not how long they fought, but the red descended and all was chaos and cutting and pain and blood.

There came a moment in the madness when Sen looked down at her hands and saw the edges of her fingers beginning to come apart, steam rising and drifting off and away. She looked to her companions, locked in furious combat. She looked at the shadow men, and it struck her that they looked much like soldiers, with rounded helmets and maille. The fallen soldiers of Brael. Kief took a glancing blow to the face and a line of blood flicked away into the steam. She saw them all beginning to come apart, all their beings and lives and souls drifting on the breeze.

It was at that moment that a question came to Senhora. *"How do I make fog become water?"*

She thought of bubbling pots and droplets rolling down her window. She thought of Mog, drenched from the rain, coming into the kitchen and warming herself by the fire, steam rising from her clothes. She thought of pies and sauce on the chins of blacksmiths, and clarity came to her. Senhora opened her mouth and music grew within her. In the joining of sound and form, she felt and heard and saw all the interlocking parts of all the world, and like plucking a string on a lute, she picked the word from the air and asked. "Can it be *cold?*"

The smoke swirled and the shadow men all stopped and looked at her. A splatter, and then another, and another. Rain fell, drenching them all, washing away the shadows. The mists dispersed and all around them began to tumble into a storm. It surged and blistered their faces so they couldn't see. Then a light above. Green, trees, and the clanging of steel. They fell, soaking and stumbling into the clearing.

Ragtail hacked and coughed and Drelle whipped around. To their right, the suit and a Darbhein were trading blows in the midst of a terrible landscape of burning and fallen trees, a flurry of brute strength and perfect movement, sparks and ash thrown into the air with every blow. The Darbhein held an axe of fire that struck out at the suit, clanging and knocking it back. The suit kicked the Baoleth in the chest and sent it sprawling. Drelle tossed aside her wooden sword and raised her voice to the forest and sang a song of power and strength, of crushing and casting and breaking, of fallen trunks and prey, of sinking fangs and locked horns. The Baoleth shrank to the sound, and as smoke, it whirled out of the way of the tree bows and roots that lurched towards it.

"A feast interrupted," the creature said, and like a passing wind it drifted into nothingness. The suit swung its sword once more at its disappearing form but caught only smoke.

When the beast was gone, the forest seemed to let out a slow breath. All the fires in the trees went out and strands of smoke rose amongst the remaining silver trunks. The sun warmed them, and grass swayed in the breeze. The suit looked about, seeming to steam with rage. Kief was on his hands and knees, water soaking him and sinking into the earth, and they in that moment were all filled with joy and triumph. That is, all of them aside from –

XV

A Moment at Court

Grappy stopped and looked up. He was out of breath, and all around him sailors and children alike leaned toward his tale. Their vessel bobbed in the waterway, and the sounds of the morning dockland permeated all. Ringing and chattering and turning of wood. The elderly spellsinger sighed, trying to find stillness within, and he looked toward the jetty. The Adder had inched closer. Only one boat was ahead of them, and as Grappy's eyes traced the pier his gaze locked upon one man. He was middle-aged, standing as a soldier would, reeking of authority. He seemed to feel Grappy's look and turned, his eyes at once finding the old man. He wore no breastplate or helmet, but all the same, it was clear what he was; a knight. Noble heraldry was emblazoned on his chest. A shield with images of a ship and rose, and he carried a high-born air. His hand rested on the hilt of a longsword, and he seemed to grind his jaw. Men-at-arms surrounded him, along with dock officials and a steady stream of sailors passing one by one.

"And then what happened?" Timmin said.

"A moment," Grappy said. He got to his feet, resting a little too heavily on his staff. The knight on the dock said something to a man beside him and a mood seemed to shudder through the crowd onshore. All bristled and the knight beckoned Kraf-Krak's vessel.

As the Adder neared, hands threw ropes to those on deck, and they tied up. Kraf-Krak stepped easily onto the pier before the boat came to a halt.

"Greetings," he said.

The knight looked the Kammarite up and down and narrowed his eyes. The man's hair was cut short, and he had a thin scar on one cheek. He strode up and looked beyond Kraf-Krak, "Gaelar, we are here to speak with you. Your companions matter not."

Kraf-Krak bristled to be spoken past in such a way, and so he turned to the knight with one hand on the pommel of his broadsword.

"Your contract is complete, Kraf-Krak," Grappy said, "You and your crew may continue on your journey." Grappy then stepped off the boat, followed by the two children. They looked afraid, but Grappy did not. Resolve studded his features, and he walked past the knight into the throng of men-at-arms and dockhands, leaving the startled Kraf-Krak behind by his riverboat. Someone called for it to move along, and a horn sounded. It seemed the search had reached its conclusion.

The men-at-arms parted, and Grappy marched onward. The Remtaun dock was nestled between two cliffs with a steep hill betwixt them. An ancient rockslide had flattened the landscape and over generations stilted houses and decking had spread haphazardly across it. Atop the hill, the town grew further still, with newer and better-made buildings peeking across a main carriage road, with bustling trader's stalls on either side. The knight, whom Grappy seemed disdainful of, marched alongside them and gestured to a large building past the fair. It had a wide gate fit for a carriage on one side and barred doors on the left and right. Carved in wood above the two doors was the same coat of arms: a foursquare with a rose top right, a ship lower left, and red-painted squares besides. The upper windows were fortified with grated shutters and there were thin arrow slits every now and again. It would have made poor defence for a siege, but the Remtaun Rathaus was designed more as a temporary stronghold in case of raiding, though such actions had not been seen in many a long year. The young knight from the pier knocked twice at the right-hand door, a panel slid back, and beady eyes peered out.

Grappy smiled genially and the knight scowled. Until that moment, the ser hadn't bothered to say much of a word but took apparent offence at not being granted immediate access. "Lord Kehn is awaiting us. Open the door," he said.

"Of course, m'lord," came a haggard voice and there was a steady sound of many bolts being drawn. After a might of huffing and panting, an elderly serving man pulled the door aside to reveal an entranceway to a long hall. At one end sat a lordly type on a raised wooden chair, with intricate carvings whittled up the back. He was greying but still carried a look of strength, and that particular shape of arm which tells of one well used to wielding a sword. This was Lord Kehn, ruler of the east coast. His clothes were rich, and his face was stern. He called across the room, "Ser Kallek, Gaelar. I am pleased that you have come as genially as you have."

Ser Kallek snorted and assumed a position to the right of the Lord Kehn. Grappy and his two grandchildren were ushered before him and the group of men-at-arms crowded in the doorway, awaiting instruction.

"I won't insult you with restraints, Gaelar," Kehn said, to which Grappy smiled. Kehn looked quizzically down on him, and for a moment it seemed as if he may smile in return but in the end, he did not.

Behind Grappy, and almost hiding in his cloak, Timmin and Saph looked on afraid. The situation appeared neither genial nor welcoming. The knight from the pier, Kallek, looked down at Grappy as if he expected a vile monster to crawl forth, erupting from Grappy's chest and devouring all present. Grappy seemed calm, but his eyes darted from face to face, taking in their mood, and seeming to prepare something within him.

"I won't curry words," Lord Kehn said. "I'm here to talk about the fire on lord Marshe's estate. The death of a king's trusted man has deeply hurt his highness, and so he has asked us to investigate matters. We were petitioned to blockade the port in hopes of sighting you. It was said that you were seen leaving by riverboat, and it was also said that with the moon's rise the fire miraculously ended."

Grappy met the man's eyes but said nothing. Lord Kehn continued, looking at the two children at Grappy's side. "P'raps we should speak in private," he looked down at Timmin, who met his gaze in a strikingly similar way to Gaelar.

"They don't leave my side," Grappy said.

Kehn paused and twisted at a ring on one hand thoughtfully. Now that they were closer, the three remaining members of the Stroongarm clan could tell he had the kind of watery blue eyes that signalled congestion in the spring and a falcon-like nose as was common among the aristocracy of Brael. There were deep lines on his forehead and at the corners of his eyes, which darted from Grappy to Saph to Timmin and back again.

After a moment, it seemed Ser Kallek could no longer contain himself and he spat, "A man who killed his own son, the hero Pauel, and his wife. We are here for your neck!" His words echoed limply across the hall.

If Grappy were a dog, his hackles would have stood high on his back. The knight went to bark more, but the lord silenced him with a hand. Behind them, the men-at-arms all seemed to intake breath as one.

"We received a letter," Kehn said. He produced a rolled scroll from a fold in his doublet. "Would you care to read it?"

Grappy sighed and nodded. Kehn passed the scroll to Ser Kallek, who stepped down and passed it to Grappy curtly. The elderly mage unrolled it and poured over its contents for a moment, and then sighed. He then looked back up at Lord Kehn.

"I wish to hear your side of events, Gaelar. You are well known to the king, and well respected by all who cross your path."

"This man should be clapped in irons and dragged before the king," Ser Kallek growled.

Lord Kehn turned to the knight and said clearly, but not loudly, "Am I not the presiding lord, nephew? Do you plan to question every twitch of my finger? You would take the word of a single witness who saw nothing but tongues of flame, and an old man fleeing?"

"No." His face reddened, and his gaze went to his feet.

Grappy raised a furry eyebrow, and Saph took a firm grip of his cloak. Grappy put one hand on her head and could feel her shaking.

"I am here," Lord Kehn said, "so today, this room is my court, and what I decide shall be final. The king has decreed it. Tell your tale, master."

Grappy's eyes moved from face to face, until finally, he glanced down at Timmin who had tears welling in his eyes. He cleared his throat and then said, "When I arrived the fire had already started." Timmin's eyes flickered and Saph looked away. "I had been sent for by my son, Pauel. He claimed that his life was at risk and that there were those who sought to do him harm. By the time I made it to his estate, it was too late."

Grappy described the sunset spreading cool and yellow across the skyline as he arrived, the rustle of grass on the hillside, the oaky scent of the trees that surrounded the carriage road that led to the door, and the look of his son's home as fire licked the windows. As Grappy's tale grew around him and filled the room, the truth and lies in it mingled, and became inseparable.

***

It was true he was sent for, but not in the sense he implied. A whisper on the water came to him, a floating leaf, a gull's shriek. Sounds that should seem ordinary, but to Grappy screamed a warning. When he arrived the house was quiet. Grappy already knew what had become of his son, and so too knew that he must first see to the children. Darkness crept on him as a cloak, glowing flecks of sunlight receding into the clouds like spatters of fire on a mountain. He climbed hand and foot up the steep slope to the silent house, crouching like some prowling candlecat in the midst of the trees. It was a cottage that Grappy had helped to build in part, had helped to thatch, and a door he'd helped to frame. Something welled in his throat as he thought of it.

All was quiet.

When Grappy arrived, the fire had indeed not started. It appeared as if nothing were happening at all within that house on the hillside. It was of southern design, dense and finely cut beams made up the exterior, tarred and painted. The roof sloped gently, and the thatch was newly trimmed, and it rustled as the breeze rolled over it.

Grappy knew that no spellsong could be uttered, lest in the growing darkness he be heard. He hardened his heart to what he must do and came to the window of the children's room, letting out a sigh of relief as he saw the latch undone.

He fumbled with his cloak as he raised one leg over the sill, and then the other, breathing shallow and heavy. He could tell they were asleep as he crept in. He carried Saph from her bed and held a finger to his lips at the shocked look from Timmin. They knew little of what was afoot, but the grave light in the eyes of their grandfather was proof enough to still their tongues. He gestured for the boy to follow and the three climbed out of the window and went to the woodshed behind the house. It was full of feed for animals, tools, and stacked firewood. He whispered to them, asking for them to be silent, and to hide amongst the hay. He told them to await him, and that he was going to attempt to save their father – yet even as he said it the words became ashes in his mouth. Again, Grappy hardened his resolve and turned back to the silent house.

* * *

In the Rathaus of Remtaun, Grappy told nothing of this and instead said, "My son owed a great deal to a very dangerous man, and as we always knew would be, he had to pay the price for his mistakes. I saw that the road had recently been used by a small group of horsemen, but when I followed the tracks down the hill, they disappeared into the woodland. Not that it matters – for I will tell you the name of Pauel's killer."

Lord Kehn listened intently, intelligence glittering in his eyes, and beside him, resentment was sharp in his nephew's. "Witnesses described someone fitting your description leaving hastily, and they say that they saw no others enter or leave," he said.

"Twitching curtains tell no lies," Grappy replied with a wry smile. "I screamed at the top of my lungs; did they mention that? I saw there were signs of a struggle, the door battered in by heavy boots – did your witness see that? Did your witness take any steps to aid my son? Or was it left to an old man, alone in the night? Seeing the flames, I tried to enter the house – afraid for the children, afraid for my son, and his wife, but the heat drove me back. I wet my cloak in a trough and returned hoping to find the children, and I did. They were in their bedroom to the back of the house. I collected them and then hid them in the woodshed until I could discover the truth."

"And did the children see anything?"

"No, they did not. The attackers must have come silently, only two or three of them – p'raps with the use of magics. The bedroom of the children was far away from the kitchen and the rooms of Pauel and his wife. Out of earshot."

* * *

Grappy had walked slowly towards the front of the house, his heart hammering in his throat. He raised his staff and rapped it thrice on the door, recognizing every scratch and marking upon it. He remembered the summer they hewed it together, shortly before Timmin had breathed his first. He recalled the fine wine that Pauel had produced, from some campaign in The West Ward, and how sweet it had tasted after they had clinked glasses by the hearth. Grappy had been there many times before, though not in recent years. He knew the shape of the decking, the row of herb plants in hanging baskets by the window. He remembered sitting on that front step smoking a pipe and telling Polly tales of his travels.

The door was thrown open and Grappy's son grinned heartily. Pauel was a stout man, with simple clothes and a genuine smile. He was pleased to see his father. It almost seemed somehow unreal, somehow ethereal, but Grappy knew it was not. He had the same thick brown hair and the same keen eyes and the same broad smile as all the Stroongarm men, but in every movement, Grappy saw something other. He could smell blood on his son and could see, in the narrowest twinkling of his irises, something that unsettled the old man to his core.

Grappy steeled himself and said, "Where is she?"

Pauel grin grew wider. He was almost unrecognisable from when he was a boy. He had been wiry, shy, and his hair had always covered his eyes. When he first ran away Grappy had looked long and hard for him, as Meeph had asked of him, and even longer still when Meeph had asked him to stop, but to no avail. Pauel had joined a marching force and fought with the Braelian guard, a long way away. Grappy knew not that he had signed up, or even if he still lived. For all he knew his son was aboard a merchant fleet among the Caliphedes. In truth, Pauel had travelled every which way across the Braelian heartland, had in some manner met the King of Brael and spent years as an agent for him. He had gained acclaim and riches and raised his own family in the lap of luxury. The next time Grappy saw his son it was on the deathbed of his mother, as Meeph coughed and hacked, and her lungs wilted like grapes in a winter breeze.

After that, they spent many years making up for lost time. Gaelar gained his new name, and they lived peaceably until once again they became estranged by matters of wisdom and opinion. At that time Grappy could never have guessed where it would lead. A simple decision to go one way at a crossroads, while Pauel went another. In the doorway, as the sun crawled finally behind the hills, Grappy recalled it all, tinged in red and reeking of smoke. Now, Pauel was muscular, and a well-groomed beard adorned his chin. His face was beginning to show the signs of ageing, and something hung from him – something the Kammarites called *talent* – but there was something different about it that day, from the last time that Grappy had sighted it.

Being a soldier, Pauel had always had an imposing presence, but at that last light of the day, there was something more sinister in his visage, something otherworldly and altogether wrong. The wind was cold at Grappy's back, and his son gestured for him to come inside. Beyond the entrance was a wood-panelled corridor, with paintings on the walls, a row of hooks for cloaks and overclothes, and an open doorway casting yellow light from the kitchen hearth. There were boots both for adults and children to the left, and Grappy looked down on them, his eyes hesitating as they crossed the smallest pair.

"I know why you've truly come," Pauel said.

Grappy said nothing.

"Don't you see, Pappy?" He leant against the wall in the corridor, "The answers you seek are not here, not yet anyways." Pauel spoke as if he were telling of the weather. "It has never been clearer. Never has a man come as close as I to restoring the world to its natural way." His voice was quiet as if he feared to wake his children, and he leant too closely to Grappy. His breath smelled of beef, and something else, wieldenflower perhaps – or cachtail.

"Where is your wife, Pauel?" Grappy's voice faltered. He tried to maintain his composure, tried to speak in a calm and loving voice.

"I go where the Nul fear to tread, and in doing so I – "

Grappy slammed his staff against the floorboards. "You cannot! If you go there, if you make deals with them, there is no coming back."

Spittle flew from his mouth, and his son started back. In the water in the air, in the water in his blood, Grappy felt a stir. He felt the realms shake and squirm, felt parasites and tiny things spinning and reeling, their sharp teeth gnashing, and their inner fires reeking and smoking.

Outside, it began to rain.

"But father, I have already been," Pauel whispered, his eyes glittering in the orange light from the open kitchen door. "Sepulchur showed me. He even told me how to open the Ethkeld. He made me see beyond what the petty masters and those armoured fools comprehend."

"Speak not that name." Grappy's gaze was hard as hammered steel and blunt as Kuh itself.

THE SUIT OF NUL - A NIGHT ON A RIVERBOAT | 271

The man who had once been Grappy's little boy stepped back and raised his hands above his head, in an almost religious beseeching. There was an element to his voice that frightened Grappy. A zeal that could most commonly be heard among soothsayers, or criers for the end of days who stand in the squares of Blae-Muk-Tur.

Pauel's hands shook, and he cast his gaze upward, "A life of true goodness must be sacrificed, and then we may ride upon its soul."

"Pauel."

Before him, Grappy could feel the heat from the kitchen, and behind he could feel the cold of the night. The wind whipped the rain against his back, and he felt it pooling on the floorboards.

Pauel looked his father in the eye and whispered, "Sepulchur is not evil. He is a wise and noble creature. He seeks only to share the truth – he knows it all too well."

Grappy was aghast, all the water around him shuddered with the sound of his voice, which seemed to grow louder than a voice should be.

"No!" he said. The rain thrashed beyond the doorway, and his son shrank back toward the kitchen. "It is the deceiver, the burner, the guide to the Baoleth! Do you think it would not lead you down the same path?! No, I will not allow it, not my own son. Not as I live."

"What you will allow is of no consequence father," Pauel said. His bulky form filled the corridor. His voice rose. "It is already done. Now you may come with me or stay behind."

The boy, his fair son, pointed through to the master bedroom, at the end of the entrance corridor. Grappy knew it. The door flapped slightly in the breeze, but the interior was shrouded in darkness. Yet Grappy could see it. He could smell it. He knew it in his bones, in the *thrumm*. The mother of Saph and Timmin was in there. Still, bloodied, a knife protruding from her chest. He felt the last of her life rising from her. A retch stirred in his throat. He stepped past his son, and the rain outside hurtled at the earth.

As he walked down the corridor he could feel the water in her blood, he felt it on the gooseflesh covering his body. He could feel it bubbling onto the floor and the heat of it escaping into the air. He could also feel a stirring in that same blood. The great mage, Gaelar Stroongarm could feel the black eye within it waiting until it could ride its hate into the middle plain. Grappy turned back to his son, "I will not allow the Ethkeld corrupted by creatures such as your *black mass*."

As Grappy walked toward the swinging doorway, his son's voice followed him down the corridor. "Your ignorance will not halt us, will not halt the return of Darbhein and Drek, and Sphvenk, and Solemn. The world needs this – mankind needs them. Alone we are weak and frightened and too often do we bloody our swords through cruelty and greed."

There was a crack in the curtains, and a thin line of moonlight cut the bed in two. The room was lavishly furnished with pillows and plants, and grand wall hangings. A charcoal sketch that Saph had done of a fish was nailed above the bed, and in blood on the floor were painted many runes, most of which Grappy did not recognise. There were shadows above the corpse of Polly; the mother of his grandchildren. A woman who could gut a fish in one smooth movement, who could sing a song of love, and who could make an old man laugh. A true and good person. Her back was arched, and her face contorted in the pain of her final moment. There was betrayal in her eyes and a long black dagger protruded from her chest – a Nul dagger. Her long hair had matted into the pool, and her eyes were glassy. There were bloody handprints on her face and the velvet of her bedclothes. The sheets below her were a puddle of blood and mess, and there were streaks lining every which way.

Grappy looked on, unflinching. He saw in his mind's eye the ravings of his son as he completed this ritual, as he had driven the blade into the chest of his sleeping wife, and as he spoke to the shadow beings that flickered up the walls around him. Grappy looked down at the rippling blood, near black in the light, and in it, he saw something move. Crossing but not yet crossed.

Gaelar Stroongarm turned back to his son, looking down the corridor and he whispered, "I will not allow this."

The open front door swung on its hinges and rain thundered beyond. Pauel stepped into the kitchen, a low room with a hearth and a table, stools made of ceder, and a store filled with dried fish. He picked up a sword from the kitchen table, a fine blade – the blade of a king's man. He drew it slowly, "Do not stand in our way."

"I WILL NOT ALLOW THIS," Grappy's voice rose to an impossible volume and echoed across the way, and as it did all the rain of the world exploded into the house. As needles, it ripped through the mortar and glass, cutting through the shadows, and impaling his son. Pauel staggered, his mouth bubbling with blood.

"I'm so sorry," Grappy said. He stepped back into the bedroom and leaned over his daughter, not by blood, but daughter all the same. He closed her eyes with the tips of his grizzled fingers. His son behind him fell to the ground with a thump, and in the world thrumm, Grappy felt his life snuff out like the glowing end of a candle.

Grappy sighed, a long and low sigh, steam pouring from his nose and his mouth, and the room warmed to it. He hummed a question of fire, and the air answered him. The ice in his son's chest melted and then evaporated and the walls peeled and caught. Fire rose from the ground and Grappy stepped out into the rain. The flames roared forth within, licking up the walls and climbing to the roof.

Panting from the strain, tears mixing with the rainwater on his cheeks, he turned toward the woodshed. The rain was soaking his hair to his head, and dripping from the end of his beard, yet the fire climbed ever higher. He walked around the house, feeling the heat of the blaze beside him and opened the door to the woodshed with haste and called out to the children in the darkness where they were hiding amongst the hay. "Timmin, Saph. Come along."

"Where's Pappy?" Timmin said, starting back, eyeing Grappy's staff.

"Your father has been lost," Grappy said.

Saph said nothing and a single tear rolled down her cheek.

"Why?" Timmin said, "How? Where's mam?"

"An enemy of your father's from long ago returned, and he killed them. I drove him off with fire and my strength, but we must leave now. I cannot stay a moment longer."

And as accepting as children can be, the two arose and followed him outside. They hiked the many miles in the darkness to the nearby town of Brill, and from there they chartered a riverboat.

* * *

In the cold Rathaus, Grappy finished his fiction, "My grandchildren had hidden, and Gemlock, a terrible and dangerous oath keeper – for I know not which lord of Pallid, had already come. He exacted his revenge on my son and his wife. I scooped up the children and spirited them away from that accursed place. His home, the place that I had helped him to build sixteen summers ago, was burning."

"What debt did your son owe?" Lord Kehn said. There was true pity in the elder lord's eyes.

"He had killed Gemlock's lover, among some others of his clan following an incident in the north. The king had sent my son, and when diplomacy had grown foul, my Pauel barely escaped. We knew that one day Gemlock would seek his vengeance. If you tell the king the name, he will surely know it, and will surely understand."

The lord knight stared at Grappy with a gaze of sadness and hardness and finally said, "I have heard enough. You may leave."

"But we came to arrest this man," Ser Kallik said. "Pauel was a great friend to King Abenthy, a great friend to me. He will not allow this unpunished."

"We came to discover the truth."

"And a tale is no truth. No one saw any, apart from this man, enter or leave."

Lord Kehn held his hand up again, "I came to look him in the eye and tell if I saw guilt and malice, and I see no malice. We will tell the name Gemlock to the king by hawk and allow Gaelar to take the children home."

In a haze, the three remaining members of the Stroongarm clan were loaded into a small wagon and they departed Remtaun. It was not far to Grappy's home, and for much of the journey, they sat in silence. As the moments trickled by Saph turned to her grandfather and said, "You lied to that man, Grappy."

And to that, Grappy said nothing.

End.

Milton Keynes UK
Ingram Content Group UK Ltd.
UKHW041820210924
448622UK00004B/184